SOMETHING TO
BELIEVE IN

Something To Believe In

Silver Series Book One

MELISSA K. MORGAN

Melissa K. Morgan

Contents

Published by Melissa K. Morgan, Edited by Cameron Yaeger, (Aurora Publicity), Cover by Melody Barber, (Aurora Publicity)
First Printing, 2013, Revised 2020
Imprint: Independently Published

For Darlene,
I miss you and love you.

Chapter 1

Mackaela

I was walking down a dark alley, trying to avoid ruining my newest pair of heels. It was just beginning to rain, so I pulled my hood up over my straightened, brunette hair and hugged my purse closer to my chest. This wasn't a place that a girl like me, well at least one who looked like me, should be hanging around. At a glance, any stranger would probably assume I was lost or in some kind of trouble. Luckily for me, I had many years of experience in being able to slip under the radar and go unnoticed.

The sound of something rustling to the right of me made me hug my bag tighter. I silently prayed for whatever the source of the noise was to leave me alone. I wasn't scared, not after years of practice at this, merely anxious to get this meeting over with and avoid the run-around with some straight out of high school junky that worked for a high. I was told that there would be a new guy picking up, but it wouldn't be the first or last time that Mickey lied to me.

I allowed a sideways glance to the area of the commotion and saw a black cat jumping into a dumpster. I let out a grateful sigh of relief that it wasn't a person who would no doubt ask questions. Looking ahead again, I saw the dim light of the end of a cigarette. The collector, dressed in black, was facing the opposite wall of the alley. His stance was casual, with one booted foot bent back against the brick of the building. He instantly turned toward me when I was about five feet away from him. A stranger, most likely the newest of Mickey's minions sent to do the bitch work. I let out a breath. I wasn't sure who to expect, but this guy didn't look like the usual junkie.

"What do you want?" he asked, his voice gruff, eyeing me up and down speculatively. I watched as he shoved away from the wall and stepped toward me, blowing smoke out of his nose and throwing the cigarette butt on the ground.

"I'm expected." As I spoke, I lifted my hands to my hood and lowered it.

Immediately, I noticed the stranger's emerald eyes widen marginally, a look that I had come to expect, especially from Mickey's people. Nobody ever thinks the twenty-something girl that looks like she is from a prominent part of Seattle would be a deliverer. This guy was no different obviously, and I rolled my eyes as he relaxed his stance and took another step closer. He was taller than me, which isn't common considering I, myself, am 5'9".

I had a couple of self-defense classes under my belt, as well as what I learned from both Mickey and Dom. If this guy wanted to play games, he was going to be in for a big surprise. I was in no mood and had other plans that if I were late for, I'd pay dearly. I offered a quick once over from booted foot to head and couldn't help but notice the hint of a smirk on his too attractive face. *Don't flatter yourself, pretty boy*, I thought to myself.

"Who's expecting you, beautiful?" A slow, lazy grin appeared across his perfectly full lips. I bet he charmed all the girls wherever he came from.

I was surprised that Mickey actually had a guy like this doing the job. Yes, I'll admit he was definitely good looking and those eyes, something about them was mesmerizing. I would never admit that though. I offered a tight smile of my own and lowered my bag from my arm.

"The name's not 'beautiful,' and I suggest you quit screwing around, pretty boy. I've got somewhere to be." I removed the envelope from my purse and stuck it out to him. His gaze slid down to the envelope and then back to meet my eyes.

He shrugged and said, "Can't blame a guy for trying." He snagged the envelope and unzipped his jacket, placing the contents in a pocket. With a wink he said, "It was a pleasure doing business with you, sweetheart."

I began walking backwards, shaking my head as I spoke. "Tell Mickey he needs to quit switching up on me. I don't like not knowing who I'm dealing with."

A wide grin formed on the stranger's lips. "The name's Simon, Simon Silver, and I can assure you that it is me you will be dealing with from here on out."

I stopped in my tracks. *Silver, as in ... ?*

"That's right, beautiful, I'm Mick's brother. What's your name?" He wore a cocky smile at the shocked look on my face.

I tried to quell the expression and take a more casual approach. Shrugging, I said, "Apparently it's 'beautiful.'" I turned around then and began heading for the mouth of the alleyway.

Simon Silver was back in his brother's life. *This should be interesting.*

*

I pulled up to the front entrance of the expensive downtown hotel and a valet opened my door for me. "Good evening, miss," he said, holding out his hand for my keys. I narrowed my eyes at him.

"No joy riding this car or you'll be eating your balls later." I shot him a glare as I dropped the keys in his hand. His smile left and he cleared his throat, nodding once as I rushedspeed walked through the main entrance to the elevators.

The tan and brown, semi-modern yet classic look of the main floor always amazed me. This place was elegant and far more than I could ever afford on my best days. The only reason I was ever here was because of the services to my clients. I had two that stayed here for our "business meetings." and oOne day I thought it would be nice if I could actually take advantage of a comfortable four-poster bed or lounge in one of the deep Jacuzzi tubs while sipping on a martini and listening to Chopin or Debussy. I love classical music and art; yet another thing that most people didn't know about me.

The steel door of the elevator opened just as I was approaching it and I stepped inside, immediately pushing the fifth floor and "door close" buttons. I pulled my cell phone out to silence it and checked the time. I had literally one minute to get to the room where my client was waiting.

I removed my jacket and used the interior mirror of the elevator to assess my appearance. I was wearing a pair of dark skinny jeans and a metallic lace top that was classy yet sexy, just how Mr. Watson liked me when I came to serve him. My heels were still in pristine condition even though I had been in an alley while it was raining. They were black leather pumps with spikey rhinestones on the toe. I figured in a do or die situation they may serve as a weapon. I was nothing if not resourceful. I was wearing a pair of dark skinny jeans and a metallic lace top that was classy yet sexy, just how Mr. Watson liked me when I came to serve him. When the elevator stopped, I took a deep breath, shaking my hair out and adding some lipgloss.

When I got to the door, I made two solid beats on its surface, letting him know it was me. The door opened almost instantly. "You're late, Kale," Mr. Watson said as he opened the door a little wider.

Offering him an apologetic smile, I stepped forward, placing a hand on his chest. "I'm so deeply sorry, Ken. I got into a little bit of traffic." I batted my fake lashes at him and watched as his brows smoothed out.

I could see the lust in his pale blue eyes as I lightly circled my finger along the front of his white dress shirt. His tie was loosely undone, his feet bare.

Mr. Watson was in his mid-forties; he wasn't completely un-attractive, but under normal circumstances I wouldn't give him the time of day. He had sandy brown hair that was thinning slightly and thin lips that felt like sandpaper when he touched me with them.

I never let any client kiss me on the lips, but that didn't mean they didn't try. Kissing was too intimate and not at all appropriate for the task at hand. I was Kale the working girl, all business now. Not the real me who was nothing like this alter ego.

I stepped closer to him and closed the door behind me. "Please forgive me?" I spoke in a too sweet tone that I knew would get him to drop it.

He nodded and put his hands on my waist, pulling me into him. I stepped out of his embrace and walked into the large suite with hardwood floors and ornate furniture, including a large black bed and white linens. I placed my jacket over the back of a chair before sitting down in it and setting my purse at my feet.

"What will it be tonight, Ken?" I asked as I sat myself in one of the chairs and set my jacket and purse down. I crossed one leg over the other, letting my arms rest on the chair.

Ken smiled as he sauntered slowly toward me. "You know what I like, baby. But we have to be quick. My wife is expecting me home tonight." He winked at me.

I nodded and stood, approaching him. I grabbed his tie, pulling it so that he followed where I led before pushing him back on the bed. He let out a grunt and grabbed for me as. I climbed on top of him, sitting exactly where I knew I would have control. I never gave that up in these situations, even though the men thought I did.

I pressed myself into him and he groaned, closing his eyes. I stroked from his neck down to his waist with one finger as I slipped my hand into his pocket. "You got the five hundred?" I asked in a seductive tone as I pulled the bills from his pocket, rocking against him once more.

He opened his eyes and smiled. "Yeah, baby, now give me what I want."

Simon

It'd been a week of working for my brother so far and for the most part it wasn't that bad of a gig. I was apprehensive at first, considering he made me fight one of his main guy's named Dom before deeming me worthy of the job. Dom was a pretty big guy, all muscle and intimidating as hell. I wasn't afraid of him, just worried that I would end up looking like a chump and Mick might tell me to get bent. I needed this job. I needed my brother. I was out of options.

Sparing with Dom ended up not being as bad as I thought. I held my own, of course. It's kind of hard not to considering I used to fight a lot while locked up. If it was one thing I was good at, it was fighting. Mick had slapped me on the back after the fight. He even said, "Good job, bro!"

It was odd hearing him call me "Bro" so easily. I had no idea when I looked him up that he would let me back into his life so quickly. The truth was, based on the bullshit lies our father told him, he had every right to assume the worst of me. I was shocked Mick had been so forgiving. It did take meeting up and explaining my entire life, well most of it, in detail for quite a few hours though.

Mick had a lot of questions about my mother and the way I was raised. Apparently, our dear old dad had made it sound like I was living it up in a huge house with tons of money and everything I ever wanted with my mom and new step-dad. Mick grew up resenting me and wondering why I'd choose money over him and our father. It was never about money for me. I didn't even reap the benefits of my step-dad's fortune. The only reason I went with my mother was because she was my mother and I loved her. Even at a young age, I felt like it was my duty to protect her and be wherever she was. I loved my brother and father, but my mom needed help. She was a lost soul that needed saving.

I didn't know what drugs were at such a young age, but I understood the effects they were taking on her and how she fought with everything she had to try to break herself from the habit. Todd wasn't much help in keeping her clean. He was just looking for a trophy wife to brag to all of his business colleagues about.

Todd didn't like me at all. I think he was afraid I was taking time with my mother away from him and he saw me as a threat. I remember when the abuse started. I was around ten years old and at first it was only directed toward me. I hated every minute of being smacked across the face and whipped with a belt. But that wasn't even the worst part. Two years later, he decided to start taking things out on my mom. I wanted to fight back. I even attempted it a few times. That was when Todd decided that I needed to be locked in my room for periods at a time and starved.

Every time I tried to help my mother or defend her, he would pull me up the stairs to my room and lock me in. Sometimes it was only a few hours, sometimes a few days. There was a point in time where I blamed my mom. She was the one who hooked up with Todd. She was the one who wouldn't leave him and made me stay when she could have sent me back to Dad's. To be fair though, I probably wouldn't have left even if I could have. Not without her.

I loved my mother despite my violent upbringing and. I missed her terribly. It was after seeing the way Todd treated her, when he'd vowed to honor, cherish, and protect her in marriage, that Imade me realized I never wanted to go down that same road. Women didn't deserve that kind of degradation. I could never understand the appeal in treating them poorly or harming them.

Which was why I was surprised to see a woman, let alone one that looked so well put together, delivering the check from the supplier. Whoever she was, she wasn't what I expected when Mick told me about his contact. I assumed it would be some tweaker guy that would try to screw me over or fight me. I wasn't sure how I felt about him hiring women for that sort of position.

I stood there in that narrow alley for a good ten minutes after she'd walked away and got into a classic black Mustang, which surprised me even further, trying to think of who she could have possibly been. She was dressed as if she was going out and said she had somewhere to be. I wondered where a pretty little number like her would be headed and how she could just walk a back alleyway in the dark with no one to protect her. She'd seemed confident and cool about it.

Now, I was headed back to Mick's place, navigating the ever present Seattle traffic. The new phone my brother had hooked me up with, claiming he needed to be able to contact me whenever he wanted, started ringing in the center console. "What's up?" I answered.

"Did you get it?" he asked in a tone that seemed bored.

"Yep, I'm headed your way now."

"Good, was there any trouble?"

"Not a bit, but why didn't you tell me your contact was a girl?"

"I didn't think it mattered," he muttered absently. "Hey, you better not have given her shit or I swear to God, Simon ... " His tone turned defensive.

"I didn't do a damn thing but get what you wanted. She had somewhere to be, was in a hurry anyway." Mick grunted in response. "I'll be there in five," I said before ending the call.

I wondered if he would even tell me her name. Other than Dom's girl Sadie, I never really saw many women around Mick's place. Well, other than the skanks that vied for his attention. I steered clear from them, not wanting to fall back to old habits.

I pulled into the parking garage at the warehouse and set the alarm on the Audi R8 that Mick let me drive. He said it was his own personal vehicle and I wasn't to come back with so much as a scratch on it or he would castrate me. It was hard not to take advantage of the thing, but I was on my best behavior. Cars were definitely a weakness of mine. I had always been interested in them. It was the one healthy hobby I could maintain and hopefully make a living with in the future.

I took the elevator up to Mick's office area in the nondescript downtown building. I was pretty certain the building used to be some sort of loft style apartments or something but it was now run down. How my brother was able to operate his less than legal business dealings in and out of here was beyond me.

I knocked on the door and was greeted by a petite blond who was half dressed in a black bikini top and jeans. I'd seen her a couple of times in the last week but couldn't remember her name. I didn't really care to.

"Who are you?" she asked, looking me up and down.

I smirked down at her, noting the way her eyes widened slightly before focusing on my lips. "I'm Simon, princess. My brother is expecting me."

She gave me a wide smile and opened the door further, motioning me to step inside. "He's in the other room."

"Thanks," I mumbled as I headed for Mick's converted makeshift office.

It might not seem smart for a man fresh out of prison to hang around the likes of assistant drug lord, Mickey Silver, but I was desperate and he was family.

I walked into his office without knocking. He was on a callthe phone and didn't look happy. Mick pulled the phone away from his ear and told me to close the door. When I turned around, I noticed the blond, thinking she could come in too, pout and roll her eyes before I shut the door on her.

I took a seat in one of the black high back chairs in front of the massive oak desk as he paced behind it. The tension in his jaw and the way his knuckles whitened on the hand that held the phone to his ear told me he was irritated with whoever he was talking to.

"I could give a shit about his idle threats. I'm not going to put up with this from him or anyone else," he practically yelled. The person on the other end was giving him an earful. He appeared to listen intently, though his face showed exasperation. "Okay!" he shouted abruptly. "Stop yelling at me, all right? Jesus. I'll take care of him." He let out a sigh and took a seat, propping his feet on the desk.

I watched as he pinched the bridge of his nose while closing his eyes. This was the first time since appearing back in my brother's life that I'd seen him almost vulnerable. He was usually a hard ass with everyone, including me. It was almost as if he feared whoever was chewing him out on the other end of the line. I studied him as he scowled, listening again.

Only six months apart in age, Mick was the polar opposite of me as far as looks went. My hair was dark, almost black, and I had green eyes. Mick had blond hair and hazel-gray eyes. He was more of a stalky, athletic build while I was leaner and taller than him by a few inches. We looked like each of our mothers more than Jack Silver. I was grateful for that. The only things we seemed to share with him were a similar facial structure and our last name, which was fine by me. I wasn't ready to speak with my father any time soon.

"You know I love you. All right, I'll see you soon," he said before hanging up the phone and tossing it on the desktop.

I raised a brow at him. I wasn't aware he had a girlfriend, especially considering the entourage of girls that seemed to flutter around the place.

"So, you got my mail?" Mick asked, ignoring my look.

I pulled the envelope out of my pocket and set it on the desk in front of me. "There you have it." Mick grabbed the envelope, opened it to check the contents, and then placed it in a drawer.

He stood suddenly and walked over to the mini-fridge that sat next to a pale yellow couch on the far wall. "Want a beer?" he offered.

I nodded and caught the can as he tossed it to me. Opening it, I took a long pull and relaxed back in my seat.

"All hell is about to break loose in this place," Mick said as he went back to his desk chair and got comfortable.

"Who was that on the phone? I didn't think you were tied down." I wasn't sure if he would actually fill me in or not, but I figured I'd ask. My brother hadn't been very forthcoming in sharing his personal life with me yet.

Mick smirked. "I'm not tied down, Simon," he replied, and then quickly changed the subject. "So your first gig was a success. How do you feel?"

"I feel fine, that wasn't difficult. Is that all you need me to do, be your errand boy?"

Mick shook his head and let out a low chuckle. "Not exactly. I'm just working you up slowly. You know, initiating you."

That was actually a relief to hear. I was willing to do whatever at this point, but being a gopher didn't seem very appealing, though the money was okay. "So what am I doing next?" I asked, taking another swig of beer.

"I've got an employee that needs some help. One of the client's is trying to fuck her over which in turn screws me, so I think he needs to be dealt with. I'm thinking about recruiting you for the task."

I sat up straighter and narrowed my eyes at him. "What exactly does this employee do?" I asked. Mick shot me a telling smile and I knew what he was getting at. It was exactly what I had suspected with all the girls around this place. "She's a prostitute. So what, some guy didn't pay?"

I was used to being around narcotics. It was second nature to me because I grew up around it my whole life,. Aalthough, I never touched the stuff. Probably because I saw the consequences first hand at what they did to people. Prostitution was a whole other ball game and something that would be sketchy territory for me, especially if I were beating up john's.

"To be honest, Simon, I'm not ready to delve into all the details with you until I know that I can trust you completely. However, this guy tried to take advantage of my best girl and I want you to rough him up a bit. Remind him that you don't mess with Mickey Silver or any of his employees."

I nodded. I could handle kicking some guy's ass, especially if he messed with a woman.

Mick continued speaking. "We're brothers, Simon. I know you have that Silver blood in you and I need a right hand guy that I can trust around here."

"I thought you had someone else in the running?" I remembered the associate he told me about when I first started. I think it was Dom's cousin, Ricky.

"I think it is time to loosen ties with that one. He's been distant lately. If you do this, I'll explain the business in greater detail. It'd be nice to keep this all in the family."

Part of me wanted to just walk away right then. It wasn't that I didn't love my brother. It was simply that I had just been released from prison. Keeping a low profile and helping out in back alleys gave me more anonymity. Becoming his main guy might increase further illegal activity. If I were to get caught, I might be locked up for good. The other part of me, it must have been the Silver side, was intrigued. More responsibility meant a higher pay grade and. I needed the money.

"All right, I'll do what you want, but if I get arrested ... " I started to say.

Mick laughed as if what I said was the most ridiculous thing he'd ever heard. "Simon, Simon, Simon ... Don't you know that you can't get arrested if you don't get caught? Besides, why would you be afraid of jail, were you somebody's bitch the last time?" He chuckled darkly.

I clenched my jaw and narrowed my eyes at him. "Don't be a dick," I gritted out.

I'd done a year for armed robbery. Todd called the cops on me when I came home drunk after my mom died. I had a gun on me for protection from that son of a bitch and he told them I was robbing his house and beat him up. I did kick his ass, but I was innocent. Unfortunately, when a multi-millionaire presses charges and pays the cops to corroborate the story, you get the raw end of the deal.

I wasn't anyone's bitch and as a matter of fact, most people feared me. Of course, that was after I was beaten within an inch of my life by some gang member. Once I fought back, people respected me.

Before either of us could say anything else, I heard shouting from the other room. Mick seemed to tense and then stood from his desk.

"That would be my favorite employee." He sighed, strolling to the door and pulling it open just as it was pushing in.

I looked up and my eyes connected with a familiar face. It was her, the girl from the alley.

Chapter 2

Mackaela

I wasn't proud of my profession, although I wasn't altogether ashamed by it, either. Truthfully, I never really cared what anyone thought of me, even though not everyone knew I was a prostitute. It wasn't like I woke up one day and decided that my dream was to use my body on rich men in order to get a fat paycheck. Actually, it wasn't my idea at all.

Mickey Silver, my best friend and boss, was the one to pitch the idea of having me become a "companion" for a few of his V.I.P. clients. At first, I was a little nervous about it, considering my past with men and what happened to me. All in all though, the pros outweighed the cons. I would be in control of the situation, simply give them what they wanted, or what they thought they wanted, and then collect the cash.

Mickey said I was creating a solid relationship with some of his best customers so that they wouldn't stray. As a bonus, I got to keep all the cash. The men I dealt with were a select few of the highest elite in Seattle. In his mind, it was a win-win. In my mind, he was using me for business, but that really wasn't anything new. Don't get me wrong, I loved Mickey Silver to death since the day I met him at the age of thirteen. He had always been that one constant for me, a true friend that I could always count on to take care of me. If I didn't have him, I would probably be living on the streets, in jail, or dead. Mickey was my lifeline. I depended on him, albeit much more than I wanted at times, but it was the truth. He took care of me, because honestly, I didn't know how to take care of myself.

Case in point, the event tonight with Watson. I should have seen it coming, I knew better. But when he pulled the knife on me and pushed me against the wall, I froze.

His hands trailed from the top of my head and slowly down my back to my ass. He squeezed gently before pressing himself against me. "You aren't leaving yet, Kale," he gritted out and turned me around to face him.

Now being in the line of work I was in, there were some rules. You never turned your back on a person, you learned to fight and defend yourself, and you always went for the balls when all else failed. I knew it was horrible that I used my body for something I didn't want to, but to allow someone to take my body without my offering it was an absolute deal breaker for me.

I reacted instantly, grabbing Watson's wrist which held the knife and twisted it in a way that made him yelp in pain. I brought my leg up and kneed him in the crotch, causing him to drop on the ground.

"That's your warning, Watson," I said calmly and turned on my heel to get the hell out of there.

I instantly called Mickey as I was leaving the hotel. There was no way I was ever going to work with Watson anymore after that. I didn't care if we lost him or not, I was not going to become someone's victim for a second time. Not for anybody, not even for my best friend.

Nobody talked back to Mickey Silver, not even his women that he had parading around all the time. I yelled at him for a solid two minutes, stating that there would be no "again."

When I walked into the area above the warehouse, I was instantly greeted by Britney, the bubbly blonde who had only been here for a few weeks and thought she owned the place. Mickey always had a flavor of the month. This month was obviously bimbo with a side of sass.

"He's in a meeting," she snapped.

"You are not his secretary!" I shouted, marching toward his closed office door. "Do you know who I am? Get the hell out of my way!" I may have slightly shoved her, but I didn't care.

I got to Mickey's door and grabbed for the handle just as he opened it. I didn't lock eyes with him though. It was the other person in the room with those damn emerald eyes. Seeing Simon there made me even more irate. Of course he'd be here with his brother.

I shouldered past Mickey and went straight to his desk, pulling out a pack of cigarettes from his drawer and taking a seat in his cushy office chair.

"You want a beer?" he asked as he closed the door.

"Yeah, that would be great," I said in a snotty tone.

Feeling Simon's eyes on me, I shot him a sideways glance. Maybe he was curious as to why I came in here like a bat out of Hell. No, I knew that look on his face. It was the same one that I got from anyone who found out that I was pretty much a call girl. Clearly Mickey had filled him in on the issue at hand.

"You got a staring problem, pretty boy?" I asked as Mickey handed me a beer.

Simon raised his brows before narrowing his eyes, looking to the desk instead.

Mickey laughed. "Pretty boy, huh? I like that," he said. "You remember him from the alley earlier?"

I popped open the beer and took a large gulp. Lighting my cigarette, I shot a look at Mickey. "How could I forget. Where did you find him?" I refused to look at Simon again. I knew those eyes were on me again and for some reason I was unsettled by them.

"He needed my help. Apparently he hasn't been living in the lap of luxury as I once thought," Mickey explained.

"You've gone around talking about me?" Simon asked defensively.

"Not to just anyone," Mickey replied. "This girl here is the only one that I confide in. She knows me more than you do and you should know better than to think I would run my mouth. She's family."

"All right, I got it. I'm sorry," Simon said.

"I should probably formally introduce you two since you may be working together in the future," Mickey said.

"We already had introductions," I responded, taking another drink.

"I don't even know your name," Simon interjected. I couldn't help it,. I looked at him and narrowed my eyes.

"I prefer it that way."

"You'd prefer it if I just call you 'beautiful?'" Simon countered with a smart-ass smirk.

"Call me whatever you want, *pretty boy*." I shrugged.

I could tell that little name bothered him by the way he tensed and looked down. I leaned back in the chair, propping my feet on Mickey's desk, smiling in victory. I didn't like being called "beautiful." I wasn't about to tell Simon that though. It was none of his business, and whether Mickey was putting his trust in him or not, I didn't have to go along with it. Trust was something that I didn't have for anyone.

"All right, so tell me exactly what happened with Watson," Mickey said.

I shook my head, rolling my eyes. "That piece of shit told me he was moving to some other dealer. He claimed they could get him a higher return for less money. I told him he was full of it. That's when he started listing off the people he'd been talking to. Some group run by a guy named Hawks," I said.

"Hawks, who the hell is he?"

"How in the hell should I know? Anyway, he dropped this bomb while I was working him and then afterward he threatened that if I didn't continue to see him even after he left, and if I told you about this new dealer, he'd silence me." I rolled my eyes again.

I wasn't afraid of Ken Watson. I was simply irritated that he'd tried to gain the upper hand on me. Plus, getting on Mickey Silver's bad side was the stupidest thing a person could do.

"They're just empty threats. You know that he can't harm you. I'll kill him before he even gets close," Mickey assured.

"Please," I snorted. "That isn't what makes me want to cut ties with him. You think I'm scared of his threats?" I asked incredulous.

Mickey shook his head. Suddenly his eyes went soft, the way they did when we were kids, when he felt like he needed to protect me. "What happened?" he asked in a soft voice.

"Maybe I should check out and let you guys talk," Simon said, standing.

I turned to look at him but his eyes were looking across the room at the yellow couch. "What's the matter, pretty boy?, iIs it the fact that I'm a prostitute, or is it because you have virgin ears to this stuff?" I quipped.

I didn't really care if Simon stayed or not. I was sure Mickey was going to enlist him or someone else to rough Watson up and they would want to know why. This way if the man for the job was Simon, he was already here to listen to the details of why he was needed for the task. He seemed to consider what I said for a moment before pinning me with a fiery gaze.

"There's nothing about me that's virgin," he said darkly. "I was simply trying to be respectful, *beautiful*." He winked at me.

I sneered at him and looked back to Mickey.

"He needs to know." Mickey shrugged.

"I figured as much," I muttered.

"He's going to handle more tasks for me."

"You're going to send pretty boy to Watson? Is he going to only threaten him or actually kick his ass?" I looked Simon up and down. He was tall, sure, but I couldn't make out much in the muscle department with the jacket and jeans he wore. "Can he kick his ass?" I teased.

"Don't worry about it. Tell me what happened," Mickey ordered.

Suddenly I felt a little uncomfortable talking about this with Simon in the room. I think his admission of being respectful made it difficult. Nobody normal respected girls like me and I didn't like feeling like I was being examined. After a deep breath and putting out my cigarette, I started talking.

"I was walking away, out of the room, and I told Watson that he knew better than to make threats. I don't know why I turned my back on him. I guess I was just amped up from the information."

Mickey's eyes narrowed as he listened to me. Simon sat back down in his chair, placing his elbows on his knees and his fingers under his chin. They were all ears now. I took a long pull of my beer before continuing. I was not going to repeat this.

"He came at me from behind and he shoved me into the wall. There was a knife that he held to my throat as he ... touched me and told me that he wasn't done with me yet." I swallowed, remembering the fear that I'd felt in that moment. It was the worst. The fight or flight, but all you do is freeze feeling. I hated it. "He turned me around to face him, and I took the opportunity to grab his wrist and knee him in the balls,." I said, shrugging and finishing off my beer.

I glanced up at Mickey, watching as a slow grin spread across his lips. "That a girl, I know you can defend yourself."

"Yeah, I can," I said as I got up and tossed the beer can in the trash. "But I don't want to defend myself, Mickey. I won't go back to him again."

Simon

There were a million things I wanted to say to Mick right then. Most telling him to shut the hell up about the girl being able to defend herself. She could have been raped or worse. I wanted to tell her that she was right to not want to do it anymore and that she shouldn't, but I couldn't say anything because it wasn't my place. I didn't know her or the history she shared with my brother. So, I sat there and kept my mouth closed. Not only would Mick give me shit, but this girl, she wasn't the saving kind. Or at least it seemed she didn't want to be saved.

Something about her was clearly defensive. I didn't know her past, but if she ran with my brother, it couldn't have been any better than mine or his. I watched her take a seat back in the chair behind the desk, gazing at her again as a person and not just another pretty girl like I'd done originally.

Her long brown hair fell below her breasts, and her face was covered heavily in makeup. Her full lips were painted red, and she had dark lashes, longer than naturally possible and thick. Now that I knew what she did for a living, I could tell she was in a get-up of sorts for the job. Her uniform.

Mick commenced talking about what the options would be to get this Watson guy back on their side. When she turned to look at him, I spotted a thin scar on the side of her neck, behind her ear. The faint pink line appeared to trail all the way down to her shoulder. I wondered what happened to her, if it was part of the reason she came off tough and moody. I wasn't trying to analyze her on purpose, it was simply second nature to me. I had this uncontrollable trait instilled in me to want to protect and help people. In a way, this girl reminded me of my mother. Likely lost and broken from years of neglect or abuse. No one without issues would be a part of this fucked up lifestyle willingly.

"So, I say we go pay Watson a visit, get him to talk. Then see who this Hawks guy is. If he's everything Watson says he is, then I would personally love to meet him. We're the only ones in this town that deal to my knowledge. Either Watson is full of it, or we have unwanted competition in these parts," Mick said.

"Do you think he's just bluffing?" I asked, focusing my attention back to my brother.

Mick shrugged. "It's hard to tell. Watson is a hard ass and one of the big time lawyers for the city. He could easily screw us and turn me in, but then my girl here would have a huge round of evidence against him. You see, Simon, I'm quite intelligent. Every person I come in contact with has a price and a secret to hide. Blackmail is a great form of collateral in this business."

"So what are you saying that we should do? Question him and then rough him up a bit?" I wondered.

Mick pursed his lips while putting a finger to his chin, thinking. After a few minutes, he turned to the girl and said, "You have to meet with him again."

"Mickey, I told you ... " She started to protest.

"Simon will go with you. I need you to see what kind of information you can get out of him and if all else fails, Simon will get the information." Mick looked at me. "I'm not happy about the fact that this dickhead tried to threaten my girl, so I don't feel like playing nice. If she can't get the info out of him, take matters into your own hands. Any means possible, got it?"

I'd potentially have to beat the shit out of this guy for information. Was it weird that the idea didn't faze me at all based on what I'd heard so far? What bothered me was the fact that this Watson guy might try to harm the girl again. I could tell she didn't want to confront him.

"Why don't we just cut the middle man? I'll beat his ass and get the info. That way she can get what she wants and not have to see him again," I offered.

Mick instantly began shaking his head. "No, Simon, I make the rules here, not you. She's more likely to get him to talk than you could due to her assets and dirt on the guy. Plus, we don't want to make waves. Remember what I said earlier about not getting caught?"

Suddenly, there was a knock on the door and the blonde entered timidly. Mick turned to look at her. "What is it, Britney? We're in the middle of something here," he barked.

"There's a guy, says he knows you and wants to discuss a matter of business," she explained.

"Well, who is it?"

"I think he said Watson." Britney shrugged.

Mick clenched his fists and I stood instinctively. I heard the girl behind me groan in frustration. "Send him in but give us about five minutes," Mick ordered.

Britney nodded and left, shutting the door behind her.

"What the hell is he doing here?" I asked.

"Probably trying to cover his ass and get to me before she does." He pointed back at her. Would I ever know her damn name?

"He doesn't know that I'm close with Mickey," she explained. "He thinks I'm just one of his women with no pull."

"So what are you going to do?" I asked Mick.

"I think we hear what he has to say. Go sit on the couch over there with her. I don't want her near him at the moment and when he sees her, he might get pissed and act out."

I nodded as I made my way to the couch.

The office door opened as she was rounding the desk and it took less than a minute for me to react. I lunged forward, shoving her behind me as Watson rushed her. He stopped short when I narrowed my eyes at him, tightening my shoulders.

"Who do you think you are?" The man sized me up with a sneer on his face. I could smell whiskey on his breath. His eyes were glazed over. I stood taller, stepping within inches of his face.

"Your worst nightmare, pal, now back the hell off before I bash your face in." I growled.

Watson backed up slightly, swaying when he did. Mick came up beside me and clapped me on the shoulder.

"Well done, bro," he muttered and motioned for me to sit down.

I backed up, taking a seat on the couch. It was a two-seater and the proximity was a lot closer than I had anticipated. and I could smell her perfume, like berries and vanilla. I glanced at her, noticing that she seemed almost relaxed, composed, as if she didn't almost get jumped by a guy. She definitely wasn't timid.

"What do you want, Watson? I have little time for your games," Mick said. He walked around his desk to sit down in his chair, looking bored. Watson continued standing, glowering at the girl next to me. "Sit!" he ordered Watson.

The man did as he was told before shooting another glance toward the girl. I sat up straighter, pinning him with a glare. He looked at me briefly then back to Mick.

"I see Kale got to you first," Watson said. Kale? Was that her name? I wondered if it was short for something or if it was a pseudonym she used for the job. The latter seemed more likely.

"You want to tell him your side of the story?" she asked in an icy tone.

Watson glared at her. "This bitch didn't deliver. Took my money and ran without even doing the work."

"You son of a bitch, you're a liar!" She attempted to stand, but I grabbed her wrist and shot her a warning look.

"Be cool, you'll only make it worse," I whispered. She looked like she wanted to deck me, but she did as I asked and sat back.

"I know for a fact she delivered and you got exactly what you paid for," Mick began. "What I don't understand, is why you don't want to do business anymore and why you attempted to push her into giving you something for nothing."

Watson looked at Mick for a few long moments. "I can't help the fact that she's a nice piece, Mick. I had the money. I'd pay her again for more."

I narrowed my eyes at Watson, disgusted by his words and regard for the girl. She shuddered slightly beside me. It was clear she didn't want him more than she had to for the sake of the job. I wondered why Mick would make her do this or why she would choose this profession in the first place.

Mick's jaw muscle ticked as he stared down the man across from him. "You better hold onto the memory of the last time you had her, because it isn't happening again." Watson began to protest, but Mick silenced him with a look. "Who is this Hawks that you want to do business with?"

Watson swallowed, his eyes roamed around the office, landing on the girl's face.

"You think I wouldn't tell?" she questioned.

"Hey," Mick said, grabbing the guy's attention again with a stern voice. "Answer the question, Ken, or I'm going to lose my patience and let this guy take care of you." He gestured toward me.

"Hawks is a new distributor. He runs an outfit out of Olympia. Ricky told me about him a few months back. Said he was moving units over here and he offered a lot more for a lot less. I'm not going to him yet. I don't even know if I will. I'm just ... researching it right now," Watson explained.

"Why would you need to research anything? Do we not take well enough care of you?" Mick's voice was measured, quiet.

Watson glanced at the girl and nodded. Mick rounded his desk, stopping in front of Watson, meeting him at eye level.

"Now you listen to me, Ken. I'm not in a place to trust your word. I want to know everything about this Hawks guy, and I want to know now. If you fuck me over, I'll make your life a living hell."

Watson scoffed. "Her testimony would never hold up in a court of law. She's a worthless prostitute."

Mickey turned his attention toward me and the girl. "Kale, be a sweetheart and get the video." She nodded and stood from the couch.

"What are you talking about?" Watson demanded.

I could see the sweat beading on his brow. Clearly, he didn't want someone to know what he'd been up to, most likely his wife and colleagues. "Kale" as they were referring to her at the moment, rifled through a filing cabinet before pulling a circular disc from one of the drawers.

Mickey turned the computer screen around to face his intended audience. I wasn't sure what was on this video, but I was both intrigued and apprehensive about it. Kale walked by Watson, shooting him a glare.

"I told you that you should know better," she muttered before handing the disc to Mick and coming back over to sit next to me.

When the video began playing on the screen, my stomach knotted. Kale was dressed in a short leather skirt with knee high black boots. Her top was barely covering her chest as she stood before Watson, her hand on his shoulder. I shifted beside her, not sure if I wanted to see this act play out.

"You uncomfortable, pretty boy?" She smirked at me.

I shook my head, I biting the inside of my cheek. I *was* uncomfortable, though I wouldn't admit it.

In the video, Watson placed a hand on her waist, pulling her against him. "I want you now, Kale," he said.

She stepped away from him, letting her hand wander from his shoulder down to his lap. He groaned as her hand moved over him before reaching in his pocket. "I want my money," she said, biting her lip seductively.

Pulling a large wad of bills out of his pocket, she shoved it into her top and then stepped into him again. I scratched at the back of my neck, looking away. Hearing the act of her begin working him turned my stomach. From the sounds of it, this particular piece of evidence left little to the imagination. I could understand the need for it as collateral, however, the fact that she'd willingly filmed herself made me wonder how often this happened with her clients. My gaze moved to Mick who was eyeing Watson, waiting for his reaction.

I then looked over at the girl who I was sitting next to, who I'd just seen and heard in the video. Her eyes were on me. She looked expectant, as if I might say something to her.

Thankfully, Mick cut the video off.

"How the hell did you get that?" Watson asked, turning to the girl.

She stood, approaching him slowly. "I bugged the room while you were taking a piss. I'm not worthless after all." Watson's face turned beet red in an instant.

I watched his fists clench at his sides and. I moved to stand, positioning myself between him and her.

"What do you say, Ken?" Mick asked with a wide grin.

Watson seemed to weigh his decision, though he had to know he was baited and there would be nothing left to do but talk at this point. "Fine," he muttered. "Hawks is this newbie, reminds me of you, the selfish prick that he is. He claims to be doing some sort of hybrid experiment with crack. Claims he can make it for cheaper and sell it for more. Ricky is the one I heard it from. I get all my info from him. He offered me twenty grand to take the girl and move on to Olympia with Hawks. It seems like they're trying to copy you."

I heard an audible gasp from behind me. Mick looked like he was about to punch Watson's lights out.

"What does this mean?" I asked.

"It means we have a rat in our system and he needs to be dealt with,." Mick growled as he turned his attention back to Watson. "Simon here is going to escort you out of the building. You will not speak of this meeting and you will not be calling on Kale anymore. Do you understand?" he asked, pulling the guy up by his jacket.

Watson nodded. "I've got it, Mickey. I won't breathe a single word."

"I don't trust you. Therefore, Simon is going to give you a little warning of what could come if you choose to tell anyone about our meeting here." He shoved him in my direction.

Watson stumbled away from me, toward the door. Mick grabbed my arm, pulling me back slightly. "Beat the shit out of him, enough to keep him breathing but not talking," he whispered.

I gave him a swift nod and walked out of the office, leaving any sense of reasoning behind.

Chapter 3

Mackaela

"He looks like he's been doing this awhile," I commented as Simon shut the door behind him. Mickey nodded.

"He's definitely a good fighter. I had him fight with Dom and he held his own. I figured we need more muscle in this place anyhow. If anything, he's good for that."

"So you actually trust him?"

Mickey narrowed his eyes at me.

"Mackaela, not everyone is out to screw us over. I hate that you're so paranoid about people. I mean I get it, but Simon's my brother. He's been through a lot and I couldn't just leave him out on the streets."

"Hey, you're the one that said he was a spoiled brat who abandoned you," I said. "I was just wondering why you'd change your mind so easily."

Mickey smiled. "I guess it's my fault you think the worst. However, he's blood. I need someone to be around when I can't be and clearly I need someone who I can trust to look out for you."

I shook my head. "I'm fine on my own, Mickey. Don't start this bodyguard crap again."

Mickey grabbed my arms gently above the elbows, waiting patiently until I looked him in the eyes. "I'm so sorry for what happened to you tonight. It's always been a fear of mine that you'd be hurt or worse. I was stupid for putting you in the situation in the first place. I've been selfish having you work the field. Maybe it's time for it to end."

"Mickey, who else can you trust but me? Besides, I need the money. Ever since Ashley moved out, I've been strapped for cash. I can't afford that apartment on my own with no income."

"You get money from the deliveries."

I rolled my eyes. "That's a high school kid's job. I don't even know why you have me do that. I could easily just hand you the money myself."

Mickey released my arms and stepped back. "I don't contact who you contact, Mackaela. The guys you work with might follow you. You would lead them straight to me. I can't be implicated if I want to stay off the radar. We have to have a collector."

I knew this already, what bothered me was that it was his brother. I didn't want to trust him. "Why is Simon your collector? What happened to Josh?" I asked.

"That damn kid went and got into college! He said he didn't need the job anymore. Can you believe it?" He smiled.

Mickey loved Josh like a brother. He was a really good kid and had a ton of potential. He just grew up in the wrong part of town and happened hustle to get ahead.

"Simon came in at the right time. I figured collecting was a good starter job for him. Although now we have to do something about Ricky."

I watched as Mickey's eyes darkened, his jaw muscle flexing. Ricky had clearly been lying to him all along. The only reason Ricky was involved in the business so closely at all was because of his relation to Dom who was Mickey's right hand. Dom had been Mickey's best friend in high school. His father was a police officer and that gave Dom some pretty important information on how to stay on top of the game. He had a few family members on the force.

"You can talk to Dom about that. I'm staying out of it."

Mickey laughed. "Oh sure, just hang out for the fun parts," he joked.

I shrugged, giving him a small smile. "You know me."

"I do, better than anyone."

"I'd like to keep it that way, so don't go telling your brother my name, all right?"

"What is that about anyway? You know he'll eventually find out."

"I know, but he seems like the cocky type and it irritates me. I just want to see how far I can push him."

Mickey's brows rose and he shook his head. "Why do you always find a reason to push people away? That is exactly what you did to Ashley," he scolded.

"Ashley started bringing her work home with her and I didn't like random guys in my place. She pushed herself away. And as far as everyone else, well I guess I just don't like people." I shrugged.

"One day, Mackaela, you're going to have no choice but to let someone in. I want you to be happy and forget about what happened in the past." Mickey wrapped his arms around me then in one of his hugs that always made me feel better.

This guy was such a hard ass most of the time. He came off as this badass drug dealer, but he was my best friend, my family, and my home. The thought of anything or anyone else knowing me like he did terrified me. My heart couldn't take any more damage than it already had. I'd be completely broken.

Mickey started making calls to Dom and a few others to organize a meeting that upcoming weekend. He wanted to discuss the recent events involving Ricky. Dom seemed to take things in stride as was usual. He, like Mickey, was tough but had a heart of gold when it came to the ones he cared about.

"I think I'm going to head out," I said.

"That's probably a good idea. You had yourself another busy night, Mackaela."

"More than I'd anticipated," I agreed. "Do you need me tomorrow?"

He shook his head. "Take the next few days off. I'll need you on Thursday to go with me to a club to meet a new dealer that you'll collect from. I'm considering lessening your responsibilities when it comes to certain business dealings now."

"Sounds like a plan." I was in no mood to discuss matters further regarding working with the guys.

Simon walked in suddenly, holding a towel around his right hand. I could see blood soaking through the flimsy white cotton.

"Is Watson taken care of?" Mickey asked.

"He won't be talking for a while." Simon unwound the towel to inspect his swollen knuckles.

"You did a good job tonight. I may have to increase your pay," Mickey said.

"Don't mention it," he mumbled.

I let out a not so subtle yawn as I walked over to the desk, grabbing my purse and jacket. "See you Thursday," I said to Mickey as I started to head out the door.

"Hold on," he said. Frowning, I turned back around. "I don't feel right about Simon kicking Watson's ass and then sending you off into the night alone."

"I'll be fine, Mickey," I protested.

"I have a few more calls to make. Simon, would you mind making sure she gets home safe?"

My eyes widened. What the hell was he doing?

"Not a problem," Simon said, shooting me a smirk. I rolled my eyes.

Of all the times for him to go all protector mode, now was my least favorite. "I have my car, Mickey. Pretty boy is not driving it back here," I said in an irritated tone.

"You think I can't handle your Mustang?" Simon asked, narrowing his eyes at me.

"It's a stick and she's a classic ... so ... no." My car was the one thing I had that was my own. I worked really hard to restore her to her perfect condition the last few years.

"I can handle a stick."

"I'm sure you can, pretty boy. I bet you know how to work all kinds of sticks," I retorted.

He pierced me with a hard gaze. I could tell I hit a nerve.

"Not going to work," Mickey said. "He'll drive your car back here. I'll return it to you in the morning." I glared at my best friend.

Why in the hell was he pressing this?

Too tired to fight it and dying for a shower, I relented even though I wasn't happy about it. I stomped out of the office, through the main loft area, and out the door. I also purposely hit the 'door close' button on the elevator down to the garage so Simon wouldn't ride down with me. Yep, I was petty.

Simon caught up to me once I got to the parking garage, walking beside me silently. I unlocked my car with my key and climbed in the driver's seat. He stood outside the passenger door, waiting for me to unlock it. I could have started the car and drove away, leaving him standing there, but something told me I would pay for it later if I did.

Sighing heavily, I reached over to unlock the door. He got in, glancing at me sideways and shaking his head.

"You're sort of mean," he said with a light chuckle.

"I'm sorry you think that." No I wasn't. I hoped he did think I was mean, and prayed if he thought that, maybe he wouldn't talk to me the rest of the ride.

I started the car, turning up the radio, hinting that I didn't want to talk. As I backed out of the spot, he reached over and turned it down. I froze, my hand gripping the steering wheel tighter. I glanced at him and blew out a frustrated puff of air, shaking my head.

Simon put his hands up defensively. "I just wanted to ask you something, Beautiful."

"What?" I gritted out, keeping my eyes on the road.

"How long have you known my brother?"

I sighed. "Since after you disappeared," I muttered. "Eight years now, I think."

"So, he told you all about me, huh?" I nodded. "What made you get into the business?"

I turned my head slightly to look at him. I didn't want to answer a series of personal questions right now. I was already beginning to crumble from the earlier events and my guard could slip.

"You really want to know, pretty boy?"

"Yep," he replied, drumming with his fingers to the beat of the song that was playing.

I rolled my eyes. "You like The Black Keys?"

He nodded and shot me a mega-watt smile that I'm sure charmed the pants off most girls.

"Do we have something in common?" he asked, feigning shock.

I rolled my eyes again. I wanted to hate him and now we liked similar music. At least he had good taste, I guess.

"So, why are you working with Mick," he pressed on.

I sighed again. He wasn't going to let this go. "Like I said, we grew up together. He kind of always helped me out when I needed it. I owe him for all he's done, so I figured why not work for him."

"Didn't you want to go to college or be something else?" he wondered.

In my peripheral vision, I saw him turn his body toward me. He was really listening. Simon seemed extremely interested in getting to know me. How weird.

"I don't know what you think you see when you look at me, but I'm not really the college type. Plus, I dropped out of high school when I was sixteen." I actually had thought about going back to school, but I wasn't about to share that with him.

Simon nodded. "Gotcha."

"What about you, why are you working for Mickey?" I asked.

"My mom died and a while after that my step-dad kicked me out. I went to prison and had nowhere else to turn. You know that whole song and dance." He sounded so lackadaisical about it,. I shot an incredulous look at him.

"'That whole song and dance.' Like it's common." I scoffed, shaking my head. "What the hell did you go to prison for?"

"Attempted murder," he said in yet another casual tone.

My heart rate spiked a little bit. Mickey let me go alone in a car with this guy, and he'd been in prison for murder? I swallowed the fear that was rising and tried to relax. Surely this was some sort of sick joke.

Simon started laughing.

"What?" I asked, glaring at him.

"I'm sorry, Beautiful, but the look on your face is priceless. I wasn't in jail for that. I just wanted to see your reaction," he admitted. That wasn't cool.

"What were you in for then?" I asked, growing irritated.

"I'm not telling you. You get to keep your secrets; I get to keep mine," he whispered conspiratorially.

"Well as long as you don't kill me or stalk me, we should be good," I responded.

We were nearly to my apartment now, and I was starting to feel the pain of being in heels all night.

"Where did you get this car?" Simon asked after a few moments of silence.

"I bought it at a junkyard when I was seventeen. Mickey and Dom helped me fix it up and restore it."

"Nice, I had a '69 Fastback for a while. I promise I can handle driving her for you."

I glanced at him briefly. "Where's your car now?"

"My step-dad took it. It wasn't worth the trouble to get it back. I'll just build a new one someday."

I pulled into the parking lot of my apartment complex, pulling into my dedicated spot. After killing the ignition, I started to remove the car key from the ring. I lifted my head and glared at Simon.

"If you so much as let a bird shit on her ... " I started to say.

Simon smirked. "I've got it." He held out his hand.

I hesitated for a minute but released my key to him. We both stepped out of the car at the same time.

"Well, thanks for taking me home," I said.

"No problem. Mick wants me to walk you to the door and make sure you're safely tucked inside for the night."

I shrugged and turned on my heel, leading the way up the stairs to my third story apartment. I unlocked the door and opened it, immediately flipping on the switch that was on the wall to the left of the front door.

"Tell Mickey that he better have my car here when I wake up or I'm coming after him."

Simon nodded and smiled. "Sleep well, Beautiful." He winked at me before descending the stairs.

I stood there for a minute with my brow crumpled as he walked away. Something about Simon Silver was different. He had a way of getting under my skin like no one else. I didn't like the way he so easily struck up a conversation with me. Most people were intimidated by me and left me alone.

Releasing a sigh, I locked the front door behind me and kicked off my shoes. I made my way to my bedroom and started undressing after removing the few items of jewelry I wore. Shaking my hair out with my hands, I wandered to the bathroom and brushed my teeth vigorously before starting the shower.

I made sure the water was extra hot as I ambled in, letting the water soak every part of my body. My muscles loosened, my body relaxing as I stood there in the stream, playing what had unfolded that evening. The way Watson pressed himself against me, how he held the knife to my throat. It was the first time in a long time that I'd felt helpless.

I shuddered as I recalled his touch and his lips at my ear saying that I wasn't going anywhere. I shook my head to release the memory as I began washing my hair mechanically. Sometimes I wished I could tell people what happened to me. I didn't like always putting up a front, but there were just some things that were so unforgivable and shameful that I didn't know where to begin to explain. Mickey was the only one who knew everything about me, the good and the bad. He never walked away. That didn't mean other people would be as accepting, though. My fear of appearing weak, being blamed for the things that had happened, was what kept me from opening up to others.

I stepped out of the shower, drying my hair with a towel before wrapping it around my body, and wiping the fog away from the mirror to inspect myself. Without the makeup and clothes, I was simple Mackaela. Not Kale the prostitute, not the pretty delivery girl. When I saw myself in my most natural state, I noticed who I really was. A tall, slender, twenty-one year old woman with scars and a nasty past of violence and unspeakable abuse. I tilted my head, running my index finger from the base of my ear to just below my shoulder, following the long pink burn scar.

There was another one similar to it just under my breast that ran to my hip. I tried to cover up the scars as best as possible, growing out my hair and never wearing a short shirt or bikini. Even when working with the men, I wore corset style lingerie to cover my ribs.

When people saw scars, they asked questions I wasn't prepared to answer. How can you tell someone that your mother set the house on fire by lighting up the curtains in all the rooms of the house? I was asleep when she had done it and thankfully woke up as the curtain's ashes began dropping on me. I didn't come out unscathed of course, but it could have been a lot worse.

I made my way to my bedroom and put on a pair of my comfiest flannel pajama bottoms before donning a tank top, then I crawled up into my tall, king-sized bed. This was the place I felt safest. But the occasional nightmare would come as they seemed to when I was at my lowest. I was sure I'd no doubt be having one tonight after everything that happened.

I tried not to dwell on that at the moment, though it was difficult. Instead, I gazed out my bedroom window at the bright crescent shaped moon. I loved this apartment with the unending view of the city and the mountain and the sky. Loved looking out the windows and, if only for a little while, dreaming of what could be if I were able to face my demons and cast my injustices aside. I sank down into my covers, curling onto my side.

When my eyes closed, I was suddenly seeing those haunting emerald eyes staring back at me. What was it about Simon Silver that mesmerized me? Before long, the green turned to coal black and the screaming came as another man, one who had wronged me years ago, infiltrated my thoughts. Suddenly I was reliving being sixteen years old again, having my innocence taken by a man that my mother told me to trust.

Simon

She was a high school dropout. That didn't seem like a big deal. I could tell she was hiding more from me, but it's not like I could fault her for that. It was obvious she didn't like answering my questions. I felt kind of bad for pressing her, but I was trying to get her to ease up with me. She was someone that my brother cared about which had me curious about her. I also liked engaging with her, even if she was abrasive. Usually the girls I met were a lot more outgoing and talkative. She was different, refreshing. I was intrigued by her.

Maybe it was growing up with a mother that was beaten and resorted to drugs as an escape, but something in me just couldn't resist the protective urge that I felt toward a girl with a broken heart. And this girl clearly had some demons in her closet. I wondered if she ever even opened up to anyone willingly. I was sure that Mick might know more about her, seeing as how they grew up together and were best friends and all.

My cell started ringing, forcing me to turn down the stereo. This Mustang had a damn good system in it. "Hello?"

"Hey, Simon, did you get her home all right?" Mick asked.

"Yep, she's safe and sound."

"Thanks for doing that. I think she was a little shaken from tonight. A client has never tried to attempt that shit before with her."

"Well maybe she shouldn't be doing that anymore. She said she's known you for a long time, man. Why would you want her doing that for you?"

I felt like Mick should be a better friend to her.

"I already have a new plan set. She won't be working the guys anymore," he explained. "I'm just leaving the warehouse right now, meet me at the house."

"Will do," I said before hanging up.

Mick had a pretty nice house just north of Downtown Seattle. It was in a little suburb, which was kind of surprising considering his job description. The house had three bedrooms, so he was letting me stay with him for the time being until I made enough to get my own place. I hadn't expected such hospitality from him, and I was immensely grateful for it.

When I got home, I made my way to the living room and tossed the keys on the coffee table. Mick was sitting on his leather couch with a beer in hand. I went to the fridge, grabbing a beer as well, before joining him on the couch.

"I wanted to talk to you about something." He looked like he was contemplating how to say something to me. I shot him a questioning look. "It's about Mackaela."

"Who?"

Mick's eyes widened. "Fuck." He shook his head, chuckling. "She's going to kill me. I wasn't supposed to tell you her name."

Mackaela. Her name was Mackaela. So Kale had been sort of a shorter version. No doubt she'd be pissed off that I knew. Why did that make me unbelievably happy? I grinned.

"Something tells me you're not joking. What about her?"

"Well for starters, there's some things you should probably know about her. I decided, after the Watson incident tonight and you doing what I asked, that I can trust you."

"Okay ... " I said slowly.

"Mackaela is a bit rough around the edges. The girl hasn't caught a break since she was fourteen and her dad walked out on her and her mom. There's a lot of other shit that happened, but it isn't my story to tell. I just want you to know, she's my best friend and I've been helping her out for a long time. I love her like a sister. I consider her family, more so than you." He shot me a smirk.

I nodded. "I get it. I'm not too sure about you either yet," I admitted.

"After talking to Dom tonight, I found out that Ricky Delgado has been stealing some product from us and claiming to give it to those guys in Olympia that Watson mentioned. Apparently, he was using the drugs he'd stolen and modifying them to expand their longevity. He skipped town within the last few hours and that Hawks guy has a hit out on him."

"What does this have to do with Mackaela?" I asked. It was weird actually using her name.

"I have to take a trip to Olympia and talk to Hawks. We've both been screwed by this asshole so I'm hoping to connect with him. That way there aren't any issues in the future. I need you to look after her while I'm gone."

"I can do that," I said without hesitation. If she meant a lot to my brother, I'd do it.

"Sticking up for family is priority number one. You're proving yourself quite valuable. I appreciate that."

"It's no trouble, Mick. I'm sort of indebted to you anyway. I'd be homeless without you. Not many people want a felon on their payroll. You're helping me out."

"Like I said, family is important," he said. "I don't know exactly when I'll go to Olympia, but it'll be soon. Just keep an eye on her in case Watson comes sniffing around."

"You think he'd do that after what I did to him?"

"I don't know. He can't be trusted and he knows how close she and I are now. I have to think of every possible threat. He could very well harm her to get to me. I just don't want to run the risk."

"I'll do it. No problem."

After squaring things away with Mick, I decided to clean my busted knuckles up and take a shower. The nice thing about the room I was staying in was that it had its own bathroom. I didn't like having to hurt people, but if they deserved it, that was a different story. Watson was a prick and I wasn't going to allow him to talk about Mackaela the way he did. As morbid as it sounded, it was worth it to feel the crunch of his nose under my fist.

I couldn't believe that I finally knew her name. I wondered how she would react when she found out that Mick told me. I needed to find a way to get her to stop calling me "Pretty boy." Maybe my looking out for her would get her to open up a little more.

Chapter 4

Mackaela

I didn't get a restful night's sleep at all and my head hurt. It was nearly seven a.m. and I'd already been up for about two hours. I was sitting in my living room on the old recliner that I bought at a thrift store. It was beat up, but one of my favorite places to sit in the apartment because it was incredibly comfortable. I had it facing the large, long windows that overlooked the heart of the city, including the Space Needle.

I was expecting my car to arrive any minute with Mickey. I wondered if he would hold true to his word about letting me have the next few days off. Sometimes he would have me running around every day for weeks at a time, but I didn't really mind since it kept me busy and helped in avoiding the negative thoughts that consumed me.

There were certain days though where I just needed to be by myself. I liked painting and drawing. When I had the time, I found it was nice to zone out and be creative.

I placed the coffee mug I was holding in my hands on the side table and brought my knees up to my chest, wrapping my arms around them. There was no avoiding the images that were plaguing me from the night before. After what happened with Watson, I knew there wasn't any amount of money in the world that could get me to sell myself again. Being strong-armed and caught off guard shook me more than I thought it would.

I spent most of the night in fits of panic, reliving what happened when I was younger. It was days like these, after hellish nightmares, when I was left alone, that I often thought about what would happen to me in ten years-time when I was in my thirties. Surely Mickey would eventually be running the whole business. He couldn't spend all his time taking care of me. I didn't want him to do that anyway. But I was afraid I'd never find someone, that I'd always be alone.

No man could possibly ever love an ex-prostitute who worked in the illegal drug industry with too many issues beyond repair. I'd either be too distant or totally clingy. Sometimes I thought I should've died the day my mother set the house ablaze. I could have just let the fire consume me, then I wouldn't be so broken now, wouldn't have to feel the lasting effects of being not only abandoned by my father and mother, but also living in fear of every man who looked at me with intrigue in his eye.

It was like everything snowballed in my life, taking a turn for the worse when my father left us. Mom had been a complete wreck when he left. I never expected her to take out her pain on me. I was nearing my sixteenth birthday and my mother was attempting to right herself after being sucker-punched into divorce by my dad. She was working as a waitress at a local diner and had even started dating again. She was seeing this guy, Jason, for a while. I didn't remember much of his face, only that he was that obviously good-looking type. It was his eyes though that stayed with me, a murky brown that seemed to turn black as night sometimes when he looked at me.

I'll never forget the night in June when he was over with a few of his buddies and they were all drinking. I was still haunted by the feel of his rough hands on my body, the sound of his voice as he told me to relax. My mom had allowed the party and was pretty drunk herself. The worst part is that no matter how many times Mickey would tell me that I was a victim and this shouldn't have happened, I blamed myself. I shouldn't have been so vulnerable. I should have known better than to trust him or accept a drink. The memory of that night still crept up on me even though it'd been nearly five years. Some days I didn't think about it at all, other days it ate at my brain like a cancer and the only thing to numb the pain and fear was to stay busy or withdraw with painting and drawing.

When I hear someone call me 'Beautiful,' it makes me cringe, taking me back to that place and time. What guy in his right mind would ever want someone like that?

I was pulled out of my self-deprecating thoughts by the sound of my phone ringing. "Hey, Mickey."

"Hey, Mack, I got your car out here."

"Thanks. I'll come get the keys, just give me a minute."

"Sounds good," he responded before hanging up.

I tossed my phone on the kitchen counter and ran to the bathroom. I was sure my face looked wrecked after my horrible night. I didn't want Mickey to see because as soon as he did, he'd be concerned. I was in no mood to talk about it with him.

Luckily, it was really sunny for seven in the morning, so I splashed some water on my face and adorned my favorite some big rimmed sunglasses. I pulled my hair out of the ponytail it was in, running my fingers through it. It was still cool in the morning and I hadn't thought to grab a sweater as I headed downstairs toward the parking lot, so I crossed my arms, shivering from the slight breeze.

Mickey was leaning against the hood of my car, which was parked in my assigned spot. He was scowling at the ground. As I stepped down from the last stair, he glanced up at me, plastering a fake smile on his face.

"Is everything okay?" I asked. I wasn't fooled.

"Sure, why do you ask?"

I narrowed my eyes at him. "Don't play dumb with me, Mickey Silver. I know when something's bothering you. Did that brother of yours do something?"

"Actually he's proving to be quite helpful. Why are you so bent out of shape about him?" he asked, kicking my bare foot with his booted one.

"I'm not. I just think it's weird that suddenly everything's great between you and him."

"Mackaela, he's my brother, what do you want me to do, just tell him to go rot on the streets?"

Sighing, I said, "I guess not. I just think he's hiding something. Did you know he was in prison?"

Mickey laughed. "Do you really think a stint in prison is going to make me turn him away? What do you think I do for a living, sell kittens?"

"I'm well aware of the business, Mickey," I snapped.

"I actually had a long talk with Simon last night. I think he's great for us right now. He can fight, he's damn near fearless. He didn't leave anything out when he told me what happened to him in the past. I know you think he grew up rich and spoiled because that's what I told you. It isn't the case though. He actually went through some serious shit. Makes my life look like a damn Disney movie in comparison," he said.

"What did he go to jail for?"

"He was wrongly accused of armed robbery by his step-father." Mickey shrugged.

"Oh.," That wasn't nearly as bad as attempted murder.

Though he did have possession of a firearm. Would he shoot someone if need be? I wondered what it could be that was so dark about Simon's past that made Mickey's seem easy. Sure Mickey had a drug dealer dad and his mother was never around, but Jack never disowned him and his mom died when he was too young to really remember. Simon mentioned his step-dad taking his car. If he'd also accused him of robbery, maybe he was mean in other ways toward Simon. A small part of my heart ached at the thought. I felt bad for him and also oddly connected in a way. I knew what it was like to have a parent that hated you.

"You should know I'm going out of town for the weekend. I've received some new developments last night on Hawks. It turns out Ricky was a nark and a thief who was using both of us."

"What are you going to do?" I asked.

"I'm going to Olympia so I can talk to Hawks. I'll see if we can work something out since we both have similar interest in finding Ricky."

"Is Dom holding things down while you're gone?"

"Yeah. We don't know where Ricky is though, so I'm going to need you to lay low for a while." I understood what he meant. Anytime there was fallout with someone in the business, Mickey feared it would somehow result in my getting hurt.

Everyone knew how close we were and how much he cared about me. It made both the girls and the guys jealous at times. Mickey was concerned that one day there might be a chance I'd be used as a pawn to get him to break down. Maybe that was the reason for his sullen expression earlier.

I nodded. "I can do that."

Mickey's car pulled into the lot, parking behind mine. I looked through the windshield to see Simon driving. He left the car running, putting it in park before stepping out. He was wearing dark jeans and a black t-shirt that showed off the biceps and chest muscles I hadn't realized he had. He was leaner than Mickey, but he wasn't scrawny by any means. His brown hair was gelled in a disheveled way, making him look rugged and good looking. He was wearing a pair of dark aviator sunglasses so I couldn't see his eyes, which I was grateful for.

My stomach fluttered when he spoke to me. "Hey, Beautiful," he said with a smirk as he approached us.

What was it about this guy that I found myself faltering and unable to keep my mind straight? I rolled my eyes behind my large shades and pursed my lips. "Morning, pretty boy," I shot back coldly.

"Well, we better head out," Mickey said. He stepped toward me, wrapping his arms around my waist, hugging me close to him. "I'll check in with you later. Call me if you need anything," he said quietly.

I nodded as I hugged him back. It was apparent the sunglasses didn't do the trick. Mickey was always able to read me like a book. The nice thing was he didn't question me about what was wrong. I didn't wait for Mickey and Simon to drive away before heading back up to my apartment.

Simon

She haunted me all night. I fell asleep with her face on my mind, even dreamed of her. However, in my dream she was smiling, something I had yet to see her do in real life. Even when Mick hugged her, I thought she would have some sort of positive reaction. Yet she seemed cold and calculated, as if she didn't want to give anything away.

I didn't hear what he said to her. I wondered if he saw something in her that I was missing. To me, she looked good. Hell, she was gorgeous even standing there in flannel pants and a tank top with her hair messy in loose waves that blanketed her chest.

"I have a meeting with one of my dealers. You down to tag along?" Mick asked as he pulled out of the parking lot. "After that, we need to go to the dealership."

I shot him a questioning look. "The dealership?"

"Yeah, you need a ride. I'm not letting you roll around in my car anymore since I'm going to need it this weekend."

I hadn't made nearly enough in the last week to afford a new car, maybe a beater off of Craigslist. Certainly not anything from a car dealership. "Mick, I've only been working for you one week," I started to protest.

"So what? I'm buying you a car, bro. Consider it back-owed Christmas presents," he said, grinning.

"Are you sure you trust me enough to do that? What if I take the car and bail?" I asked with a grin.

Mick just shook his head. "You wouldn't do that. I can tell you're trustworthy. Not everybody would spill their guts about a past like yours and be willing to help however needed."

"Mick, I didn't tell you all that shit about my past so that you'd feel sorry for me. I just need to get on my feet, then I'll be out of your hair."

"I don't feel sorry for you. I simply realized that I didn't have it so bad growing up. I mean yeah, I've never had a mother, but after seeing the fear in Mackaela's eyes from the situation with Watson and knowing her story and yours, I think I got through life pretty easy."

He shot me a sideways glance. "Look, I'm not saying you have to stay in the business forever, I know I don't want that for Mackaela. Last night solidified it. She isn't going to want to work the men anymore and honestly, after her state this morning I think she needs a breather."

I arched a brow at him. "What do you mean her state?" I asked. "She seemed her normal, unpleasant self." I was joking. I didn't know her well enough to judge her everyday demeanor but based on the last twelve hours or so that I knew her, she was definitely prickly.

"No, she was upset. I can tell. When you've known a girl as long as I have, you understand their cues. I can tell when she's angry or upset just by looking at her. She's had it rough. You probably can't even imagine the issues of her childhood. I've always worried about her, and with this fallout with Ricky and Watson, I'm afraid I'm the one who messed up her life even further. She could be in school or hanging out with better people. I wonder if she'd open up more and gain some independence if she could trust in someone else besides me. Selfishly, I've kept her around for my own piece of mind. Until last night, I wasn't thinking about what I was doing to her by having her work for me. It isn't right." Mick's voice broke in conviction.

I could hear the emotion in his voice and I was amazed by it. He loved her and only wanted the best for her. However, all he knew was this life, what he'd been dealt. I wondered if he'd leave the business and move on at some point. If he'd want something more than being Jack Silver's son with money and power and un-limited women forever.

"Why wouldn't she just leave? She doesn't seem like the type of person who lets anyone control her. Doesn't she want to be in the business with you?" I asked.

Surely she wouldn't stick around just because they were friends? Last night she'd said that Mick helped her out a lot and she owed him. Was this her way of paying him back? Even if it made her angry or scared, she would she sell herself and get in potentially dangerous situations to repay a friend? Did she really think she wasn't worth more or that she couldn't do better? I found that hard to believe, although I was beginning to think I was the one who was clueless to what this really was about for my brother and Mackaela.

"I think she thinks she has to work for me. She won't leave me because she's scared shitless of what might happen to her if I'm not around. It gets a little overwhelming sometimes, having to worry about her. I love her, don't get me wrong, but I don't know. Maybe she needs counseling or someone else to talk to," Mick said quietly.

Of course, I had that inner conscience in me to want to help Mackaela, and I wanted to help my brother, too. "I'm here for you both. Whatever you need me to do, Mick. I already said I would look out for her while you're away."

Mick let out a breath. "Thanks, man, it feels good to actually talk to someone about this." He was silent for a few beats before smirking at me. "Now don't tell anybody about this little heart to heart or I'll kick your ass!"

I snorted. "Yeah right, you kick my ass? That's hilarious," I teased and punched his arm. We both laughed, and just like that the atmosphere was suddenly less intense.

I felt my heart swell a little at the comradery between my brother and me. It felt like we were starting to form little pieces of that bond that'd broken all those years ago. In that moment, I realized that I missed him more than I ever thought before.

Chapter 5

Mackaela

I stood in the living room at my painting easel. The mid-day sun was coming in through the vast windows of my apartment, warm and bright. I wanted to purge everything from my mind. I didn't want to think about Ken Watson anymore or the man from my past. I couldn't think about my mother and the sorrow I'd been subjected to. I hated feeling broken, refused to be treated like a victim by myself or anyone else. So here I was, my shorts and t-shirt covered in watercolor splotches, with a brush in my hand.

I was working on a landscape. For my inspiration, I was using a picture clipped to the edge of the easel that my mother had taken on one of our trips to the Oregon coast many years ago. I missed the time I used to share with her back when things were innocent and carefree. A time when everything seemed brighter and the possibilities were endless. It was nice to have this time to myself where I could work out all of my sadness and anger. I spent the entire day working on the painting.

By ten o'clock, it was completed. I stretched, rolling my neck and wrists to loosen the stiff muscles. Grabbing all of the brushes I used and the wooden palette, I took them to the sink to rinse them off. Just as I finished rinsing the last brush, my hands still wet, my cell phone began ringing. I turned the faucet off and grabbed the dishtowel at the stove to dry my hands before grabbing my phone off the counter.

It was an unavailable number and my first instinct was to just let it go to voicemail. Once a month or so, I would get a call from the treatment center where my mother was staying. Maybe she'd successfully found a way to block the number so I'd answer. She would call to "check in," but it always resulted in her yelling at me for her being there and begging me to come get her out. She blamed me for her current situation and thought I had the power to release her. I didn't.

My mother was admitted to a psychiatric hospital after the fire incident. I hadn't physically seen her since the morning after she nearly killed me. I hadn't spoken to her in months. She was carried away on a stretcher by EMTs while shouting how much she hated me, saying it was my fault that no man wanted her. At the time, I didn't cry or yell. I just stood there and listened to her shouting obscenities at me while I was in a daze. Everything happened so fast that I didn't seem to have the ability to process it all at once. Thinking back on it now, there were a few things that I could have said at the time. I could have defended myself or blamed her or called her names back, but I didn't. What good would it have done me to say things that I may just end up regretting anyway? I refused to feed her anger or give her more reasons to think of me as the worst child in the world. I didn't like to deal with her.

The shrill ringing continued and I let out a shaky breath as I pressed the answer button on the screen. "Hello?"

"Mackaela Stone?" a man's voice asked. His tone was clipped, business like. It startled me.

"This is she," I replied cautiously.

"This is Dr. Clark from Harborview Medical Center. We have your mother, Lindsey, here."

My heart began pounding against my rib cage. What was my mother doing at the actual hospital and why was this doctor calling me? The treatment facility my mother stayed at was just outside of town and had medical facilities on site. If she was at Harborview, something bad must have happened.

"What did she do?" I wasn't that close with my mom anymore, but I knew her well enough to assume she may have attempted something.

"It appears that she overdosed on medication. She's unresponsive and they're currently working on getting her stabilized. We need you to come down here since you're listed as her next of kin. In case something happens."

I felt all of the air leave my body as I absorbed what Dr. Clark was telling me. My mother could possibly die. I didn't know how to feel about that to be honest. My head was spinning. I wanted to scream in frustration at her for putting me through one more thing. Would this ever end? And if it did, would it make things better? Despite the way I was treated, I didn't want to think she'd be gone forever.

"All right, I'm on my way. Where is she?"

"She's in the operating room right now. Just come in through the main entrance when you get here. I'll notify the desk staff that you will be here."

"Okay. Thank you, Dr. Clark." I hung up and grabbed at my hair, tugging it slightly as my fingers ran through it.

Damn it! What was wrong with the woman that she felt it necessary to try and end her life? How in the hell did she get ahold of enough medication to overdose in the first place? What kind of facility allowed something like this to happen? I was pissed off and terrified. What if the next time I saw my mother it was the last time? A wave of nausea washed through me as I went to my room to grab a pair of jeans and fling them on.

I pulled on a hoodie before gathering my keys and purse, making a split second decision to call Mickey as I walked out the door. His phone rang four times before going to voicemail. I left him a message letting him know where I was headed and explained what the doctor had told me.

As soon as I arrived at Harborview, I went up to the front desk and asked them where my mother's room was. I was directed to go up the elevators to the sixth floor. All that I knew so far was that my mother was still being stabilized and Dr. Clark would meet me with further information. My heart was beating furiously in my chest. I wondered if it was due to the fear that I had for my mother or the anger toward her. And that made me feel both guilty and sad. As soon as I stepped off the elevator, I was greeted by a tall man with graying hair.

"Miss Stone?" he asked. I nodded and he brought his hand out for me to shake.

I took it reluctantly before asking, "How is she?"

Dr. Clark offered me a small smile then motioned with his hand toward a waiting area. "Why don't you have a seat, Miss Stone?" His voice was cautious.

I instantly felt tears pricking my eyes as I tried to swallow the lump forming in my throat. Was this really happening? I sat in the uncomfortable blue plastic chair and began chewing on the inside of my cheek. I wished that Mickey were here right now. I didn't want to face this alone. I knotted my fingers together in my lap, letting my gaze meet the doctor's. I could tell in his eyes that he was reluctant to speak. He looked apologetic.

"It seems that the medication your mother took was a mix of a sleep aid pill and pain reliever. The combination of the two caused her heart to slow down to a dangerous level." Oh god. What had she done? "We were unable to pump her stomach, let alone stabilize her in time. I'm sorry to tell you ... that we lost her."

Nothing in life can prepare you for the feelings that consume you when you're told that somebody you love has died. It's like a mixture of anger, sorrow, and defeat. Your chest feels as if your heart is literally breaking in two and you can't breathe. You want to scream and cry and demand that somebody explain why this happened and how to fix it. But you can't. Or at least I couldn't do that. My body froze. All the things I wanted to say and all of the times I thought of going to see her replayed in my mind. A sudden pang of guilt rooted as I thought about the last time I'd spoken to her. It hadn't ended well.

I was selfish, unforgiving, and now all I was left with was a shattered heart and regret for letting it eat at me this long without doing anything about it. I thought all this time I was protecting myself by not letting anyone in. Somehow, I felt lonelier now and the solitude sent a sharp pain to my chest. "Is there anyone you need to call?" Dr. Clark asked, pulling me out of my thoughts.

"No. I'm her only family." There was of course my father, but I hadn't heard from him in years so I figured he didn't need to be notified right away. I wasn't even really sure if I could stomach talking to him at the moment anyway.

"Your mother is being cleaned up. You can see her if you'd like," Dr. Clark offered.

That was one of the things I never understood about some people. To me, when someone is dead, they're gone and their spirit is no longer here. A person isn't the body that lies there cold and hollow. A person is the soul that carries that body. Maybe it's morbid curiosity or maybe some honestly think their loved one can still hear them. Personally, I wouldn't want to willingly view a dead body. Not even my own mother's.

"No, thank you, doctor, I don't need to see her." My voice came out hoarse. I realized I was on the verge of breaking down.

"That's okay, Miss Stone. I'll talk to the treatment facility and check on what preparations your mother had for when she passed. I may need you to sign some paperwork so if you can stay here for now ... " Dr. Clark patted my hand as he stood from his seat and walked away.

My hands were shaking. The tears were bound to slip at any moment. I could feel them hot and unyielding, rising against my eyes. I peered up at the standard wall clock on the sterile white walls of the waiting room. It was nearly eleven-thirty at night.

I grabbed my cell phone out of my pocket to check for any text messages or calls. I had a text, but I didn't recognize the number.

Unknown Number: Wanted to give you my number just in case - Simon

Just a simple text message sent around ten-thirty. I didn't reply back because there was nothing for me to say. I wasn't going to talk to him about this. I took a deep breath and stood, clutching my phone tightly. I was about to try calling Mickey again, but he beat me to it.

"Perfect timing, I need to tell you something," I said as I answered.

"Mackaela, what's going on?" I could hear the concern in his voice.

Immediately, I squeezed my eyes shut, trying to stop the tears from falling. It didn't help. Several leaked out from the corners of my eyes. Damn it. "She's dead, Mickey." I choked back a sob. "My mom is dead."

I heard him let out a slow breath from the other end of the line. "Mackaela, I'm so sorry. Are you still at the hospital?"

"Yeah, I have to wait for the moment. The doctor might need me to sign papers."

"Shit! I wish I could be there with you. I'm in Bellevue, heading into a meeting. I might be an hour or more."

I shook my head, even though he couldn't see it. "Don't worry about it, Mickey." It would have been nice to have him here while I was on the verge of hysterics, but I knew that by the time he got here I would already be a mess.

I just wanted to go home. I needed to curl up in bed and let out all the sorrow and helplessness I felt. Dr. Clark came walking down the hall, approaching me with a plastic bag in one hand.

"Hey, I've got to go, Mickey. I'll call you when I'm home, okay?"

"All right, Mackaela, I love you."

I felt a tear roll down my cheek. I mumbled back a "You too," before hanging up. Dr. Clark handed me the plastic bag and told me that it had my mother's belongings in it.

A few pieces of jewelry and her slippers were all that was left of her. The nightgown she wore had to be removed due to her aspirating on it. I thanked him as well as I could. He told me that I was free to leave. There was nothing left for me here anymore. I was relieved to get the hell out of there and as I exited the wide glass doors of the hospital, I felt my resolve slipping more and more.

By the time I made it back to my car, I had tears streaming down my face. I managed to get the door unlocked before falling into the driver's seat. I didn't even close the door as the sobs broke free from my throat. I threw my arms around the steering wheel, letting my head fall against it. I couldn't contain it anymore, so I gave into the anger, the grief, and everything else that was inside of me.

Simon

Mick called to tell me that Mackaela was at Harborview Medical Center because her mother had just died. I was on my way there now, my mind racing frantically. I didn't know how she would react to seeing me. I wasn't sure if she wanted the company or just wanted to be alone, but I couldn't sit and do nothing if she needed someone.

When my own mom died when I was sixteen, I just sat there, holding her hand and trying to demand that God let her come back to me. I wasn't even coherent to other people. When they finally made me leave her side, I had to be dragged away. The pain of losing a parent, no matter what mistakes they made, was earth shattering.

While navigating through the nearly empty parking lot, I noticed her Mustang with the driver's side open, sitting in a space directly under a street lamp. I pulled in beside the car and got out immediately. Her body was hunched over the steering wheel, her shoulders shaking uncontrollably. I heard soft sobs as I came around the car and stepped within the open door.

Slowly, I reached my hand out onto her slender shoulder. I was afraid to frighten her, but the gnawing urge to console her outweighed any trepidation. Her head shot up and she peered up at me through swollen, tear soaked eyes. Initially she looked at me with a mixture of shock and confusion, but then her face fell and she was crying more. It made my chest hurt to see the pain she was feeling. I knew that pain all too well. I crouched down so that I could look at her straight on.

"Mick sent me," I said quietly. She nodded once as another sob came out when she tried to speak. "Shh ... It's okay. Let it out,"

I whispered softly as I brushed a strand of matted hair off her cheek and tucked it behind her ear.

More tears began flowing from her usually golden eyes, and then she surprised me. Abruptly, she extended her arms, wrapping them around my neck, pulling me tightly into her. Her head fell to my shoulder as she wept. We sat like that for a long time, her arms around me, clinging to me as if one of us may float away. My hands gently stroked down her back and through her hair.

I tried to soothe her as best I could. Mackaela needed a sense of security at the moment while she grieved for her unbearable loss. Eventually, she quieted and her grip around me loosened. As she sat back to wipe her eyes I stood back up, stretching my legs. Neither of us spoke for a while. I stood there patiently.

"Thank you for ... for being here." Mackaela spoke so softly that I almost didn't hear her.

"No problem." I watched her face closely, trying to figure out what might be going on in her head. "I know you probably don't want to hear this right now, but I'm sorry."

She only nodded as she stared at the steering wheel. Again, a silence fell between the two of us.

"I need to go home. I need to get as far away from this place as possible right now," she finally said.

Her head turned up and our eyes locked. "I don't know why you're here. I haven't been nice to you since the moment we met. I hate to ask any more of you, but would you mind following me home, Simon?" Her eyes were clouded with more tears, her voice thick with emotion.

She was right, she hadn't been nice at all since we met, but I wasn't the type of person to hold that against her. Considering what she was currently going through, I felt sorry for the girl. There was no way I could be mad at her or tell her no. Especially when she looked up at me with such sorrow.

Gazing into her eyes, I formed a small smile, saying, "I'm here because I want to be and yes, I'll make sure you get home safe."

I watched as her face showed a brief sign of relief and then she looked down with her brow furrowed.

"Can you call Mickey for me? Tell him to meet me at my place?"

"Sure thing, I was supposed to call him as soon as I got a hold of you anyway." I stepped back as she started the car up and placed my hand on the top of the door. "You sure you're okay to drive?" I asked, suddenly thinking that maybe it would be better to just offer her a ride instead.

"I think I'll be okay." She reached out to grab the door.

I offered a single nod before stepping out of the way and returning to my car. I waited until she pulled out and followed close behind her as we headed toward her apartment.

Mick was just getting into town after cutting his meeting in Bellevue short and had already planned on heading to Mackaela's apartment when I called him. He asked how she was holding up. I told him that it was about as good as it could be in this type of situation. I really didn't know her well enough to judge if she was being more emotional than her usual self or not. To be honest, I thought she was keeping pretty calm considering the events.

I pulled into an empty parking space alongside her Mustang. She hadn't opened her door yet, so I got out and walked over to the driver's side of her car. She looked up at me through the window, fresh tears streaming down her pale cheeks. I pulled her door open immediately and placed my hand on hers, which was still clutching the steering wheel.

"Mick is on his way, let's get you inside." She took the keys out of the ignition, glancing to the seat beside her. Her purse sat there, along with a plastic hospital bag that I figured must have contained her mother's belongings.

Without thinking, I removed my hand from hers and reached across, grabbing the items. I heard a small whimper escape her throat. "Let's get you inside," I repeated, cupping my free hand around her elbow.

Her grip loosened on the steering wheel as she let me guide her out of the car. Her body collapsed into me, so I wound my arm around her waist to support her. It was after midnight, so she was probably physically and emotionally exhausted.

As soon as we got to the door, she mumbled something about keys and then her hand came out and dangled them in front of me. I quickly unlocked the door, kicking it closed behind us with my boot. I set the keys, the bag, and her purse on the kitchen counter as she made her way to the living room. Suddenly, the front door opened and Mick immediately rushed to Mackaela's side. She broke down again as Mick wrapped his arms around her, pulling her close to him.

I stood there with my hands in my pockets. I was no longer needed here.

"Thank you for taking care of her," Mick whispered.

"No problem, bro. I'm going to head out. Call me if you need anything."

"Thanks, Simon, I really appreciate it."

I offered a quick smile and let myself out.

As I walked down the steps to my new car that Mick had purchased for me earlier this afternoon, I felt off balance. It was as if a piece of me was drifting away the further I got from Mackaela. My legs didn't want to move. I had to force myself to take each step. It didn't feel right leaving her like this. I wished I could be the one who held her right now, consoling her.

Something shifted between us tonight, or at least it did for me. She took a piece of my heart and I didn't think I'd want that piece back, ever.

Chapter 6

Mackaela

My eyes shot open and then squinted at the bright sunshine temporarily blinding me. I let them glide open slower this time as I took in my surroundings. I was lying in my bed, wrapped up in my gray comforter. When I sat up, my head instantly began pounding. It felt like my skull was about to rip open. I groaned and let my head fall back against the pillow. I stared up at the ceiling as the night came back to me like a vicious living nightmare. I lost my mother. A woman who I hadn't physically seen in four years, who I hadn't spoken to in months. And now she was dead. I was left with words unsaid and a broken heart that was far beyond repair. I must have cried all of my tears out last night because my eyes felt swollen. The skin around them was tight from drying out.

I replayed the call from Dr. Clark, the moment he told me my mother had died when I got to the hospital. It was like a punch to my heart, stomach, and throat all at once. I remembered going to my car and breaking down, feeling in that moment that the world was caving in on me. Simon had showed up somehow. Probably because Mickey asked him to. He comforted me. A man who had only known me a short time, who didn't seem at all like the sympathetic type, comforted me. I

66

managed to cover his t-shirt and shoulder in snot and tears, yet he remained, letting me cling to him for support that I so desperately needed until I was calm enough to breathe again. He even followed me home. I didn't remember Simon leaving after Mickey showed up. A new set of tears had worked their way out when he appeared and wrapped his arms around me.

The last thing I remembered was laying down, curled into Mickey's side on my couch in the living room. I was still dressed in my jeans and t-shirt from last night. Mickey walked into my room then, his face solemn as he studied me carefully.

"Thanks for staying with me." My voice came out gravelly and hoarse.

Mickey smiled and approached my bed, sitting down at the end of it. "I wasn't about to leave you alone. How do you feel?" His hand began rubbing my leg from above the comforter.

Shrugging, I said, "It still doesn't seem real, but the pain is there." I let out a staggered sigh.

"It'll probably take some time before the pain lessens. There are still days that I miss my own mother terribly." His eyes locked on mine, he knew my pain and that made me feel a little better. Of course, he never got to know his mother, so it was different.

He understood me in a way and I suddenly felt incredibly lucky to have him in my life. He always said that he never re-membered much about her, but the fact that he didn't have a mother around growing up was hard on him. I think it was one of the reasons that he resented Simon, or at least he used to. Simon ...

My gaze fell from Mickey's and I looked down at the com-forter, my brow furrowing slightly. "Will you tell Simon thanks for being there?" My voice was nearly a whisper.

I felt Mickey grab my leg and squeeze gently. "Are you warming up to him?" he teased and winked at me.

I rolled my eyes. "Please, I just don't know what I would have done had he not been there. He ... didn't have to do that, you know?"

Mickey smiled, saying, "I guess my brother is better than you thought. When I called to ask him to go to you, he didn't even hesitate in agreeing. I think he was in his car and on his way before we even hung up."

The thought of that made my heart do a funny flip-flop thing. Hearing him confirm just how good of a guy he thought Simon was made me feel bad for giving him such a hard time. If Simon was important to Mickey, and caring enough to console a stranger, then I guess maybe I could give him a shot. Or at least try.

"I suppose I need to make some calls and figure out what to do."

Mickey watched me with a speculative glance.

"You can stay in bed if you want. I can call whoever it is."

I immediately began shaking my head. "No, it's all right, I don't want to lie around and dwell on this, Mickey. I don't want to think about all of the things that are bothering me right now." Getting out of bed, I began grabbing some clothes from my dresser before making my way to the bathroom. *Just keep moving.* That's what I always did. *Don't focus on the negativity. Let it go.* "If you want, you can make me some coffee though." I shot a grin at him and his lips curved up to match my own.

"I can do that," he said and then stepped closer to me. I closed my eyes as he ran a hand through my hair and placed a soft kiss on my forehead.

I knew that it was going to be okay eventually and having Mickey here with me was the best thing for me right now. He was always here when I needed him. After taking an extraordinarily hot shower, I dressed in a pair of yoga pants and a tank top. I decided to forgo the hair and makeup thing as my eyes were still pretty puffed up from crying and my heart just wasn't in it.

I was walking down my narrow hallway when I heard Mickey's voice. I stepped into the kitchen and saw him, sitting on the counter speaking to someone on his phone. His hazel eyes met mine and with a quick smile, he pointed to the coffee pot that was full of wonderful caffeine.

"Yeah, I get what you're saying, Dom, but I don't see any reason not to believe it." So Mickey was talking to Dom, I wondered what about as I poured some vanilla creamer into my mug. "Yeah, I got the number for Hawks. I'll give him a call in a while." Ah, Ricky, of course. I wondered if they had found that slime ball yet.

I turned around to face Mickey, peering at him over the rim of my coffee mug. "She's doing okay for now," he said with a wink at me.

Dom was like a brother to me, like Mickey was. His girlfriend Sadie and I were almost friends. I say almost because I never get close to anyone, not even wonderful, understanding and genuine people like Sadie. I engaged in the small chatter of basic conversations whenever she was around, but I just couldn't open up to her fully.

Sadie and Dom had been together for a few years and she just found out she was pregnant. For being a big muscled and tattooed guy, Dom seemed over the moon about the news. He was such a softy sometimes, and it just went to show that you can't judge a book by its cover.

Who am I kidding though? I judge a book on everything from its size, to its cover, and all the pages. I'm incredibly selective about who I even choose to engage with in eye contact most of the time. Thinking about the fact that my mother was gone and how I didn't get the chance to ever speak with her, tugged at my heart. It made me now wonder if I'd been completely unfair to everyone around me. I'd separated myself, shut the world around me down. I didn't really mind before, but now I didn't like it.

My phone ringing brought me out of my thoughts and I jumped slightly at the sound before walking to the opposite end of the counter to retrieve it. It was the treatment facility. My stomach turned as last night came to the forefront of my mind again.

"Hello?"

"Good afternoon, Miss Stone. This is Margo from Open Arms. We would like you to come down here at your earliest convenience." Margo's voice was casual and not at all laced with sympathy. She must have been used to these kinds of things.

"Sure, what for?" I asked. I could hear Margo rustling papers from her end of the line before she began speaking.

"Well, we need to have you sign some release forms to the state letting them know your mother is no longer with us. We also have some belongings here."

"Okay, when do I need to be there?"

"Whenever you're available is fine, no need to rush. Does to-morrow morning work for you?"

"Sure, I can be there at ten."

"Perfect, we will see you then, Miss Stone." I let out a slow breath as Mickey stepped beside me, nudging my shoulder with his own.

"What was that about?" he asked softly.

"Just paperwork stuff, collecting belongings and all that at the treatment place."

"Are you okay with going?"

I knew what he was doing, trying to get a feel for how I was coping so far. I didn't like to appear weak in front of others, including him. I bottled things, as Mickey said, and I usually waited until I was prompted before saying how I felt. I shrugged again, taking another sip of my coffee.

"Of course it isn't what I want to be doing, but I know that I have to. I would rather just get it over and done with, to be honest."

"I get that, Mackaela," Mickey said as he sighed and then pinned me with an apologetic look. I narrowed my eyes, waiting for him to speak. "I have a meeting to be at tomorrow. I feel really shitty about you going by yourself."

To be honest, I was a little crushed to find out that he couldn't go with me, but I knew he had stuff to do. If he could get out of it, he would.

"Don't worry about it, Mickey," I said quietly.

"I don't really want you to go through any of this alone. I know you have feelings you want to get out. I just think it best if ... " Mickey trailed off, causing me to look up at him with wary eyes.

"What do you think, Mickey? Do you think I'm going to try and kill myself or something?" I was irritated that he would think that of me. He should know better.

He instantly shook his head and tried to back pedal. "No, it isn't that at all." He stared at me, concern in his eyes. "I just don't feel right about leaving you when you need me. I can imagine what you're feeling. I just want to make sure you're okay."

"Thanks, Mickey, but you can't be around me all the time and I can handle this on my own. I need to." I stood a little taller with my statement.

I'd relied on Mickey a lot over the years, and recently I had wanted to try gaining some independence. Handling things that needed to be taken care of after my mother died independently was sort of exactly what I needed.

"Mickey, I want to do this by myself," I clarified, looking into his hazel eyes. My voice was steady and sure.

"Okay, that's okay, too. I guess I just feel like I need to look out for you even more now."

"I'm a twenty-one year old woman, Mickey. I need to look out for myself. I can't depend on you all the time. It bothers me to need you to help me out so much," I admitted.

"I've noticed. You've been pulling away more lately." He looked down at the floor before sliding his gaze to mine again. An amused smirk graced his lips. "Are you ... Are you breaking up with me?" Mickey asked in mock outrage, his hand coming up over his heart.

I rolled my eyes and punched his arm. "You know that could never happen. You're too far under my skin, Silver."

"Simon said something the other night, questioning why I would make you be a part of the business. I think he looks at you and sees something more. I see that too, Mackaela. You know if you wanted to go back to school or do something else with your life, you could."

Simon was concerned about me being in the business? Why would he care? I wasn't worried that Mickey would be mad if I left, but I was afraid of being out in a new world, out of my comfort zone that I had created for the past few years. The thought of moving on was appealing yet terrifying.

"I know that, Mickey, and I appreciate Simon's concern. As far as me going to school or something, I just don't know if I'm quite ready for that yet."

Mickey raised an eyebrow at me. "You can't really prepare yourself for life, Mackaela. You just have to take every day one step at a time and hope for the best possible outcome."

"I know. I have so many issues to work through. I just don't know how to be a people person."

"Maybe you should get into counseling or something. It might help you out to talk to someone else besides me." I understood fully what Mickey was saying and I wasn't at all offended by his suggestion.

I let out a sigh. "I've thought about it. I'm just ... undecided."

Mickey put an arm around me, pulling me into his side. "Not that I don't love being your best friend, but I want to see you happy again. Like you were when we were younger, before all the shit."

I let my head rest against Mickey's chest, feeling the tears well in my eyes. "I want that too, Mickey," I whispered. "More than anything."

Chapter 7

Mackaela

My alarm clock was blaring with its god awful high-pitched shriek. I groaned, not wanting to open my eyes as I whipped my arm out to swat at the damn thing. I ended up in contact with a face instead; Mickey's face.

"What the fuck?" he moaned.

My eyes flew open and I sat up. "Sorry, I didn't realize you were still here." I reached over, carefully this time, to hit the button on the top of the clock radio. He'd offered to stay with me again last night and while I wanted to be more independent, the company kept my thoughts from overtaking me.

Mickey rubbed his face and gave me a sideways glance. "Yeah right. I bet you hit me on purpose. I'm not used to this kind of treatment when in bed with a girl." He was still nursing his cheek. I stifled a laugh.

"Yeah, well, I'm not the kind of girl you usually share a bed with. I know all about you and I'm sure you've deserved that smack a time or two."

Mickey rolled his eyes.

"Fair enough," he said and rolled out of the bed.

"I'll make some coffee if you want to shower. You have some spare clothes in the other bedroom," I told him as I wandered to the door.

Mickey yawned loudly. "Thanks, Mackaela."

I gave him a quick "Yep," before making my way to the kitchen.

I knew that today was going to be a big day for me. As I made the coffee, I promised myself that I would try hard to stay positive and not let myself get down if I could help it. I was a little apprehensive about taking on the things that went with my mother passing like paperwork, sorting any belongings she had, and burial plans. However, if I could just stay strong and get through this, I'd be heading in the right direction.

After Mickey showered and dressed, I followed suit and did the same. It was going on eight o'clock. I knew that I needed to leave within a half hour to get to the treatment facility on time. It was just outside of town, about thirty minutes away, but with it being a weekday morning I didn't know what traffic would be like. Honestly, the sooner I got this over with, the better.

I walked out to the living room, my sandals in hand when I heard Mickey on the phone.

"Yeah, pick me up in about fifteen minutes. We'll talk more about it when I see you." He hung up abruptly.

"Isn't your car here?" I wondered as I slipped a foot into my sandal.

"Yeah, but I want to check on you again before I head out of town so Simon is picking me up for the meeting."

"Okay." I straightened and went to my purse on the kitchen counter.

I began going through my wallet, making sure I had all of my identification if they asked for it. I pulled my phone off the charger next to my purse and noticed the little blue light blinking. I had a missed call and a voicemail. When I checked the number, my heart began pounding.

My father had called me. The man who chose to walk out on me and my mom's life, seven years ago. The man who started the avalanche that caused my life to spin out of control into one giant shit filled snowball. I hadn't heard a word from him since my seventeenth birthday, the same year I moved in with Mickey. The year after the horrible things happened with my mother. He knew what she did to me, he knew what happened since he'd left, but he never did a thing about it. Not once did he offer to have me stay with him and his bimbo new wife in Auburn. He never called to check in and see how I was doing, whether I was alive or dead in some gutter. Not. A. Single. Damn. Time. My jaw clenched as my heart hammered in my chest.

"What is it?" Mickey wondered. He must have picked up on my tension.

"My dad called me."

Mickey knew how I felt without asking. He nodded in understanding and placed an arm around my shoulder. "Do you think he knows?" he asked.

I shrugged., "I have no clue how he would, but I don't know any other reason why he'd call."

"Let it go for now, Mackaela. You have other things to do today. Just put him on the back burner." Mickey grabbed his wallet and keys off the counter.

He was right. I didn't have time to talk to my dad right now. I had to go take care of everything that he couldn't because he left us to our own devices. He could wait on me; he would wait on me. I wasn't even going to listen to the voicemail yet. I threw my phone in my purse and slung it over my shoulder.

With a quick hug goodbye and a "Good luck" from Mickey, I was on my way to the treatment facility that my mother had lived at. I cranked the stereo as I entered the freeway, staying focused on the music, singing along to every song on an old playlist I'd made.

It was fifteen minutes to ten when I pulled into the parking lot of the treatment center. I turned the ignition off and sat in the leather seat of my Mustang, taking a few deep breaths. The facility was nice, less like a medical hospital and more like a posh care community. The brick surface was well maintained with perfectly manicured hedges along the perimeter and potted flowers at the entrance.

When I entered the sliding doors, I was instantly greeted by a clean-cut, middle-aged security guard who offered a smile and a "Good morning" as I passed by.

Sitting behind the large slate countered desk was a woman with bright red hair and thin framed glasses. She looked up and smiled at me as I approached. "Can I help you?" she asked with a warm tone.

"My name is Mackaela Stone. My mother is—was—Lindsey Stone. I'm here to sign papers."

My voice wasn't quite as shaky as I thought it would be. It didn't match the way I felt inside, all nerves.

"Oh of course, let me call Margo for you. Please have a seat." She motioned to a small sitting area with two burgundy wing-backed chairs and a long matching couch.

As I sat down in one of the chairs, my phone beeped.

Mickey: You can do this. Call me when you're done.

I smiled at my best friend's thoughtfulness and replied back.

Me: Thanks. So far, so good.

I was just placing my phone back in my purse when Margo approached me. She was a tall, thin woman with long black hair falling over her shoulders. She wore a blue business suit and heels. Margo placed one of her hands out to me and I stood, taking it.

"Mackaela, thank you for coming. I'm Margo."

"Nice to meet you," I said.

"Please follow me and we'll discuss everything." I followed her down a narrow hallway, into a small office.

Margo took a seat behind her desk as I sat in one of the chairs across from her. With a smile, Margo pulled out a manila folder and began speaking. "First of all, I would like to offer you my sincerest apology for what happened to your mother. We pride ourselves on being a very hands-on establishment and there is no excuse I can give you for the incident. We're currently looking into how your mother was able to obtain the amount of medication that she did. The nurse on staff at the time has been terminated."

I wasn't sure what to say to that so I simply nodded.

Margo cleared her throat and continued. "With that being said, I talked it over with the director, and we would like to offer you a monetary compensation for this."

That grabbed my attention. "You mean money." It wasn't a question.

"That's correct. I know you must be devastated. Your mother was in our care and yet able to ... do what she did."

"She committed suicide, she wanted to die. It wouldn't have mattered how well you were watching her. If she wanted to do it, she would have found a way." Irritation laced my voice.

They wanted to buy me off because they were afraid I would raise hell that my mom died under their care. I didn't want the damn money. If anything, I wanted my mother back. I cleared my throat and sat up straighter.

"Look, Margo, I wasn't close with my mother. I know what she was like and though I'm sad that she's gone, I don't think any amount of money is going to help me, so just keep it."

Margo's lips thinned as she gave a curt nod. She began pulling papers out of the folder, sliding them around on her desk to face me. "These are the release forms for your mother's property. It simply states that due to the circumstances, you legally sign to agree that you took the items."

She handed me a pen and I instantly signed on the dotted line. Margo removed them and produced a small new stack of papers that were stapled together.

"This states that you're not holding the facility liable for anything involving or surrounding your mother's death. It's a legal precaution."

My hand hovered over the first signature line and I peered up at Margo. "Nothing can bring my mother back. You don't have to worry about me suing you." I spoke in a low quiet tone and then promptly signed.

Margo had me initial other pages and sign and date the last one. She then had me sign a few more things stating my mother was in fact deceased. This was for the insurance company. There were no funeral arrangements because when asked, I had opted not to have one. Who would go anyway? Margo said that the facility would pay for an urn and a chamber in a local mausoleum and inform me of the location at a later date.

After the paperwork was complete, Margo handed me a cardboard box that had been sitting in the corner. It contained all of the little mementos and things that belonged to my mom. I took her word that everything was in it. I didn't feel like going through it at the moment and was ready to leave. Besides, I had no idea what sort of things she'd kept here since I hadn't visited.

After another apology from Margo and her wishing me the best, it was done. The only sort of closure that I would ever have with my mother was over.

A small weight lifted off my shoulders, but grief crept into that now free spot.

Simon

Mick had me running errands for him all day yesterday to dealers. I hadn't been able to stop thinking about Mackaela since I'd left her apartment the other night. I was worried about her and. I wished I could have helped her deal with the pain she was going through.

Mick texted me to let me know how she was doing among telling me about other business related stuff. I felt some relief knowing that she wasn't alone, but damn it if I didn't want to be the one to wipe her tears and wrap my arms around her. Something about that girl made me feel things that I'd never felt before.

With all the issues I had after losing my mom and dealing with my rat bastard step-dad and the whole jail thing, I didn't have time for anyone else. There were the occasional drunken nights of meaningless sex and one-night stands, but I never got close to any girl or anyone for that matter. I didn't want the drama or baggage that came along with getting too close to people. There wasn't anyone I'd met that interested me enough to risk it. Until her.

Mackaela was different somehow. Mick let on that she had a rocky life, but instead of putting a wall up and not wanting to hear it, I felt the need to talk to her and help her in any way that I could. Maybe it was because she wasn't just some typical girl. She was close to my brother and despite the time apart and life getting in the way, I loved him. Anyone that he cared about, I cared about, too. That's what family did.

Mick and I were on our way back from a meeting with a new client in Burien. He had asked me to pick him up from Mackaela's and go with him. It was always best when meeting a new potential client to have another person on hand he said.

"You know how I asked you to look out for Mackaela while I was gone?" Mick shot me a sideways glance and I nodded.

"Yeah I remember. Are you still going to Olympia?"

"Yeah. It sounds like Hawks has information on Ricky's whereabouts, so I definitely need to be there and find out what's going on."

"How long are you going to be gone?"

"I'm not sure yet, maybe a day or two. Will you just check up on her while I'm away? I won't have you running any other errands for me while I'm gone. I can get Dom and some of the other guys to handle the business. I need someone to take care of her and seeing as you're familiar with what she's going through ... " Mick trailed off.

"Sure, bro, it's no problem. Does she know you're leaving?"

Mick let out a sigh. "I'm not sure she remembers since she's had a lot on her plate. She's trying to be strong, but I know she doesn't want to be alone right now."

"I get it. I'll do whatever I can for her, Mick. I know I've only known her a few days, but I want to help."

"Thanks."

Her car wasn't in the parking lot when we rolled up. Mick called her to find out where she was, drumming his fingers on his knee as I parked my new silver Range Rover in a spot and waited.

"Voicemail," Mick muttered as he began tapping along the phone, probably texting her. We waited ten more minutes without a response.

The tension rolling off Mick spread to me and a kernel of unease sprouted in my chest. He was about to call her again when the black Mustang pulled into the lot beside us. I could hear loud music coming from within the car.

When she got out, her eyes were covered with sunglasses that were almost too big for her face. She walked around to the passenger side and opened the door, pulling out a cardboard box. I approached her carefully, holding my arms out. "Let me take that for you," I offered.

"Thank you." Her voice was low and though I couldn't see her eyes, I saw the tear stains on her cheeks.

Mick fell into step beside her, pulling her to his side as I followed them up the stairs to her apartment.

"Just set that on the counter." She motioned to me and continued walking toward the back of the apartment, down the hall.

Mick followed her. They stepped into what I assumed was her bedroom and. I heard the sound of their muffled voices but couldn't make out the conversation.

I went to the living room, taking in the amazing view of Seattle through the huge window. This apartment was really nice with hardwood floors and new appliances. The view though was breathtaking. It wouldn't have mattered if the walls were a nasty shade of green and there was no stove, I could sit and stare out the window all day. I wondered if Mackaela often did that.

I heard footsteps getting closer to the living room and turned to see Mick standing with his arms crossed over his chest. He pursed his lips, glancing at me.

"So what's the plan?" I asked.

There were fresh tears pooling in Mackaela's eyes when she entered the room. My heart ached for her. I wanted to wrap my arms around her instantly and never let go.

Mick cleared his throat. "I'm heading out now. I think it best if you stay with her for a while. You two should probably get to know each other better anyway. She doesn't want to be alo—"

"I can speak for myself, Mickey," Mackaela interrupted. Her gaze met mine. She offered a half-smile. "Do you mind, Simon?"

I shook my head. "No, I'll stay as long as you need me." I meant exactly that, too.

As long as she needed me, I'd be here. That was more than okay with me. Probably more than it should be.

Chapter 8

Mackaela

Mickey had insisted on having Simon stay with me for a while. He went on and on about how important it was that I wasn't alone. He didn't have to work so hard to sell me on the idea. I was already going to agree because I knew what I was feeling and I knew that being by myself wasn't going to help.

I was scared to trust Simon, but seeing as how Mickey trusted him and Simon was so agreeable to staying, how could I not take the offer? Mickey had Simon walk out with him to say goodbye. I assumed they were probably going to discuss me but I didn't really care.

I stood in front of the large apartment window and stared out at the city bustling below. It was a beautiful day, not a cloud in the sky. It made me think of the summers with my mother and the trips to the Space Needle and Science Center.

It was thinking about the innocent times, before all of the bad, that made me miss my mother horribly now. There was no chance for reconciliation anymore. I thought about that the entire ride home from the treatment facility. I'd never have the chance to apologize for being distant, never hear my mother apologize to me. I wondered if she still held a grudge toward me for accusing her boyfriend of what he did to me. That was the whole reason for her going off the deep end in the first place.

Maybe if I'd kept my mouth shut and just let it go. Maybe if I'd been more willing to talk to her after my dad left. I wondered about all the maybes now. There was grief but it swirled with guilt and I wasn't sure how to fix it anymore.

I heard my front door open and close softly. I stayed where I was, rooted to the floor and inspecting the scenery. Simon approached me noiselessly, coming to stand beside me. Neither of us spoke for a while and that was okay with me. I didn't want to talk at the moment, yet it was nice to have another person here.

After some time, Simon finally broke the silence. I figured he'd ask how I was doing or ask me if I wanted to talk about things.

He surprised me though by simply saying, "This view is amazing."

I turned to him slowly, studying his face as he regarded the city-scape. His green eyes were sparkling, his square jaw relaxed. I couldn't help but smile at him.

"It's pretty much the reason I picked this place."

Simon gazed at me. "I would, too. What's the point of anything else in here when you have so much to look at out there?" He pointed a finger to the window.

"It's definitely a source of inspiration."

Simon's brow furrowed. "Inspiration?"

"I like to paint." I cleared my throat nervously. I didn't typically share that with people. It just spilled out naturally.

"Wow, really? That's pretty cool."

A small smile crept up my lips. "Thanks. You should see the Space Needle all lit up at nighttime. It's pretty cool from here."

Simon's face fell marginally and then he caught himself and glanced back out the window. He shook his head slowly. "I've never been."

"Like at all, ever?" I asked in disbelief.

I thought he grew up in Seattle. How could it be that he never went to the Space Needle in his twenty-some-odd years of life?

"Isn't that shitty? I mean I've lived here my whole life." Simon let his gaze fall back to mine.

I shook my head and shrugged. "Well, I'm sure you couldn't have had time if your mother was ill."

"That happened when I was older, sixteen. I remember asking my step-dad to take me when I was like twelve, but he wouldn't."

I frowned. He'd told me how he'd been put in jail because of him. "Because you didn't get along."

Simon had his own past filled with unfortunate circumstances. Maybe he was worth trusting in; maybe we were more alike than I originally thought.

"Something like that. He wasn't a big fan of me."

"I'm sorry, that must have been rough. Why didn't you just move back in with Mickey and your dad?" I was being sincere. I wanted to get to know Simon and this conversation was a welcomed distraction compared to all the other crap I was dealing with.

Simon's lips pressed into a thin line. "I couldn't. My mom started to get sick and I didn't want to leave her with him." He looked away from me and focused on the view again.

Curiosity got the best of me and I asked, "Was he mean to your mom?"

Simon narrowed his eyes at the view of the city and let out a breath. "Yeah," he said simply.

My gaze fluttered back to him. "I'm sorry."

He shrugged. "It's a part of life. Things happen. It's how you deal with them and learn from them that matters."

How true that was. How you dealt with things made all the difference. I was slowly beginning to wake up to that realization myself. It was easy talking to Simon right now. I should take advantage of this opportunity to be a little more open. I wanted to know what it was like for him. If what I was feeling was okay.

"Were you close with your mom before she died?" I asked.

Simon took a deep breath and held it before letting it out slowly. He was quiet for a while and I wondered if I had crossed a line by asking him that question. Perhaps he was still raw about losing his mother. He let out another breath before looking at me.

"I was. When I was younger, when we first moved in with Todd, my step-dad, I didn't see her as much as I thought I would. But toward the end, before she died, we were closer."

I nodded and my gaze shifted away from the intensity of his own.

"There are so many things left unsaid and I don't know how to move on. I wasn't close with my mom. I feel guilty and angry. Is that normal?" My voice was quiet, hesitant, though knowing Simon went through a similar loss, gave me the courage to express my feelings.

"I can't answer that for you, about it being normal. I do think that no matter how somebody dies, no matter what the circumstances, there will always be words left unspoken. You can't beat yourself up about it."

I nodded, feeling the tears surface and threaten to spill over. "I guess my biggest regret is her not knowing that I still loved her," I admitted.

I risked a glance back at Simon. His eyes were clear, penetrating mine.

"I can't say for sure, but I think that she knew. If you still love her now, she knows." His voice was soft; his response gave me comfort.

My tears began to fall freely now. I wiped them away quickly though it didn't help much.

"I just want to stop this ache in my chest. I want the pain and resentment to go away."

Simon slowly brought his hand up to rest on my shoulder. A flood of warmth spread through me with the contact. "It will get better eventually. It's never going to be easy and some days are better than others, but I promise you it will get better."

"Thank you," I said, trying to smile.

"You're welcome, Mackaela."

A thought occurred to me then, after hearing Simon respond to me, that he called me by my name. Not 'beautiful' like he usually did. I hadn't seen much of him, so that could only mean Mickey went against my request. Not that it mattered much now. I liked the way it sounded coming from him and that unsettled my fragile heart.

Simon watched me curiously, his brow raised in question when I narrowed my eyes at him and then pursed my lips.

"When did he tell you my name?"

He grinned at me.

That smile, his smile, was probably the most magnificent thing I had ever seen. It made butterflies swirl in my belly. I liked smiling Simon.

"Yeah, about that ... " He hesitated, scratching at the back of his neck. "Mick kind of slipped up a few nights ago. It's kind of hard to talk about you without mentioning your name."

"He's such an asshole." I rolled my eyes.

Simon shrugged, not breaking that smile of his. "I'm willing to bet it would only be a matter of time before you told me anyway."

"What makes you think that, pretty boy?" I smirked at him.

Simon narrowed his eyes. "Don't call me that."

"All right, but you can't call me beautiful anymore. I hate that term."

Simon raised a brow. "But you are beautiful."

I sighed. "Simon don't try to compliment me. You know my name now, use it."

Simon shrugged.

"Whatever you say, Mackaela." He smiled at me again and I couldn't help but smile back.

In a matter of minutes, my mood had lifted. Simon had a way of cheering me up and making me forget all the bad things temporarily. Maybe he wasn't so bad after all.

We ended up watching Top Gear on my television. I liked the show because it was entertaining and cool to see the different vehicles they tested out. Before long, we were in a deep conversation about cars and I found it incredibly effortless talking to Simon.

I was sitting in my favorite old recliner, my legs tucked against my chest while he sat on the couch. When he brought up that he used to work on his car and his friends' cars all the time, I listened intently. He admitted to wanting to own a shop one day. He said that's why he was working for Mickey now. He needed a place to stay while he tried to save up money. He was extremely grateful that Mickey offered to help him out.

When he mentioned he might move away from Seattle, I was surprised.

"There isn't anything for me here other than bad memories. Sure, I love Mick and all, but I don't need to see him every day."

"Where would you go?"

"I don't know, not too far. What about you?"

"What about me?"

Simon quirked a brow. "Don't you want to eventually get out of the business and do something else?"

I chewed on my bottom lip. I was usually guarded and had proved this to Simon already when he brought me home the other night. I let out a breath, meeting his eyes.

"Honestly, I don't know what I want. I mean, I have thought about going back to school. I like to paint and stuff so I kind of thought it might be cool to make a career out of that."

"That'd be cool. You're fairly good then?" His lips quirked up. He was teasing me.

"I'm ... decent."

"Can I see your work?"

"No," I replied automatically.

Simon's face fell slightly, and I surprised myself by laughing. He narrowed his eyes at me.

"You're so mean," he murmured. I shrugged.

"Get used to it, Simon. Nobody gets to see my work. You have a better shot at seeing me in my underwear." I shouldn't have said that.

A blush crept up my cheeks as I watched Simon's eyes go wide in shock and then darken, a look that made my heart skid to a stop. Forget the smile he had earlier, those emerald's blazing like that did things to more than my heart. My stomach clenched as heat swept through my body. Not a feeling I was used to.

Simon made a sort of strangled noise. I couldn't believe I said something like that to him. It wasn't like me to joke around with people. It was becoming clearer to me that something about Simon Silver was different. Whether it was a good thing or a bad thing was debatable at this point.

Simon

I nearly choked when Mackaela mentioned her underwear. I wasn't expecting to hear that and it threw me off balance. The visual that came to mind was not at all appropriate for the current situation. I cleared my throat, quickly racking my brain to say anything to change the subject. I was drawing a blank.

I sat there, staring into her eyes, barely noticing her cheeks darkening with humiliation at what she said. Before I was able to find my voice, her cell phone began ringing loudly. She shot up from her chair and damn near sprinted to the kitchen.

I let out a breath while running my fingers through my hair. Yeah, that was awkward. Everything had been fine up until that point. I was actually having a good time with her and was glad she'd been opening up to me. I liked talking to her without the tension like the first time we met. It was different between us now. Maybe it was because we had similar pain, a connection.

Seeing her laugh moments ago was one of the most incredible things I'd ever witnessed. The way her eyes lit up, she looked so carefree and happy. I wanted to make her laugh and smile all the time.

Mackaela walked back to the living room after a few minutes. She stopped in front of the couch, handing the phone to me.

"Mickey wants to talk to you." I took it from her, our skin touching briefly and my eyes locked on hers.

"Thanks," I mumbled quietly before putting the phone to my ear. "Hey."

"Hey, Simon, are you taking care of my girl?"

"Yep, all is well."

"Good, is she being nice?"

I laughed.

"Yeah, so far so good."

Mick laughed too.

"She sounds better. I'm glad you're there with her. Listen, I just got to Olympia. I contacted Hawks and we're meeting tomorrow. I got a tip on Delgado, so I'm going to check that out now."

"Nice, I hope it goes well. Be careful." Knowing what I did of my brother, I was certain he'd likely be getting his hands dirty in dealing with Ricky. What he said next, confirmed it.

"It will for me, can't say the same for him." He muttered something to someone before speaking to me again. "Tell Mackaela I'll call her tomorrow to check in. I really appreciate what you're doing, Simon."

"It's not a problem, Mick. I'm actually having a good time with her."

"Glad to hear it. Catch you later."

"Later."

After I ended the call, I stood and wandered into the kitchen where I could hear Mackaela opening and closing cabinets. She was standing in front of the refrigerator with the door open, bent over to grab something.

My eyes traveled the length of her, from her long hair that cascaded down her back to her long legs. Shaking my head, I cleared any thoughts of her in a non-platonic way from my mind. Not a good idea when my brother trusted me to look out for her, or when she was finally trusting enough to allow my company.

"Mick said he'd call tomorrow." I set her phone on the counter.

She straightened, pulling out a couple of tomatoes. "Okay. I was thinking of making spaghetti for dinner tonight. Does that work for you?"

"Sure, do you want some help?"

"Yeah, would you get a pot from the cupboard and fill it with water?" she asked as she set the vegetables on the countertop.

I added water to the pot before setting it on a burner for the noodles to cook. She began chopping tomatoes and adding spices into a glass bowl.

"You make your own sauce?"

Mackaela grabbed a spoon before stirring everything together.

"I don't like the pre-made stuff in the jar," she said with a shrug.

"I didn't know you could cook." I took a seat in one of the stools at the small island. She glanced at me over her shoulder.

"There's a lot you don't know about me," she said with a brief smirk before pouring the sauce into another pot.

"Why don't you tell me something about you then?" I challenged, raising a brow at her as she met my gaze, looking slightly uncomfortable.

I wanted to know every detail about her. She seemed so much more open now and I wanted it to stay that way.

I sort of expected her to shut me down, but was surprised when she asked, "What do you want to know?"

I pursed my lips, gazing around the kitchen. "Do you like me?" I locked eyes with her.

She was silent a moment, turning back to stir the noodles in the boiling water. "Yeah, I think I do. I guess it was hard to accept you right away. I mean, I only heard negative things from Mickey for a long time but it wasn't fair of me to judge you."

I smiled at her response. "I'm really not all that bad, Mackaela, and I'm not a pretty boy." I jokingly glared at her.

She rolled her eyes and then smiled. "You're sort of pretty." Her nose wrinkled and I found it adorable.

I bit my lip to stifle my grin. Narrowing my eyes, I said, "So you're warming up to me and we're on a first name basis. That's quite an accomplishment."

"Yeah." She wandered to the refrigerator again, pulling out ingredients for a salad.

I watched her as she grabbed a bowl and placed it on the counter. She lifted her hands and grasped her hair to pull it to one side. I noticed that scar again on her neck and tried to look away quickly when she glanced at me, but she caught my gaze. Her brow furrowed.

"Will you chop the lettuce?" Her tone was quiet as she pushed the sleeves of her hoodie up her forearms.

"Sure." She handed me a knife and placed a cutting board on the counter next to her.

I moved beside her to begin chopping as she grabbed another knife to cut up carrots. We stood next to each other, our elbows nearly touching. It was silent for a while and I worried I'd upset her by looking at the scar.

She cleared her throat, speaking quietly. "I was burned."

I hesitated cutting for a moment, then started again. "In an accident?"

Mackaela let out a long steady breath and placed the carrots in the bowl. "No it wasn't an accident. It was ... deliberate."

I put my knife down and looked at her, my brow furrowing in confusion. Who would hurt her that way? Anger took root inside me for her. "What do you mean?"

She looked away toward the wall before slowly letting her gaze fall back to me. I patiently waited for her response.

"My ... My mother set our house on fire when I was sixteen. She was trying to end it all, including me. I woke up but not fast enough and I was burned." Her gaze fell to her feet.

I didn't know exactly how to respond to that. I was dumbfounded, speechless, furious. Part of me wanted to pull her into my arms and tell her I was sorry. Another part wanted to fume and curse her mother to the pits of Hell for treating her own child this way. Not knowing what to do, my body reacted on its own accord. Slowly my hand came up and I tucked a finger under her chin, lifting it so that I could see her eyes. Her eyes glanced everywhere except to my own.

"Mackaela ... I'm sorry," I said quietly. I examined her face carefully.

Her lashes fanned her high cheekbones; her skin was smooth, slightly tanned. Even with the scars, she was the prettiest girl I'd ever seen. She swallowed audibly, her eyes eventually colliding with mine. I could see the unshed tears.

Again, my heart burned for her. I had no right to think of her in any way but as my brother's friend, however it was growing more and more difficult when she looked at me as if she could see inside my soul.

Chapter 9

Mackaela

I wasn't exactly sure why I told Simon about what my mother had done. Maybe it was because he'd opened up to me a little bit earlier, telling me about his mother and step-father. I felt like I owed it to him to share a piece of my own past. Or maybe it was because Simon was just so easy to talk to.

Mickey told me to be nice on the phone earlier. He encouraged me to not be afraid to let Simon in, that it may be a good thing for me. It was obvious in the last few hours there was something about him that was helping me. Everything around me was changing rapidly. Opening up to Simon even this little bit felt liberating.

His emerald eyes were focused on me intently. I felt a shift in the air between us. His eyes lowered to my lips for a moment and I automatically licked them in response. I wasn't sure if I wanted him to kiss me. That would be a huge step for me, but I knew that I wasn't afraid of him or the thought of it. Not like I usually was when it came to men.

Simon wasn't like the others. He was kind, patient. That wasn't at all like me. We continued gazing at each other, not speaking. It wasn't until the pot of boiling water began spilling over on the stove top that we stepped away from each other and I knew the moment was gone.

I rushed to the stove, turning down the burner while grabbing the dishtowel to mop up the water. Simon began putting the lettuce into the bowl as I stirred the sauce, which had nearly scorched to the bottom of the pot.

"Could you get out some plates, they're in that cupboard above you." I grabbed the colander and strained the noodles at the sink.

Simon set the plates down on the island area in front of two bar stools, and grabbed silverware and napkins, setting our places. I put the noodles back in the pot, adding the sauce and stirring it a final time before adding it to a new dish. I carried it with the salad to our place settings.

"What do you have to drink?" Simon asked as he opened the fridge.

"I was going to have a beer, feel free to help yourself." He grabbed us each a bottle and opened them before coming to sit at one of the stools. He placed the beer in front of me.

"Thanks," I said, taking a small swig. I dished his plate up first. "Tell me if you hate it." I watched his face as he brought the fork to his lips and took a bite.

He chewed slowly. As he swallowed, my gaze shifted to the way his throat moved. I quickly looked away, taking my own bite. He let out a soft groan of approval and my stomach dipped.

"It's really good."

"Thanks, maybe some time I'll make you my lasagna."

"Do you only cook Italian?" he asked before taking a sip of his beer.

"No, I can bake, too. I can also grill an amazing steak."

"Where did you learn to cook?" Simon quirked a brow at me as he shoveled more spaghetti into his mouth. Clearly he wasn't lying and really did like it.

"Your brother actually. He's the only person I know that can out grill me."

"Mick can cook?" He spoke with a full mouth.

I found it oddly cute and I smiled again. "Hell yeah he can cook. Your dad never did. Since his mom wasn't around, he had to do something to feed himself. He would have starved if he didn't learn."

"I'm impressed. Looking at him, you wouldn't think that'd be one of his talents."

I shrugged.

"Mickey is kind of a jack of all trades. There isn't much he can't do."

"Well clearly he gets that from his mom's side, because I can't cook for anything," Simon stated. "I microwave oatmeal and it burns."

I giggled at his comment.

He gave me an intense glare but his lips twitched as if he were trying not to smile. "Are you ... laughing at me?"

I bit my lip to try and stifle the laughter bubbling up and then nodded slowly.

"I like your smile. You look ... happy," he said with that grin that made my stomach feel like I was riding a roller coaster.

"Who said I was happy?" I shot back sarcastically.

Simon shook his head. He spoke in a disapproving tone. "You can be so mean."

"It comes with the territory, Silver, get used to it," I teased.

He didn't say anything for a minute so I turned to see if he was hurt by my words. Simon was eyeing me, his brow furrowed.

"I'm kidding," I said quickly. Was he mad at me?

"I know," he assured me. "I was just thinking that I'm having a good time with you. It's refreshing."

"Oh. Yeah, it's nice," I mumbled, taking a bite.

I tucked my hair behind my ear as we both continued eating in a comfortable silence. Simon later helped me rinse the dishes and put them in the dishwasher.

As I was putting the remaining food away, he said, "So you can cook and you paint, although I can't say you're good because you won't show me. What other talents are you hiding, Mackaela?" He closed the dishwasher door.

I shook my head as I set the Tupperware in the refrigerator and grabbed us each another beer. "That's two things you know about me. It's your turn. What's a talent of yours? Besides kicking people's asses of course?" We wandered into the living room and he sat on the couch as I curled up in my favorite recliner.

"Well, I'm good at working on cars."

"Oh yeah, there's that."

"I'm a pretty good mechanic."

"I may hold you to that if my car ever needs work."

"That's okay with me."

"Mickey doesn't know much about cars. I think I know more than he does and that's bad because I don't know much," I admitted.

"Good. That's one thing on my brother that I can be better at."

I smiled, trailing my finger along the rim of the beer bottle.

"Don't gloat to him about it. He can be kind of competitive. One time Dom said he could do more push-ups than Mickey and they had it out in his office. I'm not even kidding you, they made me keep score and I sat there for over two hours!"

Simon chuckled.

"Can I ask you something?"

"Sure."

Simon seemed to be weighing his question. I waited patiently until he spoke again. "You and Mick have been friends since you were kids."

"Yeah, it's hard to remember a time when I didn't know him. He came into my life at just the right time." *Kind of like you, now.*

"So, why aren't you two together? He obviously loves you and you love him. You haven't ever ... dated?"

My eyes widened slightly at the question. Me and Mickey date? That wasn't even an option I wanted to think about! First of all, I was pretty set on accepting I would be single the rest of my life. Second, he did not commit, ever, for more than a few weeks at a time. I was fairly sure he'd had enough experience with women that he could understand them more than me, and I was a woman. And third, we were more like brother and sister than anything else. It was just ... gross.

"No, we have never dated. Mickey isn't really my type for one and then there's also the fact that he kind of gets around ... a lot," I said.

"So you never even wondered?" Simon asked.

"No! I can honestly tell you that I've never ever thought of him that way. Mickey's my best friend. I couldn't risk ruining that by sleeping with him, let alone entertaining the idea. Besides, I'm not attracted to him. He's like my brother."

Simon nodded, seeming to accept that answer.

I couldn't really fault him for asking. It wasn't the first time someone questioned the relationship between Mickey and me. We both were truly platonic. There was never that awkward crush phase for either of us. Believe it or not, it's very much possible to just be friends with a member of the opposite sex. ·

"So he isn't your type then. What is your type, Mackaela?"

"My type ... " Was Simon seriously asking me this question? I wondered if he was genuinely curious or just trying to keep me distracted from feeling sad. It was definitely working.

I hadn't ever really thought about what my type of guy was. I never really looked at anyone that way because I always assumed they were all conniving and shady. Most men that I met only wanted one thing. Or at least that was the vibe I got.

"I don't know," I admitted in a quiet voice.

"You don't have a type?"

I shook my head. "It isn't that I don't have one. I just never really thought about it."

"Haven't you dated anyone? What were they like?"

"I've never dated," I said, feeling suddenly embarrassed by the confession. "Ever."

Simon's jaw slackened, no doubt in shock. I knew what he was thinking. It didn't make sense for me to have never dated considering I'd been working as a prostitute, but it was the truth.

"What's your type?" I asked, trying to change the subject.

Simon smiled. "I've never been in a relationship, so I can't really say. As far as looks go, I would say long hair and pretty eyes." He licked his lips.

I inhaled sharply, taking a healthy sip of my beer. I didn't like where this conversation was heading. "Do you want to play a video game or watch a movie or something?" I asked.

"Sure, what games do you have?"

"Take a look, most of them are Mickey's that he's left here." I nodded toward the media cabinet under the TV.

Simon made his way over, sitting down in front of the cabinet, looking through the games. "This is one I am pretty good at," he said, holding up the case for the game *Forza*.

"Okay." I had a Playstation console that Ashley left before moving out and the games were either hers or ones that Mickey brought over.

I wasn't a huge video game player, but I didn't mind playing occasionally. I got up and turned on the game console before grabbing a controller and sitting on the opposite end of the couch where Simon had settled again with his own controller. We both picked the cars we wanted on the menu screen. I picked a Mustang and he picked a Charger. I was modifying the color and details to mine when he spoke.

"What's your favorite color?"

I snorted. "Are you serious?"

"What? It's a legitimate question, Mackaela."

"Yeah, for a first grader."

Simon shook his head and chuckled. "My favorite color is green."

I finished selecting everything on my car. Simon began modifying his next.

"I guess orange is my favorite," I finally said.

"That's a good color, one of the underrated ones. It fits you."

"Fits me?" I wondered, shooting an eyebrow up and gazing at him.

He turned away from the video game to look at me and nodded. "It's unique, like you."

My brow creased. "You think I'm unique?"

"Well yeah, you aren't like other girls I've met. You seem stronger than most and you're creative."

I blinked at him.

I was opening up more than I had with anyone except for Mickey and here he was, accepting me and not passing judgment. He always seemed to know the right words to say.

"I could say the same about you, Simon Silver."

"I'm not much different than the average guy," he countered. "I'm pretty typical actually; chasing girls, picking fights, and finding trouble." He shrugged.

I shook my head. "No, you're definitely something else."

I examined those emerald eyes with long dark lashes. His hair was brown, almost black. His full lips and that masculine square jaw with a little bit of stubble was far too attractive for my liking. Maybe he'd be worth getting closer to. Maybe I could find in him a part of me that I hadn't found yet. Or maybe I was trying to distract myself so much from the pain of losing my mother that I was suddenly craving any connection I could find.

Simon

Mackaela looked at me as if she were suddenly confused. I took in the bright gold color in her eyes and those full, cherry lips that I found myself wanting to taste. Her hair was flowing over her shoulders. It was a struggle to not reach out and run my fingers through it, testing its softness.

I shouldn't be thinking about her this way. Not when she was my brother's best friend, when she was grieving the loss of her mother. As much as I wanted to touch her, I wanted to earn her trust first and make sure she was comfortable around me. Now, while she was still fragile and vulnerable, was not a time to be entertaining ideas of anything other than being her friend.

I cleared my throat, turning my attention back to the game on the screen, distracting myself from the thoughts wandering in my head.

"So ... " I began. "Are you ready to lose?" I smirked at her and she smiled widely back at me.

"You're on, pretty boy," she said with a mischievous gleam in her eyes.

As it happened, she was hopelessly bad at the game. She tried really hard to keep up with me, but at every single turn in the track, her car would lose traction and slide off or spin completely around. I was biting my lip really hard to stifle the laughter most of the game. Although a few chuckles escaped and she'd glare at me.

Occasionally, I'd sneak sideways glances at her and notice a look of pure determination, her brow furrowed in concentration. After four laps, I crossed the finish line and sat back waiting on her to finish her run.

"You have to know when to let off before the turn," I said.

"I'm trying." She blew out an exasperated breath.

"Here." I slid closer to her, bringing my arm around her.

Her body stiffened for a moment, then relaxed as my hands moved over hers on the controller. I started playing the game, guiding her movements with my own fingers.

"See, let up here," I said softly.

It was difficult to concentrate when her scent, berries and vanilla, invaded my senses, sending a jolt of electricity through my stomach. I continued to help her, basking in the warmth of her body close to mine until the car reached the finish line.

Reluctantly, I pulled away from her, my heart racing wildly in my chest. I wondered if she was equally as affected by me.

"Thanks," she said quietly.

"It just takes practice. Do you want to try again?" I asked.

She nodded and I watched as she lifted the bottle of beer from the coffee table, bringing it to her lips. I observed her delicate, pale neck as she swallowed. She slowly slipped the tip of her tongue out and ran it across her full bottom lip.

"I really appreciate you being here, Simon. It's weird, I wasn't expecting this. I mean, I feel better now than I have in a long time." She gave me a sidelong glance, setting the bottle back down.

I refocused my attention to her eyes, praying that she didn't notice me checking her out. I made her feel better than she had in a long time? Why did that make me extraordinarily happy?

"I'm glad." And I was, but I was also well aware of the growing attraction I felt for her. I needed to quell these errant feelings quickly.

For all I knew she wasn't interested. No, I knew she wasn't interested. If she loved Mick like a brother, wasn't sure on her type, hadn't dated, she didn't want me. Why did I find the challenge of changing her mind so intriguing? I was all kinds of fucked up.

Chapter 10

Mackaela

I didn't know what was going through Simon's mind at the moment, but I could feel his heartbeat pounding against my back as he showed me how to play the game. My heart was doing the same thing. I wasn't used to the feelings that rushed through me with his body so close. The flood of warmth that filled my lower belly, the dizzy sensation in my head.

I was attracted to Simon Silver and as the seconds ticked by, I found myself considering what it might be like to experience him.

Simon smirked at me after putting some space between us. "You ready to lose again?"

"You aren't going to beat me twice."

"We'll see." I scowled at him and he laughed, actually laughed at me, and the sound did nothing to quell the new feelings rushing through me.

"Your evil eye needs work, sweetheart."

My mouth dropped open feigning shock. "I'm losing my touch with you, Simon Silver."

A smile slowly spread across his lips.

My gaze dropped to his mouth and suddenly I was transfixed with it. I swallowed audibly as his jaw muscle tightened;

my eyes darted up to meet his. The emerald darkened through his hooded lids and in that moment, I knew I wanted to kiss him. I not only wanted his lips on me, but I also felt like I needed it.

"Mackaela," Simon whispered, and my eyes darted back to where his voice came from.

His head began to shake slowly, his mouth opened to speak again but I cut him off. "Kiss me," I whispered, angling my body toward his.

I tilted my chin as I leaned closer, almost as if I weren't in control of myself at the moment.

A low growl rumbled from his chest; the controller dropped from his hands. In an instant, those hands, warm and strong, were on me. He cupped one around my cheek and the other stroked down my neck, making me shiver. He lowered his forehead to mine. Our lips were so close I could feel his warm breath against my own.

"You don't want this, Mackaela," he breathed.

"Yes, I do. Kiss me, Simon. Please, kiss me," I begged.

"Fuck," he murmured before pressing his lips to mine.

It was feather light and he pulled back for a moment. I blinked my eyes open, ready to demand more until his hand lowered to my waist, grasping it tightly. His mouth was on mine again, this time more deliberate as he parted his lips and glided over mine with more urgency. I gasped in surprise at how his touch was making me feel. Suddenly his tongue flicked against my own and a fire erupted within me.

I found my hands dragging themselves up on their own accord over his strong arms, to his shoulders. He guided my body closer to his and I let out a small moan as I ran my fingers through his hair. His hand was gone from my cheek now, winding into the hair at the back of my head. He groaned, lightly biting down on my lower lip. I immediately felt the heat flood between my legs.

Holy shit, he could kiss!

He guided me until my back hit the cushions. I needed him closer. I fisted his t-shirt, pulling him until he was hovering above me, with one knee planted between mine. One of my hands trailed to his hip to urge him down on top of me but he didn't move. Instead, he drew back from me, studying me with an intensity that left me feeling stripped bare. His chest was rising and falling heavily, matching my own.

"Tell me to stop," he demanded in a gruff voice.

I didn't want him to stop. This felt good, too good. It was exactly what I needed right now. I peered up at him, my hand moving to the back of his neck, shaking my head.

"Don't stop, Simon."

And just like that, his lips were on mine again. This time, the kiss wasn't quite as urgent, it was slower and more deliberate. It was as if he were savoring me. I matched his pace, letting my tongue trail across his bottom lip, earning an intoxicating moan from him.

"Mackaela," he spoke between kisses. "I can't, we can't." He lifted his head, planting his hands on either side of my shoulders.

I tried not to let the rejection that I felt show. I closed my eyes and Simon rested his forehead against mine. His fingers ran through my hair as our breathing began to stabilize.

"I want you so bad right now, but we can't do this," Simon's whispered.

"But I want this, Simon. I need this." Simon shook his head gently, leaning back so that he could look at me again.

"Sweetheart, you think you want this right now, but it isn't going to help." I opened my mouth to protest, but Simon continued. "I wouldn't feel right about it. If I sleep with you, I want it to be because you want me, not just the distraction."

I furrowed my brow, letting what he said sink in. He was right. I shouldn't use him to fill the void I was feeling. It would be a temporary fix, a Band-Aid over a bullet hole, and I'd be left feeling just as empty if not more. He moved off me and I sat up, dragging a hand through my hair, loosening a frustrated breath.

"You know I'm right, Mackaela. You'd regret it in the morning."

I glanced at him, cursing myself for shitty timing. It would just be my luck to actually want a guy when I'm at the lowest point of my life. Could he be any more perfect? For God's sake, the man had looks, compassion, and a conscience. Where the hell did he come from and how was I lucky enough to be in his company?

"You're right," I started. Simon began to smile. "About me using it as a distraction, I doubt I would regret it,." I finished.

His brow crumpled. He opened his mouth to speak, but I continued. Feeling compelled to continue whatever sudden communication we had going all night.

"You need to understand this isn't normal behavior for me. I've never wanted a guy, never *desired* a guy before." I spoke slowly, hoping he got what I was trying to say. "I don't regret what you just made me feel, Simon. I've never felt that way before." It was unbelievable that I was actually opening up to him about this, but after what we just shared, I figured it was necessary to let him know.

Maybe part of me was afraid that he'd think I was a whore. He did meet me as a prostitute and experienced one of my clients to vouch for it. He needed to understand that "Kale" wasn't me. That I was so much less experienced in certain ways than what the job involved.

"What are you saying?" Simon's voice was careful, his eyes searching mine. I let out a steady breath, locking my gaze with his.

"I've never been kissed. You're ... my first kiss. I've had sex, but I've never enjoyed it." Peeling my gaze from his, I waited for him to say something, anything.

I couldn't believe that I'd just admitted that to him. Simon's hand stretched toward me and he lifted my chin with his index finger.

"All I could think about earlier was how bad I wanted to kiss you." His lips kicked up in a small smile. "I don't want you to think I was trying to take advantage of you. I couldn't help the thoughts running through my head when my arm was around you. But you've been through a lot, not just the last few days, and right now you're dealing with one of the hardest things imaginable. I'm here for you, not because I have to be but because I want to be. I don't want to take things too far. It wouldn't be fair to either of us."

"You're seriously the only guy I've ever met with a conscience. What is wrong with you?" I teased.

Simon snorted. "I'm far from innocent, sweetheart. I just know how much Mick cares about you. I know what you're feeling, wanting to find a distraction."

"What did you do to cope?" I asked, desperate for insight.

Simon chewed his bottom lip. Watching him made the butterflies in my stomach erupt again. I almost asked him to stop it, but he began speaking.

"I was sixteen when my mom died and within the same week, I was thrown out of my step-dad's house. I turned to drinking and partying, trying to forget. I crashed on people's couches, worked odd jobs to pay rent. One night, a little over a year ago, I went back to my step-dad's house. I don't know why I did it, I was drunk and angry. There was an altercation and it resulted in my being arrested. I suppose it was a blessing because while in jail I was forced to deal with my problems and work through them."

"Do you mean like counseling and stuff?" I wondered.

"Yeah, I was in a really dark place at that time. I didn't willingly participate in the therapy at first, but eventually I figured I might as well play along. It helped, but I still hurt. I'll always have the scars and memories, Mackaela. Those won't go away, but the ability to forgive and move on can change your entire outlook on life."

Forgiving and moving on were not ideas I practiced regularly. In fact, it was my past, the demons that haunted me, that created me to be the person that I was. Cold, accusing, and judgmental fell into the category of what described me best. What would it do to me to forgive the people who wronged me?

My father, my mother, the man that took my innocence; could it create in me a new, better person? I believed change was imminent. People, places, and things could always be replaced in life. I guess how we dealt with the change was what made us who we are. If I could accept the things that altered me and embrace myself, maybe my future could be brighter.

Simon

Mackaela wasn't in a clear thinking state and as much as she thought she wanted something to happen between us, I knew she would ultimately regret it. I'd been in this place before and for me, chasing a fix to forget became an addiction in itself and it wasn't healthy. No one knew about the shit I went through in jail that caused me to turn my life around. To be honest, I was still ashamed of the steps I took to push others away and ultimately harm myself in the process. I couldn't let her go through the same thing. Wouldn't let the darkness that once poisoned me, take her. She didn't deserve it.

"I wish I knew the words to say to take some of this burden off you. I honestly don't have any advice on how to cope. Everyone handles grief in different ways. But I can promise you I'll be here for you. I want you to trust me. I'm not bullshitting you."

I attempted to keep my voice even as I spoke to her. I was nervous to admit I wanted her trust. I refused to be one of the people she pushed away.

Her eyes drifted to the coffee table. She ran a hand through her soft long hair, letting out a sigh, and then nodded, turning back to look at me again.

"I don't know why you came when you did, Simon. But Mickey told me to trust you so I can try."

I smiled and moved my hand to wrap with hers.

I felt a deeper connection to her now. There was an understanding that passed between us. We were on the brink of a real friendship, and as much as that meant to me, I knew it meant more to her.

The shrill sound of her phone ringing from the end table filled the room. She reached for it, sighing as she frowned at the screen.

"Is everything okay?"

"It's just my dad. He's called me twice and now just sent me a text to call him as soon as possible."

"You're not close with him." It wasn't a question.

"Nope, haven't spoken to him since I was seventeen, right after I moved in with Mickey."

"So your parents are divorced?"

"He left my mom and me when I was fourteen. You know that old song and dance."

I smirked at the choice of words she used, just like I had when explaining my problems to her in the car a few nights back. "That's rough, he must have heard about your mom somehow." She was still holding her phone in her hand and starting at the screen.

"Yeah, I'm just not ready to talk to him yet." Mackaela didn't speak any further about the subject and I didn't want to press her.

She began rubbing her temples with her fingertips.

"Are you all right?" I asked.

"Yeah, I'm good, just getting tired." Her voice was low when she spoke.

Seeing messages from her father had changed her mood significantly. There was no doubt she was emotionally drained.

"Can I ask you something?" she suddenly asked.

"Of course."

"Would you mind spending the night with me tonight? I have a spare room. It would just be nice to feel like there is someone else here."

The thought of sleeping over with Mackaela made my heart nearly beat out of my chest, even if it was in separate rooms. She needed me and at the moment, I couldn't imagine leaving her yet.

"I wouldn't mind."

"Thank you, Simon."

Chapter 11

Mackaela

Just knowing I wasn't all alone in my apartment tonight might help me sleep better. Simon was being extremely nice and I chastised myself again for not having faith in him when I first met him. I thought about how many other people I'd come across in the past few years that I shut down before getting to know. That bothered me more and more as it crossed my mind. After finding out my father was still trying to get in touch with me, my mood soured.

I was thoroughly exhausted and ready to crawl in bed. It had been a surprisingly good night, all things considered. But reality came crashing back when I realized I'd have to eventually face my father and talk to him about Mom.

Simon helped me pick up the empty beer bottles from earlier and shut off the game console and TV before I showed him where he'd be staying for the night. As he followed me down the hall, I heard my cell phone beep again from the kitchen counter. I ignored it. I opened the door to the room that Ashley used when she lived here. It was smaller than my room, but not terrible.

There was a window overlooking the courtyard of the complex. Simon glanced down at the twin mattress and box spring along the wall. It was covered with a pale pink quilt.

"I'm sorry the accommodations aren't great, but when Ashley, my old roommate, moved out, this was all she left behind. I don't have much," I explained, suddenly feeling like asking him to stay was too selfish.

"It's fine," he said, eyes meeting mine. "I can sleep anywhere."

"Maybe you should take my bed and I'll sleep in here," I spoke quietly, thinking out loud.

"No, Mackaela, it's fine, I promise."

I shook my head. "I have a king-size bed, Simon. It's the least I could offer considering you agreed to stay with me. I forgot how sparse this bed was. Please, take mine."

"No way, I told you that I want to be here. I'm not going to take your bed away from you," Simon argued. I let out an exasperated sigh.

"Then you can sleep with me."

His eyes widened, darkened, and then fell in a matter of seconds. He swallowed audibly.

"I can't sleep with you, Mackaela. You and I both know, especially after we ... that wouldn't be a good idea."

"My bed is huge, Simon. I'll lay a blanket in the middle if it makes you feel better. I don't want to have sex with you. I just want you to sleep with me ... " I trailed off thinking how ridiculous I must have sounded.

Who the hell was I becoming? Here I was practically begging Simon to sleep beside me like a child afraid of a monster in her closet. He probably thought I was pathetic. He seemed to consider my proposition. Finally, after what seemed like several long minutes, Simon sighed and relented.

"Okay, but if Mick knew about this, he'd probably beat the shit out of me."

He was worried about what Mickey thought? That hadn't even crossed my mind until now. Would Mickey be upset to know I was taking comfort in Simon's presence? Would he be angry that we kissed? Mickey was my best friend and only wanted the best for me. He loved his brother and trusted him. My gaze flickered to Simon's, then to my hands in front of me.

"I don't think Mickey cares, but if it makes you feel better, I won't say anything. I just need a friend," I spoke quietly. Simon's hand lifted to tentatively touch my cheek. My eyes lifted up to his again.

With a half-smile, he said, "I'm here for you. Whatever you need, I mean that."

"Thank you."

He followed me toward my bedroom and I flicked on the light, completely forgetting that I hadn't made the bed this morning and my clothes from last night that I slept in were strewn about the floor. I immediately bent down to pick each article of clothing up, shoving them into the hamper in my walk in closet.

I pulled out a pair of my comfiest boxer-like sleep shorts and a black tank top. I almost picked the white one I usually slept in, but remembering that I would sleep sans bra, I didn't think that was a good idea considering Simon was sleeping next to me.

There happened to be a spare pair of flannel pajama bottoms that belonged to Mickey in the bottom drawer of my dresser. I tossed them to Simon and he made his way to the bathroom to change. I was re-making my bed when I heard Simon come out.

I glanced up at him as he sauntered into my bedroom clad in only the pair of flannel pajama bottoms that hung dangerously low on his hips. All the air in my lungs left my body and my mouth went dry. I tried and failed to avert my eyes. I took in his stomach with abs that looked unreal. My eyes traveled up to his chest where I saw a tattoo on his peck, right where his heart was. It was a scene of a dark, starry night with a full moon. The shading of it was done extremely well making it look more like a painting. I let my gaze linger on that spot a moment before slowly looking at Simon's face. He was gazing back at me. A lazy smile spread across his lips.

I shook my head, trying to rid myself of the thoughts that began swirling. What did I get myself into? I pulled the comforter up to the pillows then folded it down.

"Making the bed before you get in it?" Simon questioned.

"I like the feeling of getting into a freshly made bed." Once I was done, I walked toward the door.

Simon turned, lifting the blankets with one hand. I had to bite my lip to stifle the gasp when I saw his other tattoo. His shoulders and upper back were just as glorious as his front. From just above the low part of his shoulder blades and out to the back of his biceps was a set of large, inked wings like that of an angel. Each feather was intricately detailed. If he were to spread his arms out, it would appear as if he were truly some kind of ethereal creature. I shook my head again before darting for the bathroom.

Standing behind the closed door, I took in a few deep breaths. What the hell was happening to me? I wasn't the girl that got all jumbled and giddy over a guy's appearance. I felt foolish for the feelings coming over me, yet for some reason I couldn't help it around Simon. I turned to the sink and brushed my teeth. I then pulled my hair up into a ponytail. Since Simon was already aware of my scars, I didn't feel the need to hide them anymore. At least not from him.

When I padded back into the room, Simon was sitting up in the bed, one arm lifted behind his head and the other holding his cell phone to his ear.

"What time tomorrow?" His gaze shifted to me as I walked around the bed to the other side. He mouthed that it was

Mickey. I pulled down the blankets on my side, sliding under the covers. Simon's eyes didn't leave me as he continued to listen to whatever Mickey was saying.

Suddenly he cleared his throat and shook his head. "Huh? Oh sorry, bro, what did you say?"

I tried to hide my smile, realizing that I had distracted him. Instead of being repulsed, I sort of liked that I had that effect on him.

"Yeah, eleven, perfect. I'll call you after the deals are made. What time are you coming back?" Simon waited for Mickey's response, and I peered up at him. He was still gazing at me with a look in his eyes that made my heart beat faster.

"Okay cool. No problem. Later." Simon set his phone on the nightstand. "Mick should be back tomorrow afternoon sometime. He wants me to do some deliveries for a few hours."

"Okay." I climbed back out of the bed to turn the light off. "Are you ready to go to sleep?" I asked with my hand hovering over the switch.

"Yeah, I'm sure you're exhausted."

I flicked off the switch, immediately enveloped in darkness. There was a faint bit of light coming from the moon and the city outside through my open window. I managed to walk back around the bed without stubbing my toes and curled back under the blankets, facing Simon. He was lying on his back with both arms tucked behind his head. I could make out his form but not all of the details of his body.

Simon's head turned toward me and he spoke softly. "Get some rest, Mackaela."

"Goodnight, Simon. Thank you for staying with me." I closed my eyes, already beginning to drift.

I thought I felt Simon's hand reach out to tuck a strand of hair behind my ear. My body shivered at the touch.

"Sleep well," he murmured.

I opened my eyes, finding him now lying on his side, gazing at me. We weren't that close considering the size of my bed, but it still felt intimate.

Simon kept his fingers behind my ear, gently stroking my hair. I closed my eyes again, relishing the soothing effects of his touch. Within a few minutes, I was sound asleep.

Simon

I laid there, watching Mackaela sleep while stroking her hair. She was so beautiful like this, less of the tough exterior, and more innocent, peaceful. I knew it wouldn't take her long to drift off. Her breathing evened out almost immediately after she closed her eyes.

It was strange being so content here next to her like this. I'd never slept beside a girl before without doing other things first. Yet I felt more connected to her than I ever did with anyone. It wasn't that totally inappropriate thoughts weren't swirling around in my head. I was a gentleman when I had to be, but I was no saint.

Especially when I walked in the room earlier and she made no effort to hide the fact she was checking me out. I'd done the same though. Those shorts of hers and that tight tank top made my body react and I had to muster up some self-control quickly.

What I was feeling seemed deeper than just the physical. I wanted to help her find the peace she needed. Her happiness was most important to me right now. My hormones could take a back seat. And that was new to me, to not be selfish and take what I wanted.

I failed to mention to Mick that I was sleeping in her bed. I did tell him I was staying over to keep an eye on her just in case she needed someone. I didn't know what was going to happen between me and Mackaela, but I hoped whatever connection we had would continue after tonight.

My hand had trailed down her side, stopping at her ribs. I felt her body rise and fall as she breathed lightly. It lulled me, and I closed my eyes.

*

The feeling of a warm, slender body curled into my chest woke me up. Somehow my legs were tangled with Mackaela's and she was pressed against me, her back to my front. My arm was draped over her hip, my hand resting on the mattress in front of her. My body had reacted in sleep. Her perfect ass pressed against me as she shifted slightly, forcing me to swallow a groan.

My hand flew to her hip, gripping it gently as I attempted to put some space between us. A small moan escaped from her pouty lips as she lazily rolled onto her back in the most adorable way. I chuckled softly, untangling my legs from hers. She stirred further and I propped my head in my hand, watching her slowly wake up. I couldn't seem to get enough of looking at this girl.

As soon as her eyes blinked open, she turned her head and caught sight of me. She had a small smile on her face for a brief moment, and then she frowned. She shifted her gaze to the ceiling and let out a sigh.

"What's wrong?" I asked quietly.

She remained silent for a while, breathing evenly. If I hadn't seen that her eyes were open, I would have thought that she'd fallen asleep again. Letting out another sigh, she rolled to face me.

"I forgot about things for a minute. I felt you before I was fully awake, and my mind filled with thoughts, good thoughts." She brought a hand up to wipe at her eyes. "But then I remembered why you're here and that my mom is gone. It just still hurts." Her voice wavered as she closed her eyes.

"Hey," I said softly as I placed a hand against her cheek. "It's okay, Mackaela. Each day will get better, I promise. Nothing about this is easy but you can get through this. You will get through this." Her eyes opened, there were tears pooling in those golden orbs. She nodded.

"I know it'll get easier with time, I guess it's just when I was asleep, I could escape reality for a while. It's strange ... " Her voice trailed off and her brow furrowed.

"What?" I hedged.

"I've always had nightmares in the past when my emotions were high."

"You didn't have a nightmare last night?" Mackaela shook her head and her eyes met mine.

"I dreamed of ... something better. It was nice."

My lips kicked up and I removed my hand from her body, worried I'd do something stupid if I continued touching her.

"What time are you delivering?" she asked.

I stretched and yawned, sitting up slightly against the pillow. "I have to be at the first place at eleven, one of the dealers up town." Mackaela sat up fully.

I caught a glimpse of her bare stomach before she readjusted her tank top. Impure thoughts immediately crept into my mind and I closed my eyes, trying to think of anything else other than how her body felt just moments ago pressed against mine.

"What are you going to do today?" I asked, trying to keep the mood casual.

"I'm not sure. I should probably figure out what my dad wants. I can't really move forward if I don't cover all the bases."

"That's a good idea."

"Are you hungry? I can make breakfast," she said as she popped out of bed.

I watched her pull the hair tie from her hair and run her fingers through it. I stared at her, dumbstruck. My mouth went dry and I lost all train of thought. What was she doing to me?

"Simon?" Mackaela raised a brow at me.

"Yeah," I cleared my throat. "Sure, breakfast sounds good. Thanks." She smiled and left the bedroom.

I got dressed and checked my phone to make sure I had no messages from Mick or Dom. I could already smell bacon wafting down the hall from the kitchen after using the bathroom.

"Damn girl, I might just have to move in with you," I joked as I entered the kitchen.

She was standing at the stove, plating up some food. She laughed and handed me the plate.

"I'm sure with your burning skills you must starve all day."

I took a seat in one of the bar stools at the counter and shrugged.

"I get by with a lot of cereal and peanut butter and jelly."

Mackaela laughed again.

After breakfast, I got a text from Mick with the locations of each delivery. There were five of them in total all around town. He said it shouldn't take more than a few hours and by the time I was done he should be back in town. I helped clean up the breakfast dishes and before I knew it, it was time for me to head out.

"I should get going so I'm not late." My voice came out less resolved than I wanted.

"Thanks again for everything." Mackaela's voice was quiet.

We both stared at each other a few minutes. After everything that had passed between us in the last twenty-four hours, I wasn't sure how to say goodbye to her. I didn't really want to leave.

Loosening a breath, I headed for the front door, Mackaela trailing behind me. I stopped suddenly, whirling around. I didn't realize how close she was and suddenly we were toe to toe with each other. I gazed down at her, tucking an errant strand of hair behind her ear. Her lips tipped up in the corners.

Damn, she was beautiful when she smiled.

"I'm glad I could be here for you, sweetheart. I'm happy to help you out any time. You can call me or text whenever you need."

I felt her shudder softly as my fingertips traveled down her ear to her neck. Why could I not stop touching her? She was like a magnet for me and I didn't want to lose hold.

She nodded and then surprised me when her arms came up abruptly, wrapping around my neck, pulling me into a hug. I immediately folded my arms around her waist, tugging her tightly to me. We stayed that way for a long time. I squeezed my eyes shut, convincing myself I'd see her again, that we'd have more moments. I had to pull away. She stepped away from me and we exchanged goodbyes before I left.

The chilled morning air greeted me once I was alone outside, seeping into my veins and numbing me. I already missed her.

Chapter 12

Mackaela

If it weren't for Mickey having to leave and for me needing the comfort of a shoulder to cry on, I don't know that I'd ever gotten to know Simon Silver. Even if I wanted to resist initially, I had to admit it was actually nice having him stay with me. He didn't expect anything of me and I didn't feel pressured to act like someone I wasn't. I was my sad, broken self and he didn't once make me feel bad, like I was useless. Instead, I felt warm, safe, and almost happy.

I still couldn't believe I'd actually had a dream last night that didn't involve the demons of my past. There were no dark, leering eyes that wanted to take my innocence. No fires where I was burned alive, no heartache of feeling abandoned. Instead, I dreamed of being free of all the burden and heartache and finally living.

It was an overwhelming feeling, and that brought me back to thinking of my mother. I had to force myself to let go the pain, the anger, the hurt that she caused for myself and her. There was literally nothing I could do about it now because she was gone forever.

I always thought I wasn't good enough. My mother didn't want me, guys only wanted me for one thing, and any girls that

I spent time around seemed to be bimbos who only wanted money and a guy to grant them all of their wishes. That guy was usually my best friend and those bimbos were usually whatever girlfriend he claimed for the time.

I admit I didn't really try to form relationships, but it's scary to unleash your past on someone. Especially when you're ashamed and afraid of judgement. I wasn't proud of my past; didn't want to openly admit I wasn't worth a damn to the woman who gave birth to me or the father that abandoned me. I felt weak. I just wanted to write everyone off and disappear. Mickey helped me do that.

When I was seventeen, I moved in with Mickey in a tiny little one bedroom apartment downtown. He was just beginning to run his own end of the business and enlisted me to help him with collections and deliveries. I didn't mind it at all at first. I had nothing else to do anyway, being a drop out and the fact that I had nowhere else to turn. As far as I knew, there was no other family out there other than my father. The ship had sailed on that relationship after he stopped calling me. I didn't even know his address.

Mickey and I worked well together and eventually, business started booming for him as his dad, Jack, gave him more responsibilities. Then he bought the house he's in now. He offered to have me live with him, but once I was eighteen, I wanted independence. To live on my own and have something for myself. I was perfectly content alone and after living in that tiny apartment with him, I was ready to get away from him. Unfortunately, I let myself become so far detached, I now feared I'd taken it too far.

Being with Simon last night made me wonder if I'd been sabotaging myself. Turning myself into a hermit or recluse of sorts and alienating myself from people. I didn't want to live that way forever.

I decided to spend some time cleaning my apartment and doing laundry. When I had a lot on my mind or was frustrated, I tended to clean and reorganize. I'm not talking simple tidying up. This was an all-out war against any germs or dust bunnies hiding in every little crevice. Like with my art, cleaning was helpful when trying to purge my mind and gain perspective.

After a rigorous session of tile scrubbing in the bathroom, I found myself thinking about the missed calls and texts from my dad. I should probably call him back, I just didn't feel like getting into an over the phone spat, but I knew I would feel better once I was free from the "What if" thoughts. Still, I couldn't bring myself to make the call yet.

I went into my bedroom next, deciding the sheets needed washed. Not only had Simon slept on them, but also Mickey the night before. Two guys in my bed in two consecutive nights? I didn't even know who I was anymore. I began stripping the bed, tossing everything to the floor. As I bent to retrieve the bedding, I caught sight of something reflective.

Dropping the linens to inspect, I knelt down, eyeing the silver chain with a ring around it. It was a simple ring, just a silver band, but when I picked it up to look closer, I noticed there was engraving along the inside. It read: "Unconditional." This must have been Simon's.

I placed the jewelry in my pocket and went about doing the laundry. I figured either he would reach out to me looking for it or I would just give it to him the next time that I saw him.

After my house was totally spotless, I decided to take a shower while the laundry dried. I still hadn't really made sense of anything in my contemplative cleaning other than deciding I wanted Simon as a friend. Though seemingly small, that was a pretty big step for me. I was blow drying my hair when my cell phone started ringing. I strolled out of the bathroom, only wearing a bra and panties and grabbed the phone off the kitchen counter.

Letting out a sigh, I answered just before the call went to voicemail. "Hello?"

"Kales! Hey baby, how are you?" I immediately cringed at the sound of my father's voice.

I attempted to pull myself together and ignore the tension building inside me. I was planning to call him back eventually, but I guess fate didn't want me to wait. I couldn't very well just hang up on him even though I immediately regretted answering. That would only make me feel worse than I did. I took a deep breath.

"Hey, Dad, I'm doing okay, I guess. How are you?" I wandered back down the hall to my bedroom and sat on the bare mattress.

"Doing fine. Listen, I heard about your mom. My attorney called me and told me the news yesterday. I'm really sorry, kiddo."

So that's where he learned the news. I should have figured that his attorney would be who he found it out from. Even though my parents had been legally divorced for seven years, they both still had lawyers. My mom tried to really stick it to him when he left us but all she came away with was the house and court-ordered child support for me until the age of eighteen. Her attorney stayed with her throughout the years because she had an attempted murder and child endangerment case against her from the fire. She won that trial for being deemed clinically insane, thus the permanent stay to the facility.

I could feel the tears start to pool up in my eyes. As much wrong as she did, I missed my mother horribly and talking to my dad only reminded me that she would never come back.

"It's okay, I'm dealing for now," I managed to speak with a clear voice.

"So are you having a funeral or anything?"

"No, the facility is taking care of burial arrangements. I really didn't know who to invite to a funeral." A lone tear escaped from my eye and rolled down my cheek. I quickly wiped it away.

"Yeah, that's tough for you to take on." *Tell me about it,* I thought with an eye roll. "So do you know what brought this on? I mean surely she had to have been showing some sort of signs."

This is exactly what I didn't want to talk about with my dad. How was I supposed to tell him that I hadn't spoken to my mother recently and had no clue that she would do something like this? I felt more tears start to fall and sniffled.

"As far as I knew, there were no signs. I actually hadn't spoken to her in a while. It came as just as big of a shock to me."

"Really? I wasn't aware you weren't communicating with her." He actually sounded surprised.

"Yeah, well, it was a pretty strained relationship." I was irritated with the man's lack of thinking before he spoke. He knew exactly what happened to me and he never once offered more than a "sorry." If he genuinely cared, he would have done more.

My ire was piqued and I really didn't want to continue this conversation. "Mom never really called much and I got busy. I have my own life now."

I heard my dad sigh into the phone. "Well I hate the way it had to end, Kales, but I'm sure she's in a better place now. That woman never was quite right. Her soul was just tortured." I bit down on the inside of my cheek to stop from screaming.

I closed my eyes and counted to ten. Did he really just say that she was *tortured*?

"You know, Dad, I really don't want to talk about her right now. It's still pretty fresh and it's going to take a while for me to process this." I tried to quell the anger in my tone but I don't think I was that successful.

"That's fair. I just wanted to make sure you were holding up okay. So are you working?"

My father, the king of subject changes when things started to get heavy. I more or less felt like he just didn't want to deal with me. Of course, why would he have time for his damaged daughter when little miss prissy and her princess daughter were his world now?

"Yeah, I'm working with my friend, Mickey Silver. You remember him?"

"Oh yeah, that kid you moved in with years back. So are you two married now?"

I shook my head at his idiotic question.

"We never dated, Dad. I'm not with anybody." This right here proved how much the man invested in me and my life.

"Oh, well that's a shame. I'm sure you're just beautiful." I frowned when I heard two loud female voices in the background.

I could hear someone whisper something and then my dad say, "I love you so much."

That was it. I was done with this conversation and with him. "Hey, Dad, I've got to go now."

"Oh, sure thing. Call me sometime if you ever want to talk."

"Okay, bye." At least that was over with now.

Surprisingly, I did feel less of a weight on me. I guess it's true what they say. What doesn't kill you makes you stronger. I stared out the window, thinking about where my life seemed to go wrong. I felt like the moment my age changed, my world changed as well.

It was that year, on the night before my fourteenth birthday, when I discovered that my father had decided he would no longer be gifting us with his presence. We had a really good day before he dropped the bomb on us. I was allowed to open one present that night, and instead of going for the biggest one like I usually did, I went for the smaller of the gifts.

When I opened it, I found that it was a copy of *Wuthering Heights*, a book that I'd wanted for my own since we'd read the book in English class and watched the movie. I was so excited and wanted to start reading it right away, so I sent myself to my room. It was about an hour later, when I was lost in the world of English moors and young, mischievous playmates, that I got this unsettling feeling in my stomach. I couldn't shake the nausea that began to grow.

I left my bedroom and headed for the bathroom at the end of the hall. I could hear the muffled voices of my parents talking and stopped, tucking into the shadows to listen. My mother was crying and my father was speaking in a hushed tone. I slowly allowed myself to peek at the two of them sitting on the couch and saw that my father had his hand on my mother's shoulder. The feeling in the pit of my stomach grew.

"Why are you crying?" I asked my mom, who wiped her face swiftly and looked up at me with a broken smile.

She shrugged and shook her head. "It's nothing, sweetie, don't worry about it," she said and promptly stood, walking to the bathroom.

I turned to my dad who just sat there, his eyes in a faraway place. I narrowed my eyes on him, knowing that whatever was going on was somehow his doing. I loved my dad, I really did, but I just never could get close to him. Maybe we were too much alike, but something about him bothered me and it caused an unspoken separation between the two of us.

"What's going on?" I asked speculatively.

He looked at me and sighed heavily. "Sit down." He motioned with his hand to take the place that my mother had just vacated.

I sat and crossed my arms around myself. I could feel my pulse racing, my stomach was in knots.

"Mackaela, there's something that I have to tell you. Unfortunately sometimes these things happen, and nobody is wrong or right, but it's just the way life goes."

"What are you talking about?"

He hesitated for a minute and cleared his throat before speaking again.

"I love your mother, I really do, and I love you, too ... It's just that sometimes you have a connection with someone and you can't help but be drawn to them. They say that everybody has a soul mate, and as much as I love your mother, I just don't think that I can be with her anymore. There's someone else that I met and I just feel like it's in everybody's best interest if I pursue this. I don't want to hurt either one of you, but I can't lie to your mother anymore or you for that matter."

I sat there, across from my father. On the outside, I was cool, calm, collected, and looking every bit attentive to his conversation. Inside I was crumbling. Every single wall that was lowered began to rise up against this man and people in general. My beautiful view of the world and happily ever after was now gone and all that was left was a heart that felt like stone and a mind that was bound and determined to never trust in love again.

I didn't like to dwell on that night, on my father's words when he'd basically admitted to having an affair and choosing his mistress over my mother. I'd always thought they were happy until then. Thinking back on it now, helped pinpoint where my trust issues started. I had been so lost in my thoughts that the sky had changed to pink and orange. I started to feel chilled and remembered I wasn't dressed yet. I pulled on a pair of jeans and a loose fitting black t-shirt before grabbing my sheets from the dryer. As I made the bed, I thought about last night when Simon was here. How he looked in those pajama pants and those tattoos would forever be imprinted in my mind. I immediately shook my head of all thoughts of him. I couldn't go and get a crush on Mickey's brother. What was I thinking?

I wondered if this was normal behavior for girls since this was my first time experiencing these emotions about a guy. Just as I was finishing making the bed, Mickey called me.

"Hey, Mackaela, what are you doing?" It sounded loud in the background wherever he was.

"I'm at home, where are you?" I had to raise my voice to make sure he heard me.

"Huh? Oh, I'm at home. Hang on a second!" he said loudly. I waited for him to speak again, the background noise lessening as if he'd walked outside or in another room. "Sorry about that, do you have any plans tonight?"

"No, I thought you were going to head over when you got back in town."

"Yeah, well Dom wanted to throw a party so change of plans. I got some great news in Olympia and we need to celebrate. I want you here!"

In the past, I'd go over to his place and hang out when he'd throw parties, but I'd typically steered clear of the whole house party scene the last couple months. It was just too many people and too much drama.

The last time I'd gone, his flavor of the week at the time had flipped shit because I hugged Mickey. She accused me of sleeping with him and tried to fight me. I found it more hilarious than anything because I totally could have kicked her ass, but I didn't want to be around any of that nonsense so I started declining his invitations.

Eventually Mickey stopped asking. It would make sense for him to invite me tonight though. He was looking out for my best interest and making sure I wasn't alone. However, I wasn't entirely sure I felt in a party mood.

"Mackaela, are you there?" Mickey asked, pulling me out of my thoughts.

"Yeah, yeah I'm here. I don't know, Mickey. You know that's not really my scene."

"Come on, Mack! You more than anyone need to let loose and have some fun. Plus, I want to tell you all about the news."

"Can't you just tell me the news tomorrow or something?"

"It's seven o'clock! Why are you acting like an old lady? You're coming over. I'm sending Simon to get you now. Simon!" He didn't bother to remove the phone from his ear while yelling and I winced at his booming voice. "You're going to get Mackaela."

"I am?" I heard Simon say in the background.

"Mickey! I can drive myself," I interjected.

"Yeah, take my car," Mickey told Simon, completely ignoring my protests. "I'm sending Simon because I already started drinking and if you drive yourself, you'll show up late, if you show up at all."

I sighed. "Whatever, Mickey, fine I'll come to your party."

There's no way he was going to let me out of this one. I supposed it wouldn't be the worst thing anyway. What else did I have going on? I could practically feel Mickey's smile through the phone.

"Thanks, darlin', I'll try and save you some rum," he said before hanging up.

I tossed my phone on the bed and let out a heavy sigh, walking back into my bathroom to begin applying some makeup. Once I was presentable enough, I slid into some flip-flops.

My phone pinged with a new text.

Simon: Hey I'll be there in 5

Me: Okay I'll meet you outside

I shut off my bedroom light and grabbed one of my zip-up hoodies from the closet. I shoved my phone into my back pocket and went to my purse, pulling out a few twenty-dollar bills and my driver's license, stowing them in the other pocket.

Suddenly I remembered the necklace I'd found earlier. I went back to my room where I'd laid it before my shower and slipped it over my neck so I wouldn't lose it.

I walked out into the night air and saw the headlight's from Mickey's car. Simon was looking directly at me as I approached the vehicle. I opened the passenger door and slid into the black leather bucket seat.

"I can't believe he made you come get me," I said immediately.

Simon shrugged. "It's cool, I don't mind."

Simon looked good in his long sleeved, green t-shirt and dark jeans. His dark hair was perfectly disheveled and he smelled like soap and rain. My stomach dipped, my body responding to him. Jesus, I had issues.

"Well, thanks for indulging him," I said as he backed out of the parking spot and headed for the exit.

I studied his face as he drove. His lips were mumbling the words to a soft rock song playing from the stereo. I glared at those stupid lips; I wanted those stupid lips. Ugh! This newfound attraction was a bit unnerving. I let out a sigh as I stared out the windshield. At least this was another distraction. I needed something after that phone call with my dad earlier.

My mother crossed my mind again, it was inevitable, but I tried to keep the sorrow tamped down. I had cried so much in the last few days. I didn't want to anymore.

Simon

I hadn't stopped thinking about Mackaela since I left her apartment earlier. I wanted to call her up or text her to see how she was doing. I knew that she was used to living alone and that she was probably doing fine, but after being able to talk to her and after the night we spent together, I felt like I wanted to keep that connection going.

Part of me was afraid she would close herself off again. Maybe she'd think what happened between us was a mistake and she would try to push me away. She was so vulnerable right now that it was hard to guess where her thoughts would be. I didn't know her at all really, but I wanted to.

After I made the deliveries Mick needed, he told me to go to the liquor store and get some alcohol because he was throwing a party tonight. I didn't really think much of it until I got back to his place and he informed me it was going to be a welcome party for me being in the business and a celebration of new beginnings. It felt a little awkward at his place when people started showing up. I knew Dom and Sadie and a few of the other guys there, but soon more people arrived and it set me on edge.

I wasn't typically an unfriendly person, but my defenses were always higher since my jail time because I was used to having to watch my back. Also, I'd partied enough in the last few years to last a lifetime. I had a feeling that Mackaela wouldn't want to be there. Selfishly, I didn't think it was best for her to be around the temptation of drinking her problems away. But my brother wanted her at the house and it seemed what Mickey Silver wanted, he got.

She looked damn good in those tight fitting jeans. Her hair was down past her shoulders and stick straight. Her golden eyes were lined with dark liner making them stand out more than normal. I glanced at her as I drove, my eyes wandering from her face to her hair and then lower where I saw my chain around her neck. My fucking heart squeezed tight at that.

"You found my chain."

Her hand came up and she fingered the ring, turning to look at me.

"I found it on the floor in the bedroom." She began to pull it off, holding it out to me. "The ring is pretty, where did it come from?"

I took it from her, my fingers brushing hers. "I'm not sure. It was my mom's. Her mother gave it to her."

"And she passed it down to you?" Mackaela's gaze was fixed on me.

"No, I took it. I didn't want my step-dad taking it. He wouldn't have given it to me."

"I'm glad you were able to get it."

"I am, too," I said quietly and placed the chain back around my neck.

We were a few blocks from Mick's house now.

"So you really don't want to be at this party do you?" I asked, changing the subject.

"No," Mackaela muttered irritably. "Mickey says I need to give it a chance, but the last time I was at a party here, I nearly got into a fight."

"What?" I knew she wasn't like most girls, but fighting? I just couldn't picture it.

She raised a questioning brow at me. "You don't think I can handle myself in a fight?"

I smirked at her and shook my head.

"I'm sure you could, but you don't seem like the type to start a fight," I clarified.

"Oh I can. I didn't start it though. The girl called me a whore, accused me of sleeping with Mickey. Like I would want to sleep with him!" she snorted. I chuckled.

"So you said you nearly got into a fight. What made you stop?"

She sighed. "Mickey talked her down. You can't fight someone after they apologize."

"True, but sometimes people just deserve a good ass kicking."

"You would say that wouldn't you?" She pursed her lips and narrowed her eyes at me.

"Why are you looking at me like that?"

A slow grin crept up her lips. "I bet I could take you," she said confidently. I scoffed.

"Yeah right, all one hundred and twenty pounds of you could take a six-foot-two ex-inmate. You do realize I was in prison, right? I had to fight to prove myself and some of those guys were huge."

I pulled into the driveway of Mick's place and shut off the car.

"See that's your problem, Simon, confidence is important but so are brains. Fighting just to throw fists can't make you win every time."

"I know that, trust me, but you're ... " I trailed off, looking her up and down. "A girl."

I watched her face turn hard and she glared at me. I liked riling her up. It was fun. I smirked and cocked a brow.

"What did I tell you about that evil eye?"

She continued to glare at me for a few minutes and then her face relaxed slightly as she shrugged.

"That cockiness is exactly what would make you lose."

"Oh, so now I'm cocky? Do you want to fight me, Mackaela? Because I promise you I would definitely win." I watched her as she seemed to weigh something and then her eyes met mine and that gorgeous half-smile graced those lips I couldn't stop thinking about.

"Let's do it."

My mouth gaped slightly, stunned. "What?"

She unbuckled her seat belt and turned her body toward mine. Leaning close enough that I could smell her, she said, "Fight me, Simon."

"No. I can't fight a girl," I said, shaking my head.

"Well obviously we wouldn't throw punches, wouldn't want to hurt that pretty face." She sat straighter. "We could wrestle."

"I could so take you," I said, chuckling. I liked this playful side of hers.

"You're on!" She began to open her door.

I stepped out as well, rounding the front of the car toward where she was standing near the lawn. I began shaking my head.

"I'm not going to wrestle you in the front yard."

"Why?" Mackaela probed. "Are you scared that people would see you get beat by a girl?"

"You're a smartass. You really think you can take me?" I asked in a low tone as I stalked toward her, causing her to back up a few inches.

"I can take you, Simon." She matched my tone and narrowed her eyes.

The way she said "'take you'" sent an electric current through me. Fuck me, I wanted her bad. I swallowed, trying not to look shaken as I advanced. My gaze traveled down to her throat. I watched her swallow before her lips parted, her tongue sliding along the bottom one.

I lowered my head, my lips at her ear, taking care not to let my body touch her. We were only inches apart, the air felt suddenly thick. "Are you scared?" I asked, drawing back to look in her eyes.

She was staring at my mouth. I clenched my hands into fists at my side, trying like hell not to touch her. If I did, that'd be game over. I wouldn't be able to stop. Her gaze fell and I was suddenly unsteady. Those eyes, the way they devoured my neck and the way her soft, pink bottom lip tucked beneath her teeth as she bit down ... My breathing grew heavier as her eyes lifted back to mine.

"I'm not scared," she whispered. "Are you scared, Simon?"

I had two options here, to take a step back or give in to the urge to kiss her. I took the last step toward her and closed the space between us. My hand flew to her hip, grasping it tight like she'd float away if I let go. I pressed against her, aligning our hips. I knew she could feel me, what she did to me. She moaned softly and I almost came undone. I swallowed hard, lifting my face away from hers.

"I'm terrified."

Chapter 13

Mackaela

When Simon stepped away from me, I felt a cold rush of air in the void between us that made me shiver. Mickey chose that moment to open the front door and stagger down the stairs toward us.

"You're here!" he said with a huge smile on his face.

He wrapped his arms around me, picking me up and swinging me around. I grabbed him, hanging on for dear life.

"I'm here," I mumbled after he set me down.

He smelled like tequila which meant he was already well on his way to being hammered. Mickey turned to Simon who was standing on the lawn, hands in his pockets, jaw muscle working in the twilight.

"Thanks for bringing her over. Come on you two, let's drink!" He cheered as he bounded toward the porch.

I caught Simon's gaze and rolled my eyes, shaking my head a little. He smiled and winked at me. My stupid stomach flipped. What just happened between us still fresh in mind had me all kinds of hot and bothered.

He didn't kiss me and that disappointed me. I wanted him to kiss me, to feel him against me again. I tried to clear my head as I followed Mickey into the house, Simon trailing behind me.

The music was loud, blaring out of the high tech sound system that Mickey installed in his living room a few months back. A loud rap song with too much base bled through the speakers. My gaze shifted to the living room where the furniture was pushed back and a group of scantily clad girls jumped up and down, dancing and singing along with wild abandon.

Mickey continued on into his kitchen which was past the small foyer to the right. There were a few people standing around the island talking. I recognized Dom and Sadie immediately. Her gaze lifted as we entered and she offered me a smile. I returned it naturally. Sadie was kind of like me, quiet and simple. She was a nice girl and didn't always beg for attention like most of the other girls around did. She was also stunning. She had long, thick, dark hair that was always styled perfectly. Her height and naturally tan skin made me envious. I wanted to be as naturally gorgeous as her.

Dom adored Sadie and even though he was in this less than wholesome life full of plenty of violence and drama, he always wanted to settle down and live a quiet life with her. I envied the ease at which he felt he could just step away and do that at any time.

"Look who made it!" Mickey announced as he grabbed two empty red solo cups, passing one to Simon.

Dom looked away from Thomas, the guy he'd been talking to, and directed his attention toward us. He stepped forward, opening his arms to hug me. Dom was like my big brother, protective and loving. He was always looking out for me like Mickey was. I embraced him quickly and pulled back smiling.

"Hey, long time no see."

"Yeah, are you doing okay today?" he asked, his dark eyes full of concern and remorse.

"I'm good. I have the Silver brother's to lean on." I glanced at Mickey and then behind me where Simon stood.

During our little exchange of greetings, Mickey had made me a drink. He shoved the cup at me and winked.

"Drink up, girl."

I rolled my eyes at him, bringing the cup to my nose, sniffing it first.

It was some sort of fruity rum cocktail. I took a cautious sip and grinned at Mickey. "This is good, thanks."

"I want to propose a toast!" he declared. Everyone looked at him expectantly. "To the start of new beginnings," he began, focusing on Dom and Sadie. "To the best, best friend ever." He turned his gaze to me. I shook my head and giggled. "And to my brother for being here, you couldn't have come at a more perfect time." Mickey lifted his own cup up in the air and we all cautiously clinked plastic together.

"So what's this good news?" I hollered over the loud music.

"I'm starting a new venture with Hawks in Olympia. He's a really great business man and smart as hell. Hopefully in the future, I'll be able to retire," Mickey said.

He looked genuinely happy about the prospect of being out of the game. It made me feel good to see him that way. I'd always thought he'd be in it for life and follow in his father's footsteps.

"Well I'm happy for you."

Mickey embraced me.

"I love you, Mackaela. We're going to be okay. You're going to be okay. I just know it," he whispered before making his way out to mingle with other guests.

Dom, Sadie, Simon, and I were left in the kitchen. Dom and Simon started talking with Thomas about some car he was thinking of getting.

"How are you feeling?" I asked Sadie, deciding to make small talk and avoid anyone asking me questions about my mother.

"I'm great, I actually feel healthier now than I did before I got pregnant." Her eyes softened and the dreaded conversation happened anyway. "I'm sorry about what happened. Are you really okay? I know it's hard ... " She trailed off.

If any other person were to talk to me about the situation, I would politely change the topic, but Sadie meant well, I knew that.

"I'm trying to deal with things day by day. I wasn't really close with my mom so it's hard to fully realize she's actually gone."

Sadie brought her arm up around my shoulders, giving me a gentle squeeze.

My heart seized at the affection she was showing me and I felt tears prick my eyes. I thought maybe it was just Simon who was making me feel different, but the way Sadie was acting showed me just how much she cared. After Sadie released me, I let out a sigh and said, "Thank you, Sadie. I know I can be kind of ... cold, but I want you to know that I appreciate you."

"Thanks, Mackaela, and don't worry about it. I know it can be tough around a bunch of guys. If you ever want to talk, you can call me anytime."

"Thanks, I may take you up on that."

"Speaking of guys ... " She trailed off and raised an eyebrow at me. I looked at her in confusion.

"What?"

Sadie grinned devilishly.

"Simon's pretty hot huh?"

My mouth popped open in shock.

What could I say? I didn't want to admit to making out with him, though it would be nice to ask her if it was normal to feel this way. She had way more experience than I did. Casually I said, "Simon's cool."

"Cool? Girl, are you blind? He's six foot something of hard hotness. I heard you spent the night with him." She waggled her eyebrows and my cheeks heated.

I tried, really tried to keep a composed face but Sadie narrowed her eyes, examining my reaction. I could feel the heat of her curious stare and I rolled my eyes.

Suddenly she leaned away from me gasping, her mouth dropping open. My eyes went wide and I automatically looked to where Dom and Simon were.

"Do you want to talk about it?" she whispered.

"No," I whispered back, but my head was nodding.

I think that first drink was starting to fill my head already. Engaging in girl talk wasn't typically my thing but I desperately needed to spill my guts about what happened.

Sadie grinned and grabbed my hand, tugging me out of the kitchen and into the living room where people were still dancing and drinking. She continued to drag me through the house, up the stairs, and then into a bedroom. As soon as we were behind the closed door, she flicked on the light and pinned me with a hard stare.

"Tell me everything." Her eyes lit up like a Christmas tree.

I looked around the room for a minute, trying to think of where to start and then it dawned on me that this wasn't just any room. I took in the duffel bag at the foot of the queen-sized bed that was poorly made.

"We're in Simon's room!" I whisper shouted and tried to step around Sadie to open the door. She blocked me.

"Nobody's going to come up here right now. It's fine."

"You better swear not to tell Dom or anyone else!" I demanded with a finger pointed at her nose.

Sadie smiled and nodded.

"You're lucky I need someone to talk to about this."

"Just spill it, Mackaela!" Sadie said and stepped around me to sit on the end of Simon's bed.

"Okay," I started. "So, Mickey wanted Simon to stay with me yesterday while he was out of town."

"And so he did, I know all that. Give me the details. Did you kiss him?" She was way too excited about this.

I nodded and looked down at my shoes, feeling the heat creep up into my cheeks again. "I asked him to kiss me," I said quietly.

Sadie gasped. She didn't know the whole story of my past, but she'd been around me long enough to know my aversion for the male population. I met her eyes and smiled slightly.

"I think it was partially due to the stress of the last few days and my urge to forget for a while. There was a moment where we were talking and I couldn't stop staring at his lips, so I asked him." I shrugged.

"And he just kissed you?"

"Yeah. It was nice."

"Do you like him?"

"Well, that's kind of the thing. I want to like him, I do as a friend, but I have my reservations. Simon told me that I wasn't sure what I wanted. He said that I could be using him as a distraction from everything." Sadie nodded, seeming to agree with that. "There's also this part of me that's curious and wants to, I don't know, explore I guess. I've never had a guy take interest in me for more than just my body. Simon's different, but it's also scary because I really don't do the whole trusting thing very well."

"You seem to trust me," Sadie said with a smile. I rolled my eyes.

"You're different and maybe I'm a little buzzed," I teased.

"I promise I won't say a thing, Mackaela, but can you promise me something in return?"

"What is it?" I eyed her skeptically. Sadie smiled and then she hugged me.

As she pulled back, she said, "Feel free to come and talk to me anytime, especially about boy stuff. I think you need someone to vent to, and Mickey doesn't count. Plus, we girls need to stick together."

I actually felt better being able to talk to someone about the Simon situation and once again, her hug made my heart soften more.

"Thanks."

Sadie winked at me and stepped forward, opening the door.

I turned to follow and ran right into the back of her. Simon was standing there with a confused expression. My mouth dropped open, shocked at the fact that we were caught in his room. Sadie giggled.

"Sorry, Simon. Was just having a little chat with my girl here. You don't mind?" Simon's eyes locked on mine for a moment before sliding over to Sadie.

He regained his composure and smiled. "Not at all, Dom was looking for you."

Sadie turned toward me. "I guess I better go back out there. I'll talk to you later, Mackaela?"

"Yes, definitely."

She smiled and walked around Simon, disappearing down the hall.

"What were you talking about?" Simon asked, stepping further into his room, causing me to back up.

"Nothing," I replied quickly and then shook my head. "It was nothing … Just girl talk." I shrugged.

"Oh, girl talk." He scratched at the slight stubble on his chin.

I finished off the drink I had in one long pull. Why was I suddenly nervous?

"Uh huh," I said after swallowing the contents. It was pure alcohol at the bottom and it kind of burned going down my throat.

Simon narrowed his gaze at me. I tried to avoid his eyes. "So why did you ladies decide on my room?" he asked, his lips twitching.

"We didn't realize it was your room until we stepped in here." That was the truth.

"Oh, well that's understandable." Simon began walking around me, heading to a door, which I realized was the bathroom. "What I don't understand though," he started as he flicked on the light switch in the bathroom. "Is why you needed to be alone to talk. Is everything okay?"

His voice was softer, a look of concern etched on his face. I nodded and chewed on my bottom lip, thinking of what to say.

After a few moments, I braved a look into his eyes. "Sadie was just telling me about some of her pregnancy stuff and asking me how I was hanging in there. It's kind of hard to hear downstairs," I lied.

"Well as long as you're okay. I swear it looked like you'd seen a ghost when the door opened. I thought for sure you were talking about me." Simon winked.

I shook my head, biting down on my lip again and looking away.

Terrible, terrible liar!

So fast I barely had time to register it, Simon was in front of me, hands on my shoulders as he narrowed his eyes. I gasped at the way he manhandled me. Simon eased his grip slightly, but still held my shoulders.

"You told her!" he said in a gruff whisper. "Are you trying to get my ass beat? Do you want to see how Mick reacts?"

I rolled my eyes at him. What was his deal with Mickey being this upset about it? "Seriously, I don't think Mickey would kick your ass. I only told Sadie because I needed someone to talk to about it. The things I'm feeling ... " I trailed off.

I was talking too much.

"You have feelings?"

I pushed his hands off me. "Not like 'I like you' feelings. I just ... you know that was my first kiss. It's just ... I had questions," I stammered.

Simon's slow grin irritated me. I shoved him in the chest and he stepped back. "What sort of questions?" He was still smiling at me.

"I'm not telling you. I don't want you to know what I'm feeling, was feeling." Still flustered at the look he was giving me, I crossed my arms and pinned him with a glare.

"So let me get this straight," Simon started. "You kissed me, wanted more; though I know it was mainly as a distraction. But that's still pretty intimate." My gaze flicked to his again.

"What's your point?"

"You can't tell me what you felt about it, about me? Isn't that sort of contradicting?" He cocked a brow and those emerald eyes sparkled in what looked like amusement.

"I'm not used to this," I admitted. "I've never had a guy interested in me like you are. I've never been interested." Simon nodded and let out a breath.

"I realize that. I guess I'm just worried that if Mick found out, he might think I was trying to take advantage of you. I don't know if what happened can happen again. Maybe later on, down the road."

I swallowed the lump that formed in my throat.

"I get it, Simon. I can't say exactly what Mickey might think, and I know full well that it shouldn't happen again. It's just that when I'm around you, knowing ... " I swallowed as my heart started to beat faster, my pulse pounding wildly in my throat.

I didn't know why I was admitting this, but I couldn't stop talking. "Knowing what you feel like, what you taste like and not being able to touch you. I just don't know how to deal with that." I kept my eyes on his even though I really just wanted to run the hell out of that room and disappear.

I put myself out there to him, stupid alcohol making me all loose and uninhibited.

"I know what you feel when I touch you because I feel it, too." His voice was a soft whisper as he drifted closer to me.

Our eyes locked. I could feel the pull between us again. That longing to have him breathe life into me again. Like he was some kind of ether for me. Simon's eyes shifted to my lips and I held my breath. My eyes fluttered closed as he dipped his chin, his lips dangerously close to mine.

"You should go," he said gruffly.

I opened my eyes, watching his chest rise and fall rapidly. We hadn't even kissed and yet our bodies were reacting as if we had. I let out a groan, partly due to my frustration of being denied him and partly because of my damn luck in this world.

"Sadie won't say a word. I'll make sure of it," I spoke quietly, barely glancing at him as I headed toward the door.

"I won't tell anyone, either. It's just between us."

I left the room, leaving Simon behind and all of the new feelings that surfaced between us. This was what was best for both of us. At least that's what I had to keep telling myself.

Simon

I wanted to kiss Mackaela one last time. But I couldn't do it. I had to cut this off now. Not only to keep Mickey from finding out and kicking me to the curb or worse, but for Mackaela.

She had no idea what he'd talked to me about earlier, how he told me he trusted me with his life, with hers. That kind of responsibility had me feeling like a gigantic fucking asshole for even entertaining the idea of being with her. It was lust, nothing more. It had to be. I barely knew her and if I convinced myself of anything else, I'd hurt her in the end. I'd disappoint my brother after finally gaining a relationship with him. I had to resist. She was too fragile right now anyway.

I needed to forget about the pull between us and let this go. Maybe Mick would be around more for her now and she wouldn't need me as much. He was her best friend after all and there was Sadie. I wasn't sure how close the two of them were, but maybe Mackaela needed a female friend to confide in. Not me, not a man with nothing but a record and the inability to properly take care of her.

She had plenty of other people to occupy her time and make her better. I had it all figured out, but that didn't mean it wasn't killing me to purposely put distance between us.

Chapter 14

Mackaela

It had been three weeks since my mother's death. Three weeks spent contemplating how I could have done things differently. Wondering if I should have tried harder to make amends with her when I had the chance. Each day, little by little, I grew stronger.

It helped to finally realize I had people around me that only wanted the best for me. People that genuinely cared about me. Mickey was great, checking in with me during the day and coming over at night to have dinner and hang out. I was able to sleep, but the nightmares, which I thought might be gone for good, still came occasionally.

Sadie and I began talking more. This morning she called me to tell me she really needed a pedicure and shopping trip. I had nothing else to do since Mickey still had me on light duty, so I agreed to go with her. It was actually fun to spend time with Sadie. I wasn't ready to open up about my entire past with her, but it was easier than I thought to engage in conversation.

We'd just left the nail salon and were headed to the mall when she brought up Simon.

"So what's going on with you and Simon?" she prodded with a grin the size of Texas.

I rolled my eyes and glanced in the rear-view mirror before merging into traffic. "Not much to tell. He found out I told you about the kiss and he sort of freaked out." Sadie's brow furrowed.

"Why does he care if I know?"

"I guess he's afraid that Mickey will find out and think he was taking advantage of my vulnerability or something." I scoffed.

I was a big girl, and if anything, I may have been the one taking advantage. I'm the one who begged him to kiss me after all.

"I get it, but I'm an adult and entitled to kiss whoever I want without Mickey's say so," I added.

"Maybe Simon doesn't want to let Mickey down. Dom mentioned that Simon really wants to start his own shop; you know make something of his life. He's probably afraid that anything between the two of you might rock the boat."

I frowned at the road ahead.

"You're probably right." Of course, she was right.

It made sense that Simon would need his own stability. He was going through as much of a lifestyle change as I was at the moment. Being with him, even casually, would likely lead to more issues for the both of us.

"I'm not going to lie though. It has to be hard not to fall into temptation with that boy, especially after already getting a taste of the forbidden fruit." She winked at me.

I couldn't help but laugh at her choice of words. "Honestly, I haven't really talked to him since he took me home that night. Even then, he was casual with me, a normal, regular friend." I sighed wistfully.

"You've got it bad for him."

I only shrugged at that.

I wasn't exactly sure what I felt for Simon Silver. I hoped whatever it was would pass.

Distance was important in seeing if that happened. In the last three weeks, I'd only seen Simon a handful of times and mostly just in passing. I met Mickey for lunch at the office one day and Simon was there, dropping off money from a collection. He offered a friendly smile and asked how I was but that was it.

Yesterday, I stopped by Mickey's to pick Sadie up because she was there with Dom. We were going to go catch a new movie. Simon was in the garage, shirtless and bent over Dom's truck under the hood. I didn't know what kind of work he was doing, but I couldn't help but stare at the way his arms moved, the muscles flexing in a wicked, delicious way. I took in the sight of the tattoo on his back and my mouth went dry thinking about how those angelic wings seemed so fitting for him. Ethereal, good hearted, powerful. I was walking up the driveway when he straightened and turned.

He gave me a wide smile as I approached him. "Hey, stranger," he'd said as he walked over to a large toolbox and pulled out a socket wrench.

"Hey." I offered quietly.

Damn, his hands were all dirty, covered in grease, and I was caught off guard by how incredibly sexy I found that. Simon's eyes met mine as he made his way back to the truck.

"How you doing?"

I shrugged. "Not too bad, taking things one day at a time." Simon nodded and then ducked back under the hood.

"That's good to hear. Mick told me you've been painting."

I nodded even though he couldn't see me.

I was perfectly content to just stand in silence and enjoy this view.

Suddenly as if Simon could read my mind, his body tensed and he slowly straightened again, turning his head toward me. Our eyes locked and I noticed the emerald darken, lashes lowering.

"Mackaela," his voice had been a whisper and a warning.

I bit my lip, my cheeks warming at being caught ogling. My gaze fell to his chest, not helping. I took in the scene that was so intricately done, the moon and the stars and the night sky, and I blurted out the first thing I could think of.

"What does your tattoo mean?"

Simon's jaw clenched briefly before he glanced down at the ink on his chest.

"It's for my mom. Her name was Layla. She told me it meant "'dark beauty.'" In some origins it also means "'night'" so I had this drawn up and done in remembrance of her."

"It's really beautiful, Simon."

Simon's lips curled into a half-smile.

"Thanks, Mackaela."

Sadie and Dom had come walking out to the garage after that, essentially cutting off any further conversation between Simon and me. All I got was a wave as Sadie and I left.

Sadie and I spent the afternoon at the mall and by the time I got home that night, I couldn't seem to get Simon Silver off my mind. Maybe it was from talking to her about him. The desire that I felt for Simon continued to grow even with time apart and I wasn't sure what it meant.

It was not only consuming my reality, but also my dreams at night. I'd been lying in bed for the last two hours, wide awake. It was now after ten in the morning and I decided it was time to shower. Maybe the scalding hot water would wash away the memories of the damn dream I had the night before right down the drain. It felt like each night the dream would intensify and it unnerved me to the point that I almost felt like confronting Simon and punching him in the face. That might help since he was the new star taking up my headspace.

I got up out of bed and made my way to the bathroom. I was just starting the water in the tub when I heard my phone ringing. I was in no mood to talk at the moment so I decided to ignore it. The steaming shower had proved disappointing for ridding my mind. I was sure I was thoroughly scrubbed clean though. I'd lingered, shaving my legs and everywhere else that needed it. I shampooed twice and let the water run until it was cold.

I couldn't forget the dream I had, but I tried to rationalize it in my head as best as possible. I finally concluded that I had so much emotional turmoil going on the last few weeks that my mind needed to focus on other things that were far from that. Therefore, my mind conjured up steamy dreams with Simon. Not sure that Dr. Phil would agree with that reasoning, but it was all I could come up with. Well, besides the fact that I might actually want to explore things with Simon. But that couldn't and wouldn't happen. At least not anytime soon.

It was another Saturday and I wasn't sure what I had on the agenda today, but I figured I would further distract myself by making myself presentable. I wasn't filled with grief as much anymore and the guilt of my past seemed more like a distant memory than a monster hiding just below the surface. I think it was safe to say that I was breathing again; or maybe for the first time.

I put some music on as I did my hair and makeup, dancing around a little while it played loudly from the bedroom. As I was getting dressed, I glanced at my dresser where my cell phone sat and remembered that I had a missed call waiting for me. Picking up the phone, I saw that not only was there a missed call from Mickey but a text telling me to call him. I shut off the music, wandering out to the kitchen as the phone rang in my ear.

"It's about time," Mickey answered.

"Sorry, I was showering. What's up?"

"I need you to collect for me today. It's a small amount from James downtown. You're closest and I have Simon running some deals so he's out."

"Sure, so Simon's a dealer now?" I wasn't really surprised that Mickey was getting Simon into more of the business.

Dealing was usually Dom's department since he was well trusted and could smell a set up from a mile away. It was probably one of the more dangerous parts of this job. It was one task that Mickey never sent me on.

"I'm testing him out in all facets just in case he decides to stick around longer. Anyway, I have to run and meet with Hawks, he's in town. But I told James I was sending you over to pick up. When you're done, drop it by the office. I'll be there."

"Okay, I can do that. See you later." I let out a breath and slipped on my shoes.

James was a really nice guy and I'd dealt with him plenty of times before, so I didn't mind at all collecting for Mickey. I was grateful that he had me working again. I needed a distraction from my other distractions.

Chapter 15

Mackaela

Collecting was just as I predicted, simple and quick. James had the money for me and I didn't even have to get out of my car. I sent Mickey a quick text, letting him know I was headed over to the office.

As soon as I pulled into the parking garage, I noticed Simon's Range Rover next to Mickey's car and my stomach dropped. Damn. So he was here, and I would see him. My stupid heart beat faster at the thought.

I sighed, locking the car as I got out. I walked into the glass doors and was waiting for the elevator when I heard the sound of tires squealing out in the parking garage. I instantly I looked through the door and saw a black Escalade pull up to the curb.

Before I had time to comprehend what was going on, a guy with dark hair and a scruffy beard opened the passenger door swiftly and stalked toward me. My heart was racing like crazy and it took me a minute to register his hand was lifting, a gun in it and pointed directly at me.

Suddenly it dawned on me that this wasn't just anybody. This was Ricky Delgado.

"Well, look who it is!" he said smugly, eyeing me up and down with a wicked grin. I couldn't find my voice. I just stared between him and the gun. "You aren't who I was looking for, but you'll do just fine," he said, stepping mere inches away from me.

The gun was pointed at my chest. I attempted to swallow back the bile rising in my throat. I was frozen in shock, trying like hell to think straight and form a plan of action.

"W-What are you doing?" I stammered in a choked whisper.

"Mickey Silver messed with the wrong person. We're tired of his shit and want revenge. I know Hawks is here with him, they will pay," he explained, not the least phased by the fact that he was holding me at gun point.

"Ricky ... You don't want to do this," I said softly. "Please?"

"Nah, I definitely want to do this. Although, I think I'll have some fun with you first." He grabbed my wrist harshly and I automatically stiffened and resisted as he pulled on me.

"No!" I screamed.

The elevator doors opened but it was too late for me to get in. They closed after a moment and my chest tightened. I prayed someone would come down soon. Hopefully whoever it was would be armed too.

"Mickey can't keep you all to himself. I want a piece of that sweet ass of yours." As he twirled me around so that my back was to him, he shoved the gun between my shoulder blades. His free hand snaked around my waist and drew my body against his. "Why don't you show me what you do to your clients, you can be my whore."

I struggled to break free from him. "Please, no!" I shrieked as his hand started to slide lower, down my waist to my thigh.

I struggled against him, but it was no use. I continued grappling with Ricky when suddenly the elevator doors opened up again and Simon stepped out, oblivious to the current situation. His head was lowered, eyes on his phone. When he lifted his gaze, his eyes shifted between me and Ricky.

The anger in those glistening emeralds was terrifying. Simon charged toward Ricky and me. Ricky drew the gun up, pointing directly at Simon's head.

"Don't move!" Ricky barked and Simon immediately stopped, his hands coming up to his sides in surrender. "Who the hell are you?" Ricky demanded.

Simon narrowed his eyes at him. "That's none of your business. Let her go," he said through clenched teeth.

My eyes widened at Simon. *What are you doing?* I wanted to scream at him. Simon glanced at me briefly and then back to Ricky.

"Who are you?" Simon growled.

"I'm the guy that's going to blow your fucking head off if you step any closer. You one of Mick's guys?"

Simon swallowed and nodded slowly. His hands still hung mid-air. "Good," Ricky stated. His tone seemed less hostile. "I want you to tell that bastard I'm taking what I want from him just like he did to me." He began to drag me back toward the door as he attempted to leave.

"No!" I screamed again, struggling to free myself.

"Wait!" Simon yelled. "You're Ricky, aren't you?" Ricky stopped.

"What's it to you?"

Simon took a cautious step closer and Ricky cocked the gun.

I squeezed my eyes shut at the sound and flinched.

"My name is Simon ... Silver. If you leave the girl, I can get you anything you want."

"Yeah right, what can you offer me?" Ricky asked skeptically.

"Anything you want," Simon said and then his eyes locked with mine. "Except for her. You can't have her." He spoke surprisingly calm for a guy with a gun pointed at him.

I was in awe of how unruffled he seemed. "Yeah, because she belongs to your prick of a brother. He made that clear from day one."

"I can give you ten thousand right now if you let her go. I'll even pretend nothing happened," Simon offered.

Ricky seemed to mull it over for a few minutes and then spoke in finality. "No deal, Silver. Tell your brother I'll see him in Hell." He began backing us out the door, towing me with him.

Panic bubbled up inside me and I screamed again. There was no way I wanted him to take me and if it took me getting shot to stop that from happening, then I would accept my fate.

I turned as much as I could and grabbed Ricky's wrist that was attached to the hand holding the gun. Suddenly I was falling toward the ground. I landed hard on the concrete floor, my knees smacking the ground. As I scrambled to get back up, I realized Ricky no longer had hold of me.

I turned to find Simon crouching over Ricky's body, punching him mercilessly in the face. The driver of the Escalade took that opportunity to help Ricky out and came bounding out of the vehicle, clutching at Simon's waist and throwing him off. I didn't recognize this guy, but he was stalky with dark skin and dark hair. He must have been working exclusively for Ricky.

Simon was dazed for a minute but began standing to finish off both of them. Watching him attempt to fight these two and throwing bone-shattering punches was fascinating and frightening all at once. He fought with confidence, like someone who was practiced and knew his body very well.

The new guy threw a few punches and one connected to Simon's jaw causing him to stumble back. My eyes were glued to Simon as he smashed his fist into the new guy's face, making him drop with a loud thud. Ricky staggered a little as Simon approached him cautiously, eyes scanning the area anxiously. He was looking for the gun, I realized. I noticed Simon had blood trailing down the corner of his mouth and he brought his hand up, wiping it away before it trickled down his chin. Suddenly, Ricky darted toward the elevator, dropping down to retrieve the gun that he'd released while being pummeled by Simon.

"Get back!" Ricky roared.

Both of his hands came up in front of him, gripping the gun fiercely and pointing it directly at Simon's chest. I reacted without thinking. It was that fight or flight moment and I decided to fight. I didn't care if I was risking my life. I started running at Ricky, my hands out in front of me, attempting to push him down or get the gun out of his hands.

Everything happened at once. It was like slow motion as I approached Ricky. He turned his head and his angry eyes found mine. He glared at me before turning his attention back to Simon who was rushing him at the same time. The deafening sound of a shot being fired flooded my ears. I was still, silent as I stopped just short of Ricky and closed my eyes.

I prayed that I hadn't just heard the gun shot, prayed that if it did go off, that Simon wasn't on the other end of that bullet. But my ears were ringing and everything was muffled. My eyes opened slowly and I turned toward where I had last seen Simon. He was curled into himself, lying on the concrete floor, a pool of blood forming from within him somewhere and out toward the door of the elevator.

"Simon!"

Ricky frantically picked his buddy up off the floor before they both hobbled out the door and back to the SUV. They drove off in a cloud of burning rubber, thankfully leaving me behind. I dropped down to my knees beside Simon, searching desperately for the wound.

"Simon, where does it hurt?" His eyes were half-open as he gazed up at me, beginning to cloud over.

His throat moved in an attempt to swallow. There was still blood pouring from his lip and I hoped like hell it wasn't coming out of his mouth. He opened his mouth as if to speak but then closed it, wincing and sucking air through his teeth. My hands were shaking uncontrollably as I began roaming them over his body, searching for the source of the blood. There was so much of it.

"My ... stomach ... God ... My stomach ... " he choked out in a graveled breath.

I pulled up the dark t-shirt he was wearing and my mouth gaped open in horror at the hole that was gushing crimson from his ribs.

"I need to call Mickey. I need to call 911," I said more to myself than to him.

"Mackaela ... " Simon started and then coughed.

"Shh, don't talk anymore, don't move." I ran a hand down his cheek. Simon closed his eyes.

"God it hurts!" His voice was hoarse as he winced at the pain.

I crawled over to where my purse had fallen during the confrontation and reached for my phone. I dialed Mickey's number first.

"Hey, Mack ... Are you here yet?" he asked.

"Simon's been shot! Get down here now!" I hung up the phone.

I immediately dialed 911 this time and gave them all the info that I could. I was told to apply pressure to the wound, so I ripped off the scarf I was wearing and pressed it flat against his abdomen. Simon groaned louder and I shot him a brief apologetic look.

Before I could hang up with them, Mickey was coming off the elevator. His eyes widened in disbelief as he took in the scene. He immediately dropped down behind Simon, lifting his head into his lap.

"What happened?" I could tell by his tone and the look on his face that he was scared and confused.

I ended the call with 911. They were on their way. "Ricky, he showed up. Tried to take me. Simon stopped him."

"Ricky?"

"Yes." I nodded. "He said something about taking something from you because you shut down his business. He shot Simon." Simon coughed again and his eyelids fluttered.

"Hey, hey, Simon, it's okay," Mickey said, placing a hand on his shoulder.

"The ambulance is on its way," I added.

"I ... Can't ... Mick, don't let me die." Simon's voice was detached as he looked into Mickey's eyes, the emerald more like a light sea foam color.

"I'm not going to let you die, bro. You're going to be fine." Mickey tried to comfort him, but I could tell he wasn't sure if he believed his own words. His gaze shifted to me. "I need to make some calls and find Ricky."

I understood he wanted to be with his brother, but he wanted revenge more. Mickey wasn't particularly good at the heavy stuff. But he could raise hell when needed. He gazed at Simon and then me again. "I'm sorry," he said in a gruff whisper before he stood abruptly, not wasting any more time as he pulled his keys out of his pocket and ran to his car in the garage.

I could hear the sirens now and within seconds, they were parked in front of the doors. An EMT hurriedly stepped out of the ambulance and approached us.

"What happened?" he asked as he set down his medical bag and began checking Simon over.

"He's been shot in the stomach, near his ribs," I said. My voice was wavering.

The EMT saw that my hands were applying pressure to the area and he nodded. A few other guys came in. One of them started asking Simon questions. He wasn't very responsive, and that worried me. They were checking for his pulse and rattling on to each other about his vitals.

"Can you feel your legs?" one EMT asked.

"Yes," Simon grunted.

"We can take it from here, miss," the EMT said and then started to gently move me away. I didn't want to let go of Simon, but I knew I had to so that they could take care of him.

They began to bring a board over to put him on the stretcher and I stood back, huddled in the corner, my body shaking and my breath coming quick. When they rolled the stretcher out the doors and started to put him in the ambulance, I followed behind. There was an oxygen mask over his face and his eyes were closed. I wasn't sure if he was coherent or not anymore.

More sirens sounded as two police cruisers pulled up next to the ambulance. The last thing we needed was the police involved and at Mickey's office. This was bad. Sure there was some pull to keep things covert due to Dom's family connections on the force, but these officers weren't related to Dom.

One of the officers walked to the medics, asking questions while the other approached me.

"Good afternoon, miss. What happened here?" the officer asked.

Swallowing, I blinked at him then glanced in the ambulance at Simon. "Some man came out of nowhere. He shot my friend. He was trying to rob me." My voice was mechanical sounding.

"Do you know who the man was? Can you describe him?" I could give him Ricky's name, tell him what he looked like in hopes they'd find him and make him pay. However, Mickey was already on the hunt and might get caught in the crossfire if cops were involved.

I couldn't risk him being apprehended in the process. He'd spend the rest of his life in jail if they found out who he was and what he did for a living. So I lied. And maybe it was a stupid decision, but I didn't have time to worry about that right now. Simon's life was on the line.

Shaking my head, I said, "It all happened so fast. I don't...remember. I didn't know him."

The office nodded, placing a hand on my shoulder. "That's okay. I'm sure you're in shock." Just then, one of the medics and the other officer came over.

"We're taking him to Harborview. Do you know him personally?" the EMT asked me.

I peeled my eyes away from Simon and looked at the guy talking to me. "Yes."

The EMT nodded. "Okay, head on over there, the front desk will let you know where he is."

I looked back to Simon. His eyes were now open, watching me.

"Mackaela," he whispered.

I tried to offer a small smile, but it was watery and my cheeks were numb. "You're going to be okay now."

"Stay with me." He gave me a pleading look. I began shaking my head.

I wanted to stay with him, I really did, but this was too much, it was too close even though he'd just been shot. I needed to wrap my head around this.

"We'll need to ask you a few more questions," the officer that originally spoke to me said.

"I'll meet you there," I choked on a sob.

Simon nodded and his eyes closed. I stood there, watching the ambulance drive out of the parking garage with its sirens blaring, the noise enveloping me.

I stepped back into the glass doors and grabbed my purse and phone. There was blood on the floor, on me. Simon's blood. My body shivered at the sight of it. I had to believe that he was going to be okay. And Ricky, well I was sure that if

Mickey didn't find him first, I would, and I'd make him pay for what he'd done.

I couldn't lose someone else. Not when I'd only just found him.

I had to stay behind for another twenty minutes while the police asked for my information and Simon's. I played dumb when they asked again who might have committed the crime. After they left, I called Dom who said he was already talking to his uncle at the precinct. They'd take over the investigation and make sure no one was implicated. Not even Ricky.

The reason for that was simple enough. If they apprehended Ricky Delgado, he'd sing like a canary. Justice would be served a different way. One that didn't involve jail time.

Chapter 16

Mackaela

I sat in the dimly lit waiting room for what felt like forever. Once I'd shown up to the hospital and found parking, I hurried to the front desk and asked an orderly where Simon was. I was told that he was rushed into surgery and when they knew anything, they would tell me. That was over an hour ago. So here I sat, chewing my nails and nearly bouncing up and down in my seat, waiting. And waiting and waiting and waiting.

This feeling was all too familiar and I kept praying over and over again that the outcome would be different than three weeks ago with my mother. It had to be. I couldn't take anymore loss and once again I was alone.

Mickey had business to attend to. He wouldn't rest until Ricky Delgado paid for what he'd done. The punishment would fit the crime as it always did when Mickey sought justice.

Another two hours went by and still nothing was said to me. No one had come out of the large double doors from the Operating Room. No one had said anything to me about how the surgery was progressing or if it was finished. I began to pace. I just couldn't sit still as the fear and anxiety took root, leaving me restless.

Finally, after another half hour, a tall man with dark hair and scrubs walked out of the double doors and approached the desk. He began speaking with the woman who I had previously talked to. I studied them both carefully, trying to gauge what was happening. Suddenly she offered a tight smile to the doctor before pointing directly at me. I instantly stopped pacing and nearly ran to them.

"What is it?" I asked. My body was still trembling, the shock wearing off slightly but I was a bundle of nerves.

"It appears that Mr. Silver had been shot at point blank range in the abdomen. His rib was grazed. He's extremely lucky there was no rupturing of internal organs."

I couldn't help the sob that broke free as I brought my hand up to cover my mouth, trying to hold back tears.

"We had to do surgery to stop the bleeding and remove the bullet. He's stable now and will remain here for a while so that we can monitor his healing."

I nodded, afraid to say anything because I thought I would break down. The doctor placed a firm hand on my shoulder.

"He's sleeping right now, but as soon as he wakes up you can see him."

"Thank you," I managed to say quietly.

The doctor smiled. "Of course. I'll let Greta know when to call you back." He smiled at the woman behind the desk who in turn smiled at me.

"Thank you," I said again.

Simon was stable, which was a good thing; it was a great thing. I walked back to my seat and pulled my phone out. I hadn't heard from Mickey yet, but I needed to let him know how Simon was doing. I dialed his number and he picked up on the second ring.

"How is he?" he asked in a gruff voice.

"They had to perform surgery on him. The bullet needed to be removed, and they were able to stabilize him. I can't see him yet, but when he wakes up they'll let me back there." My voice was still unsteady.

"That's good news." He released a heavy breath. "Hey, you don't have to stick around. I'm heading up there now."

"I'm staying." There was no way I'd leave without seeing him again.

"Okay, I just know this might be rough for you after ... " He trailed off for a moment. "I'm sure you don't want to be held up in a hospital all night."

"It's fine, Mickey. I want to be here." It was silent for a few moments and I heard Mickey take a breath. Afraid he was going to argue, I spoke again. "Mickey, can we not worry about me right now, please? I'm trying to get better, to be better. Yes, this is a painful reminder of a few weeks ago, but I can't leave him."

"Okay, Mackaela. I'll see you soon."

I knew that Mickey was worried about my emotional state, but I didn't need him focusing any attention on me at the moment. His brother was more important right now. Simon was there for me when I needed it, and now I would be there for him.

Twenty minutes later, Mickey came strolling into the waiting room with a pensive look on his face. As soon as he saw me, he reached for me and pulled me into a hug. It was nearly another hour before the doctor came out.

"You can see him now, but just know that he's been through a traumatic experience. If he seems different to you, it's normal seeing as how he's trying to process all that happened."

Mickey and I followed the doctor through the double doors. My heart began to speed up. My hand was trembling. I needed to be near him, to touch him. I had to make sure he was alive and well. Once I knew for certain he"d be okay, I'd leave. There were four other rooms that we passed before we came to a corner and saw Simon's room.

I could hear the beeping of the machines inside and it made my stomach turn. Unexpectedly, I felt immobilized. I was suddenly afraid to see him. My last memory of him flashed in my mind. He looked so pale and weak. His eyes glazed over in pain. Inhaling a deep breath through my nose, I blew it out slowly and shook my head. I needed to pull myself together. I could do this, I needed to do this. Mickey went into the room ahead of me with the doctor.

"Hey, man, how are you?" I heard Mickey ask. I held my breath, waiting to hear Simon's voice.

"Hey." His voice was weak but steadier than earlier.

I inched closer into the room. I was standing just inside the door now as I let my gaze travel from the end of the bed where Simon's feet were, to his legs, and then his knees. I took a deep breath again and continued my perusal to his waist, which was covered by the blanket, and then to his chest, neck, those full lips, and then finally ... the emerald. His eyes were sparkling back at me, much clearer than when I last saw them, and my heart faltered. We stared at each other for an immeasurable amount of time and then he smiled at me, a breathtaking grin.

"Don't be sad, sweetheart. I'm okay."

I took another step in.

"So, when will my brother be released?" Mickey asked the doctor who was poking around Simon, checking his vitals.

"It's hard to tell right now," the doctor replied. "We need to keep him monitored for at least a week, maybe longer, to make sure we didn't miss any internal injuries. I also want to ensure that the wound heals properly." Mickey nodded. The doctor smiled at him. "I'll let you guys visit for a while."

Once the doctor left, Mickey stepped closer to Simon's side and put a hand on his shoulder. "You had me scared, man."

"Yeah. I was just doing my job, right?" His lips tipped up.

Mickey nodded and smiled back. "Yeah, I guess you were. You may need a raise."

Simon's brow shot up. "No shit."

I was glad he seemed to be acting normal and joking around with his brother. It helped ease some of the tension flowing through me.

"Look, I don't want this happening again. I've got people looking out for Ricky. He won't get away with what he did to you," Mickey said.

Simon's face turned serious. "Good."

"How are you feeling?"

Simon shrugged and then winced at the movement.

"Not too bad, a little tired. I was pretty disoriented when I woke up. I feel fine for the most part, except for the hole in me now." He waved his hand down his side where he'd been shot.

He was taking this more lightly than I would have expected. If it'd been me, I didn't think I'd be as calm. Simon was definitely stronger than I was, but I already knew that. He turned toward me, his brow crumpling.

"What?" he asked as I continued staring at him.

"You just seem to be taking this extremely well," I said with a shrug.

"I'm lucky to be alive. Nothing really matters to me other than that at the moment."

I nodded.

"I'm going to go talk to the doctor about visiting hours. I want someone here to check on you every day. I'll probably get Dom or one of the other guys to case the place, too, just to be safe," Mickey said.

This was one of the times that Mickey's over-protective side and connections came in handy. Once it was only me and Simon in the room, I felt awkward standing so far away. He brought his hand up, curling a finger to gesture for me to come closer. I hesitated for a moment and then sighed before moving to the foot of his bed.

"How are you holding up?" he asked. I shrugged as I stared at the floor.

"Fine, I guess."

"Hey," Simon probed. "Mackaela, look at me. Please?" I slowly lifted my head and blinked at him. "Come on, don't lie to me. You're trembling, you watched me get shot, were almost kidnapped. You're far from fine."

I began shaking my head. I really didn't want to unleash my feelings right now. I was trying to stay calm, stay focused on being there for him. "I was so scared. I thought you were going to die," I admitted, my voice cracking.

The tears were already forming. I tried to blink them away, but that only caused them to escape, dripping down my cheeks rapidly. I sniffed and looked down again.

"Come here," Simon said in a gruff whisper.

I looked back up at him, noticing that his eyes were misted with their own unshed tears. I lost it then and began to cry harder as I walked to his side of the bed before throwing my arms around his neck. The arm on the opposite side of his wound wrapped around me, his other hand lifting up slower to stroke my hair.

When Simon spoke, his voice was thick. "I have to tell you something." I reluctantly let my arms slide away from his shoulders and took a step back, meeting his eyes. "When I saw you, when I came off the elevator," Simon's eyes were still glazed and he swallowed hard. "That was the scariest moment I've ever experienced. That gun pointed at you, the fear in your eyes." He began shaking his head and closed his eyes. When he opened them, a single tear rolled down his cheek. "You don't deserve this life."

My breath hitched. His concern for me was overwhelming.

"I've missed you these past few weeks. I can't stay away from you any longer." He was quiet as he spoke but his admission was steady and sure.

I swallowed the lump in my throat and spoke no higher than a whisper. "I can't figure out what it is about you, Simon, and that scares me because I feel the same way. I want something with you that I've never wanted."

Simon brought his hand up and palmed my cheek, using his thumb to wipe away the tears that had fallen. I closed my eyes and took a deep breath, relishing his touch for a few blissful moments. Pain was far too existent in my life and after losing my mother, I knew that I didn't want to lose anyone else. I couldn't bear that pain again. I wanted to let people in, I'd just been learning how to. But after witnessing Simon nearly being taken away from me, I wasn't sure if it was a better way to live or not. Either way I seemed to get hurt.

"I'm sorry, Simon, but I can't do this. You may think that I deserve better, and you're probably right. But you deserve your dreams, your garage, and a quiet life." I reached my hand up to wrap around his, still against my cheek. I let out a shaky breath as I lowered both of our hands to his side. "You can't have that with me. I'm tied to all of this negativity. I can't see you anymore. The thought of losing someone again, losing you, it's just too much."

I didn't stick around to see the look on his face. I ignored the heavy exhale and the moan that passed his beautiful lips as I left the room. I walked away and kept going. I didn't stop until I got to the double doors. Mickey was there talking to the doctor. He looked up and frowned at me.

"Mackaela ... " he started to say but I put my hand up.

"I need to go home. I've got to get out of here."

"Okay. What's wrong?"

I began shaking my head.

"Everything," I whispered and then turned, pushing through the double doors, away from him, away from Simon, and away from the feelings that rushed through me.

My heart hardened as I walked out of there, the loneliness was awful, but the agony was far worse. I didn't want to say goodbye to Simon, but this was safer for me and better for both of us in the long run. He didn't seem to be strong enough to let go of me, so I had to be. I needed to fix me before I'd ever let anyone else in.

Simon

Being shot is an indescribable feeling. At first, you feel the immense pain and simultaneously, you hear the deafening blast. The bullet enters your skin. You don't think about how fragile your body really is until you have lead going into it at a ridiculously high rate of speed. The next thing you feel is pressure. And then your ears begin to ring and your heart rate spikes in shock or panic, whichever registers first. After that, it's like your entire body is on fire. The pain is agonizing and you don't know where it's coming from, but you just want it to stop.

This all happens within a matter of seconds. You welcome the blackness as your eyes start to lose focus and the blood drains from you, pouring out onto the floor. Anything to not feel and be rid of what happened. Then everything goes cold, hollow, silent.

I wished that I'd been shot again. I would have gladly welcomed that kind of agony a million times over than what was going on inside my chest right now. She left. I couldn't believe that I told her how I felt. Admitted I wanted her, and then she just disappeared. It crushed me.

I rested my head back against the overstuffed pillow and closed my eyes. There wasn't much I could do laid up in this damn hospital bed. This was the worst kind of torture imaginable. If I had the strength, I'd hunt down Ricky right then and kill him without hesitation for putting me here.

It was nice to know Mick was trying to track down that sketchy bastard. But it wasn't enough. It wouldn't be until I walked out of here. The way my heart beat frantically and the feeling of rage that consumed me at seeing Mackaela in danger terrified me.

Whether he wanted to shoot her or take her didn't matter, it was enough for me to react. Looking back, I probably could have handled it differently, but I knew that no matter what the circumstance, I would take a bullet for her again if I had to.

It shattered me when she said she couldn't see me anymore. I didn't expect her to have this effect on me in the beginning. For some reason, I was consumed with her from the moment we met. Maybe it was the fact that she had so many secrets that she held back all the time. The walls that she'd spent years constructing were like layers that I wanted to peel back one by one. Maybe it was the pain that I witnessed in her eyes when she lost her mother. The situation resonated so close to home because of my own loss. There were so many things I could connect with her.

It became my own personal challenge, to break her down. She had me curious and I couldn't rest until I was able to fully understand her. I should have talked to her sooner. I was giving her space to grieve and move on from her mother's death. Mick kept me pretty busy anyway, but I thought about her every day. I even dreamed of her. For once, I was actually being cautious and thoughtful toward someone else instead of being the guy that just acted selfishly. The thought alone of me changing, wanting to change for her, opened up something inside of me. I wanted this girl, I wanted her entirely. I opened my eyes and scowled at the stark white wall in front of me.

I groaned in frustration and muttered a curse.

"You should get some rest," Mick said.

I turned my head to see him leaning against the door frame. "That's all I'll be getting, I'm not even tired anymore." My voice wavered and I instantly cleared my throat. "Well, maybe I am kind of tired. I just hate this."

Mick smiled at me as he approached my bedside, arms crossed. "Yeah, I bet. I appreciate what you did though. I mean it. If you hadn't been there ... "

"I know and you're welcome." I didn't want to talk about what happened anymore. "Did you get a plan in place?"

"Yeah. I'll have a few of my guys scoping out around town regularly to see if Ricky is lurking somewhere. She's not going to like it, but I may have Mackaela move in with me temporarily. That is if you don't mind giving up your bed for a while."

"I'm not using it at the moment," I said. "What about you?" Mick's eyebrow shot up in question.

"What about me?"

"As far as protection, if this was you here … " I let my hand swoop up and down my body. "The whole business would probably go under. Who's watching your back?"

"I can save my own ass, Simon. I'm not scared of Ricky Delgado. I'll have Dom on bodyguard duty with Mackaela. She's close with Sadie now so that helps."

"That's probably a good idea. Did she go home?"

"Yeah, Dom is meeting her at her apartment and then escorting her to my house. She seemed really shaken."

I stifled a sigh.

I hated that I couldn't be there for her. "Almost being kidnapped and witnessing a shooting will do that to you."

Mick's brow furrowed and he studied me carefully, pursing his lips. I didn't like that he was studying me as if trying to figure something out. I wasn't sure what to say, so I just went back to glaring at the wall.

"What did you and Mackaela talk about?" he finally asked.

I slowly met his wondering gaze and cleared my throat. "I asked her how she was doing. She kind of broke down for a minute. It's been an overwhelming few weeks for her, Mick," I lied.

Mick nodded. "It has, but she seemed more upset when she left you than before. Are you sure there isn't something else I'm missing?"

I immediately looked away from my brother. It was hard to lie to him, especially knowing how much he trusted me. What was between Mackaela and I though was private. I couldn't break what little trust she had for me by explaining the situation to him. Besides, at the moment, there truly was nothing going on between us.

"Like I said, she's probably tired and emotionally exhausted. I think what happened to me makes her think of her mom."

Mick looked thoughtful and then sighed. "I don't know what she's capable of and that scares me."

"Do you think she'd harm herself?" I asked quickly, too quickly. Concern laced my voice.

"I honestly don't know, Simon."

The doctor came in before I could say anything else. "It looks like all your tests look good after the surgery, Mr. Silver. You're extremely lucky. However, your body needs rest and I'm afraid visiting hours are over." He offered an apologetic smile to Mick who nodded.

"I guess I'll see you later, bro," Mick said and bumped his fist with mine.

"Okay." My head was starting to hurt. Sleep was probably the best thing for me at this point because I was too overwhelmed with reality.

After Mick left, the doctor checked my vitals once more. "Because of what happened to you, the circumstances and all, I have to ask if you want to speak with the police," he said, giving me a speculative glance.

I swallowed and began shaking my head. "I don't know who it was that shot me," I lied.

The doctor smiled briefly and nodded. "Well, if you want to explain to them what happened, maybe they could do a composite sketch or something," he offered.

I shrugged. "Maybe, I think I need to rest first before I talk to anyone."

"Okay, just let us know if you want to talk."

"I will. Thanks."

I wasn't speaking to the police at all about this matter. I knew that Mick had it covered, and seeing as how everything about this was illegal, I wouldn't risk the chance of Mick being questioned.

After the doctor left the room and dimmed the glowing lights that made a steady humming noise, I closed my eyes. I was sort of paranoid now and flashbacks of the gun popping and the feeling of the bullet going into me surfaced slowly.

After about an hour of not being able to let my mind rest, a nurse came in. She was a woman in what seemed to be her sixties with bright green eyes and auburn hair. She said that her name was Alice. Her smile was kind and she reminded me of my mother and what she might look like if she were still alive.

"How are you doing, kiddo?" Alice asked. Her voice was kind and soothing.

"I can't stop replaying what happened to me."

"That will happen with a traumatic event like what you experienced. I brought some meds for you that should help." She produced a syringe from her well-manicured hand. "This is going to make you pretty groggy. It'll help you to sleep."

"Thank you."

Alice smiled at me again and began injecting the syringe into the IV that was attached to my hand. Within seconds, I felt a calm come over me and my body relaxed. The faintest sensation of her patting my arm registered before the peaceful blackness overtook me.

Chapter 17

Mackaela

Seven days ago, I walked away from Simon Silver. It was a week full of reflection, decision making, and daily pep talks to myself stating that I could make it through and move forward. I'd get over the way he made me feel, the good and bad things that I witnessed since meeting him, and the hurt of saying goodbye. But it wasn't easy considering I was staying here at Mickey's house in Simon's room. It was a disturbing reminder that Simon Silver existed and the memories of him were very much real.

I could smell him here, especially in the queen-sized bed that I slept in every night. The pale blue comforter kept me warm yet chilled me to the bone as the scent assaulted my sanity, causing me to dream of striking emerald eyes and soft lips. His clothes were here, mine now sharing space with his. The first two nights were the toughest because I just wanted to forget about Simon and all of the things that we'd been through. I felt like everything about this room was taunting me.

When Mickey had come home on Sunday night from the hospital, I was sitting on the couch in his living room, changing channels absently on the TV. He sat down next to me, wrapping an arm around my shoulder. I wanted to recoil from him but thought better of it because I didn't want to answer any questions for my new sullen mood.

"How are you doing?" he'd asked.

I shrugged but didn't speak. I was getting tired of being asked that and frankly wasn't in the mood to reply with a lie.

"Do you want to talk about what happened? I know it must've been terrifying being in the middle of that."

"I'm fine, Mickey," I said quietly, still staring at the television.

"Is there anything I can do, Mackaela?" he'd asked in a too delicate tone that only lit a fire in me.

I didn't know if I was simply tired or frustrated with the emotions running through me, or both, but I reacted and it wasn't kindly. My head snapped toward Mickey and I narrowed my eyes.

"Can you take away the last month, Mickey?" I asked in a bitter tone. "Better yet, can you take away the last seven fucking years?"

Mickey's eyes widened and I stood abruptly, stalking off toward the stairs. "I know you're upset, but I don't know what you want from me. You know I would take it all away if I could." His voice was still calm, concerned for me.

That irritated me further. I turned back around and glared at him. My anger was piqued and I didn't know what else to do, so I just let it out.

"How about you start treating me like a normal person, Mickey? Why are you always so careful around me, making people babysit me and asking how I'm doing?"

His eyes narrowed and he began to shake his head. "Mackaela ... I just ... "

"I'm fucking tired, Mickey! I'm tired and I'm angry and I'm scared. I don't know what to do anymore. All I want ... All I freaking want, is for someone to just treat me like I'm not broken, like I don't need help. Maybe you should have kicked me to the curb a long time ago! I think I would've been better off. I'm dependent and I hate it! I don't want this anymore. I don't need this and I don't need you or Simon or anybody!"

He approached me cautiously, a look of confusion warred with sadness across his face. "I understand you're frustrated and I'm sorry if I've treated you ... carefully all this time. I just don't know what to do. I was young, too, and the things that happened to you were new to me. I didn't know how to react, I still don't. You've had a rough month and I know it brings up more of the shit you dealt with when you were a kid. I'm sorry."

My eyes began to pool with tears. I was so over crying. Tired of being a wreck all the time. "I'm just ... So discouraged, Mickey. I don't know what to do, what to think anymore," I choked out, trying to swallow a sob.

He pulled me into a hug.

"I know, Mackaela, I know," he soothed and rubbed my back.

We ended up talking for three hours that night about what happened to me and what Mickey was feeling at the time. I'd never thought once to consider what was going on in his mind throughout the years. I felt like a shit friend because of it.

I began to understand Mickey better and realize why he trusted Simon so willingly and how stressed he was with the business. I couldn't apologize enough to him. I told him my fears of getting too close to anyone, especially now, and how I didn't want to suffer another loss. Mickey listened and explained that loss was a part of life., Band being able to identify with people and have connections with them was important regardless of the consequences.

I wasn't sure how I became so lucky to find a genuine best friend in this world. I had someone who loved me completely and wanted only good things for me. That wasn't something that everybody had, no matter how great their lives supposedly were. I was grateful for Mickey and grateful for what my life had become despite the crap I'd been through. I needed to start focusing on the good instead of dwelling on the negative.

The following night, I was left wondering what to do about Simon. I was completely confused by how attached we were so soon, and I wasn't sure what to make of it. Simon took a bullet for me, literally. From day one, he'd always been looking out for me. He'd comforted me when my mother died. The main reason I felt connected to Simon was his honesty with me. He opened up to me too about his mother, his step-dad, and how he felt about me. Simon trusted me. That meant everything to me.

Mickey had been going to visit Simon every morning and every night the entire week. He'd come home and tell me about Simon's progress. We still didn't know when he'd be released from the hospital.

Yesterday, I'd appointed myself the task of playing secretary with Shelly. She helped run things for Mickey at his office. We talked to each of his clients about potential false product. It sounded like Ricky had been trying to steal quite a few loyal customers. I also put out calls to every dealer we had, telling them to look out for Ricky. No one had found him yet and that scared me. The longer he was missing, the harder it would be to find him.

I didn't want to be locked away in the house, especially Simon's room, dwelling on my feelings. I kept myself working and it helped, even though from time to time the void I tried to fill was ever present. It felt like a part of me was missing with Simon's absence. When I wasn't with Dom or Mickey, I'd hang out with Sadie. We didn't get to shop and have dinners as much under the circumstances, but it was nice nevertheless to have her over and just laugh and hang out.

I slowly began to feel more normal, like a regular twenty-something woman. Dom and I were just getting back to Mickey's after a delivery when I noticed a newer Lexus parked in the driveway. I cautiously pulled to the curb, waiting a few minutes before turning off the car.

"Do you know who that is?" I asked Dom.

He shook his head, peering at the car, just as curious as I was. We both stepped out of my Mustang at the same time, Dom staying close to me as we wandered the path to the front steps.

When he opened the door, a deep voice sounded from one of the spare rooms that was Mickey's home office. Curious, and a little concerned, I followed Dom toward the office and stepped in, my eyes widening.

Mickey leaned against the front of his desk with his arms crossed. The man standing in front of him wore a charcoal colored suit. His hair was gray and when he turned his attention to me, bile rose in my throat.

"Hey guys," Mickey greeted.

"Hey," Dom replied cautiously, glancing between the two men.

"Guess who decided to pay us a visit?" Mickey glanced at me.

Jack Silver smiled as he extended his hand to shake mine. His build was all Simon, but the facial structure and eyes were Mickey's.

"Mackaela, you've grown up a lot since I last saw you." His hazel-gray eyes sparkled at me.

I shook the daze from my head as I reached out to take his hand. He squeezed lightly before letting go. I couldn't speak yet. I was totally thrown by the fact he was here.

"Good to see you again, Jack," Dom said and shook the man's hand easily. "What brings you here?"

Jack's square jaw tensed and he tipped his head toward Mickey.

"I called him about Simon," Mickey explained.

I narrowed my eyes at Mickey, trying to quell the irritation bubbling just under the surface. This man was the reason Mickey hated Simon for so long. Why would he call him and tell him that Simon was shot? Why would Jack care to see Simon if he told all those lies about him while Mickey was growing up?

I suddenly felt incredibly protective of Simon, not wanting him hurting more than he already did about his past. Something told me that Simon wouldn't be as happy as Mickey to see their father. Jack began speaking and it pulled me from my thoughts.

"I haven't seen the kid in over twenty years and then Mick tells me he showed up nearly two months ago and has been working for him. After I found out he'd been shot, I decided maybe it was time to forgive and forget the past and get reacquainted with my other boy."

How was Mickey okay with this? Had he asked Simon if he even wanted to see the man?

"We're heading out to see Simon right now. Mackaela, do you want to come?" Mickey asked.

I wasn't ready to see Simon yet and though I almost wanted to be there for him when his dad showed up, I knew it wouldn't be a good idea.

"I'm good, thanks though," I mumbled.

Jack said goodbye to both Dom and Me and then followed Mickey out of the house. I let out a long breath and looked at Dom.

"To be a fly on the wall in that hospital room … "

"No kidding," Dom agreed.

Simon

I'd been stuck in this hospital bed for over a week now and was beginning to go stir crazy. The medication they kept administering helped with the flashbacks and I was able to sleep, but some days I would just sit and stare at the wall, not really looking at anything. My mind would drift off to the past, to the present, to the girl with long hair and honey colored eyes that seemed to haunt me. I was bored off my ass and trying to forget about Mackaela.

Every time he showed up, I'd kind of hoped Mick would slip up and tell me how she was doing or say that she'd asked about me, but he rarely mentioned her. The only time he had was Monday morning when he came by. He'd fallen into the chair next to my bed, nodding off several times. I finally managed to punch him in the arm, getting his attention.

"Rough night?" I'd asked.

"I was up late, talking to Mackaela. We had some things to work out. It's all good now."

I wanted to ask him what he meant and to explain further, but I couldn't do that without sounding too interested. She didn't want me, didn't need me.

My brother came to see me every morning and night. He'd said that he missed having me around to knock some people straight which made me feel a little better. The doctor's said I was healing perfectly and that I'd hopefully be released sometime by the end of the following week. I would still be bed-ridden for a few weeks, but at least I'd be out of the hospital. I was sick of the unnatural florescent lighting and the stark white walls.

I was daydreaming about being back in my own bed when I heard the door to my room open. I knew it was Mick but I wasn't expecting anyone else to be with him. Imagine my surprise when I saw the man he came in with, staring at me with a look of curiosity and superiority. The same man that I tried to forget all these years. My father was here.

Was he happy to see me and did he care that I was part of the business now? It was hard to tell by the way he was looking at me. He didn't really give much away. I tried to remain composed as I took in the man that helped give life to me, who looked so much more like me and my brother than I thought.

"Hey, bro, how you feeling?" Mick asked, wandering to my bedside and bumping fists with me.

"Good, I get to go home by the end of next week hopefully."

"Nice!" Mick shot a glance at our father before turning his attention back to me. "So, I called him. Told him about the shooting and that you're in the business."

I nodded.

"I see that." I risked a glance at my father. My jaw muscle clenched.

"It's been a long time, Simon." He stuck his hand out.

Narrowing my eyes, I took his hand briefly before dropping it. "It has, what are you doing here?"

"I wanted to make sure you were okay."

Funny how he didn't bother to check up on me in the last twenty years. I wasn't sure how genuine he was being.

Cocking my head to the side, I said, "I'm alive."

"Yeah, that's a good thing. Mick told me you've been working for him the last few months."

I really wasn't in the mood for small talk with my father.

"Yeah. Needed to get back on my feet after serving a yearlong sentence," I bit out.

He had no idea the amount of time I spent locked up, thinking I could have been free if he would have fucking given me the time of day. If he'd cared enough to bail me out. He cleared his throat and scratched at the back of his head.

"I'm sorry, son." He placed a hand on my shoulder and the contact filled me with blinding rage.

A low growl rumbled from my throat and I shot an angry glance to Mick. His eyes widened and he cleared his throat.

"Hey, um ... Why don't we let Simon get some rest? I think maybe I brought you here to soon."

Our father glanced at me, keeping his eyes locked on mine for a few minutes. I continued to glower at him. He looked away and back at Mick with a smile. "I don't think so, son." He turned back to me. "I understand why you're mad, Simon. I'm sorry I turned your brother against you."

"You told him lies," I snapped. "Do you understand that I had less than him growing up? Sure, it looked pretty on the outside, but inside was a mess. Did you beat Mick?" I seethed.

Those eyes, so much like my brother's turned down, darkening. "Of course I didn't."

"I was beaten daily and so was my mother. I was locked in my room for hours, starving and thirsty. Did it ever occur to you to check in?" My fury was boiling over at this point but I didn't care.

I was going to say everything to him that I never had the chance to before. If he planned on staying, it would be on my terms. He's lucky I was tied to this bed or I'd be kicking his ass.

"I called a few times but your mother told me you were fine. She didn't want me talking to you."

"Bullshit!"

"Hey, Simon, take it easy," Mick said, placing a hand on my shoulder.

My hands were balled into tight fists at my side. I wanted out of this bed so bad I started to sit up, shifting my leg, ready to swing it over the side when I heard a female voice clear her throat.

All three of us looked to the door and took in Alice who had a tray in hand with some crappy hospital food on it. She smiled slightly at me.

"Time for some dinner, kiddo, are you hungry?"

"No." Alice sighed and walked in anyway, stepping between my father and Mick.

She set the tray down on a side table before lowering it to my lap. "Try to eat something. All that muscle of yours is going to go away if you don't eat," she gently scolded.

Alice was the only nurse here that mothered me and I couldn't help but appease her with a few bites of the rubbery chicken on the plate. She smiled at me and then promptly left.

"We should go," Mick said quietly.

"You don't have to, just him," I said as I glared up at my father.

"I don't want to fight with you, son. Look, I should have tried to contact you. I assumed you were better off. I was mad at your mom for taking you away from us. I guess I punished you instead of her for how angry I was."

"You expect me to believe that? I can forgive Mick because he had no idea. But you, you're supposed to be my father. I won't accept any excuse from you."

"I'm sorry you feel that way, Simon. Maybe someday you can forgive me. I think it's great that you're helping your brother with the business. It's nice to see you two together again," he said and then turned away from me, walking out of the room.

I let out a long breath before raking a hand through my hair, tugging lightly at the ends. "Dammit."

"I'm sorry. I don't know what I was thinking bringing him here. He said he wanted to see you," Mick explained.

"I'm not mad at you, Mick. I just wasn't prepared. There's so much I've wanted to say to him. I want to punch him in the face."

Mick nodded. "I know. Maybe one day you two can have it out, after you're released."

"I can't wait to get out of this fucking place. This food sucks!" I pushed the table aside.

"I'll come back tomorrow. Maybe I'll bring Dom or Mackaela."

My heart thudded against my ribs just hearing her name.

The monitor I was hooked up to actually beeped unsteadily before easing back to normal.

"How is she?" I asked quietly, taking another bite of chicken.

Mick was silent. I shifted my gaze to him and saw that he was staring at the cord from my IV. "She's better than she has been. Dom's been taking her out to collect. She even volunteered to take some calls for me at the office. She keeps herself busy." Mick smiled vaguely.

"That's good."

His eyes slid to mine. "I get the feeling she's preoccupying herself from feeling anything. I'm happy she's coming into her own and discovering how to cope, but I still worry about her. I'm afraid she'll come close to being better and then fall back to where she was again."

"I'm sure she's stronger than you think. I don't know the details of what happened in her past, but what I do know is that it takes a special kind of person to be able to wake up every day and keep going like she does."

His brow crumpled.

"So insightful, bro, been watching a lot of Dr. Phil in here?" he joked. I snorted.

"No, I just get it ... get her. We aren't that different, Mackaela and me." I shrugged.

"I guess you're right. Hey, I'm sorry you had to grow up in a shitty situation, Simon. I wish I could have done something about it."

It wasn't his fault our father was a piece of shit.

"You're doing something now by helping my ass get back on my feet," I said.

I was grateful for my brother. Even though I'd been pretty pissed off to see my father come in with him, I couldn't blame Mick.

After he left and Alice came back in to take my empty tray away, I closed my eyes and thought about the one thing that didn't make me angry. Mackaela. She was keeping herself busy and attempting to move on. I was happy for her and it made me smile to think that some of what I may have said to her helped her to get to this point. I only wished I could speak to her again, see her again.

I opened my eyes and glanced at my phone on the side table. I wondered if she'd respond to me if I texted her. I'd been trying to let her go and give her space, but now that I knew she seemed to be handling everything, maybe there was a chance she'd talk to me. I took a deep breath as I typed out a text to her.

What if she didn't respond? Or worse, what if she told me to go to hell? Why did Mackaela drive me so crazy? I couldn't deny how I felt any longer and no matter what, I wanted her to talk to me again. I would do whatever it took to make that happen.

Chapter 18

Mackaela

Simon: Hey...How are you?

I stared at my phone for a good five minutes. I wasn't expecting him to text me. I figured Mickey would still be there with their father. My hands trembled as I responded.

Me: I'm ok. How are you?

Simon: Hungry. The food here sucks. Want to smuggle in some of your spaghetti?

Me: Lol...I don't think they'd let me.

Simon: Damn

Me: Sorry. Is Mickey still there?

Simon: No they just left.

It'd been difficult not being able to talk to Simon. I missed him. It clearly hadn't gone well with his dad if Mick and Jack had already left. Simon might need someone to talk to about it. Was I ready to be a friend to him again? Being a good friend meant laying down your own troubles to be there for another. I could do this for Simon. There's a lot I'd do for him, but I was so afraid of whatever pain might come.

Me: How was it?

Simon: It wasn't pleasant.

Me: I'm sorry. You know Mickey wouldn't intentionally hurt you.

Simon: I'm not mad at Mick

Me: What did Jack have to say?

Simon: Not much other than saying sorry for being an asshole all these years and neglecting me.

Me: I'm sorry Simon

Simon: It's okay. I'm okay. Mackaela?

Me: Yeah?

Simon: I sort of miss you

My heart started to pound in my ears as I read the last text over again. He missed me, too. There was so much more about me he didn't know and even though I was trying to work through my transgressions, I didn't want to drag him down with me. I had worked on talking to Sadie a little more and even telling her about the things that happened with my mother. It wasn't easy and I was scared shitless, but I felt improved afterwards. I wasn't sure I was ready to do that with him.

Me: You do?

Simon: Yeah...pretty bad actually.

I bit down on my lip, watching as the little dots blinked as if he were texting something else.

Simon: Sorry, I shouldn't have said that.

Me: I miss you too.

Simon: Really?

Me: Yeah, but it doesn't matter.

Simon: Why not?

Me: Because I have a lot of shit to get right. I'm a mess. You don't need that.

Simon: I want to help you.

Me: Why?

Simon: Because you help me.

An audible gasp escaped. How did I help him in any way? He's the one who's always full of advice and comfort. What could he need help with? I couldn't even stay at the hospital after he nearly lost his life. I was no good for him. A coward, too afraid to face my fears.

Simon: More than you know. Come see me tomorrow?

Me: I don't know...

Simon: Please? I just want to see you for a minute.

I couldn't stop the small smile that spread, shaking my head.

Me: Ok pretty boy. But only because you asked so nicely.

Simon: Thanks

Me: Get some rest.

Simon: I'll try. Have a good night sweetheart.

Me: Night Simon.

So there it was, in a matter of a few text messages I was going to see Simon tomorrow after trying to keep myself away from him. I should have known it wouldn't last long. Life kept bringing us to each other. Instead of fear and worry at the thought of seeing him, a warmth spread through my chest. Maybe it was time to get over myself and let him in. Something told me I'd be happier for it.

*

My stomach was in knots when I woke up. I showered and dressed slowly, trying to gain control of my nerves. I was going to see Simon today and though the thought of that made me stupidly happy and freaked out at the same time, I couldn't bail. I wouldn't.

I made my way downstairs and grabbed a banana from the kitchen. Mickey was watching the news in the living room, completely enthralled. He may be a badass drug kingpin, but he was smart as hell and always aware of current events. He'd graduated high school, passed all his classes with flying colors.

I'd sometimes imagine where he might be in life if Jack Silver hadn't dangled the business in front of him and made it sound so appealing. He could be some corporate big shot in a legal business instead. I peeled the banana and took a bite, wandering into the living room. Mickey turned away from the television and looked at me.

"What are you doing?"

"I'm eating breakfast." Mickey rolled his eyes before shooting me a questioning look. "I'm going to the hospital to see Simon," I said.

"You are?"

I shrugged.

"What's the big deal, Mickey?" I knew he didn't know about the dynamic between Simon and me.

Would he really care if I went and saw the guy who took a bullet for me? Mickey began shaking his head.

"No big deal, really, you just haven't been to see him since that day."

"I know," I said quietly. "I feel like shit about it. I mean, he did protect me after all."

"Yeah, he did. I think it's great. I actually have a meeting that I need to make. I'll drop you off and then I won't feel bad for ditching out on Simon's visit because he'll have you there."

I nodded. "Perfect."

Simon

They lowered my dosage of medication on one of the worst possible nights. After seeing my father yesterday afternoon and having to revisit all of the aggression and pain I felt toward him, I had a lot on my mind, making it difficult to fall asleep. The only thing that kept me from trying to make a break for it was knowing I'd get to finally see Mackaela.

It was nice to have Mick show up every day, don't get me wrong. I was appreciative that he'd visit me so that I didn't get too lonely. However, seeing her was far better. Plus, Mick was the talk of the entire nurses station and there were times I wondered if he'd spent as much time chatting them up as he did me.

I'd heard a few of them talking the other day about the "hot blond guy" who came to visit the shooting victim. They made all kinds of stories up in their heads about what he did for a living and whether or not he was single. They thought it was "so sweet" that he'd visit his brother every day.

Alice came in at nine-thirty to help me up to the bathroom. She said the doctor gave the go ahead to allow me to try small tasks like walking short distances and brushing my teeth. She'd also allowed me to change into a pair of scrub pants instead of the hospital gown.

Honestly, it hurt like hell to try and sit up fully, let alone actually walk, but I managed. I was determined to get better so I could get the hell out and move on with my life. I don't think I'd ever sat still this long. I hated it.

"Be gentle as you brush, kiddo. You don't want to strain your muscles on your wound side," Alice said as I stood at the small sink in the bathroom.

I glanced at myself in the mirror, seeing the weeks' worth of growth on my face, my eyes sunken and hollow. Damn, I was in rough shape. I couldn't wait to shave again and take a proper shower.

She helped me get settled back in bed, settling the blankets over my lap as Mick walked through the door, Mackaela trailing behind him. She looked amazing in a loose-fitting gray sweater that hung off her narrow shoulder and dark jeans. Her hair was slightly curled on the ends that hung down below her chest.

Alice hooked me back up to the machines as I followed Mackaela's every movement advancing toward me. My heart beat faster and the damned monitor I was connected with beeped several times in rapid succession. Alice's eyes grew wide as she fumbled with the machine. Mick quirked a brow at me. I shrugged.

"Stupid machine, always acts up."

Mackaela bit down on her lip to stifle either a laugh or smile. Either way it was adorable, and I grinned wide at her.

Alice quieted the machine and shook her head exasperated. "There, that's better. I see your company is here. Good job this morning. I'll be back in a few hours to bring you lunch, kiddo," she said as she walked toward the door.

"Thanks."

"What did you do this morning?" Mick asked, moving to stand beside me.

"I was able to get up and walk."

"Nice, hopefully that'll get you out of here quicker."

Mackaela seemed to be picking at invisible lint on her sweater, standing at the foot of my bed.

"You showed up," I said. Her head slowly lifted and her eyes met mine.

"I did."

"Someone has to keep you company. I can't hang out today," Mick announced.

I wasn't expecting to be left alone with her. "What?" I asked in a breathless voice. I cleared my throat and tried again. "What do you mean?"

"I actually have a meeting with Dad in about thirty minutes. She'll stay with you until I can get back." He gave me a quick smile, then turned to give her a hug. "I'll be back in a few hours," he said before heading out.

I stared at Mackaela, taking in her ivory skin, those pink, full lips. Damn if my body didn't respond to her the way it always had. If I had the energy, I'd swoop her up in my arms and kiss that pretty mouth.

"Thanks for coming," I murmured.

She nodded, taking a step closer, moving to the side of the bed. "Of course, how are you feeling today?"

"I'm good. They say I might be out by the end of the week."

"That's great, Simon."

"I'll have to have my bed back, though."

"Yeah, I suppose you will."

"Maybe we could ... share it," I suggested quietly. I was kidding of course. Unless she agreed, then I'd be all fucking for it.

Mackaela's eyes widened. "Don't, Simon."

"It was a joke. Of course we couldn't share a bed." She tucked her hair behind her ear.

"You look good." I whispered.

"Thank you," she said quietly. "You look ... better." Her eyes drifted to my chest and stomach before meeting my eyes again.

I smirked and cocked a brow at her. "Better than bleeding out. Saw myself in the mirror, I look like I'm still knocking on death's door."

"It's nice to see you out of the hospital gown." A faint blush crept up her cheeks.

"You still think I'm a *pretty boy*?"

Mackaela furrowed her brow.

"Not quite pretty anymore." Her lips twitched. I feigned shock, letting my jaw drop slightly.

"You don't think I'm pretty?"

She giggled, her shoulders loosening.

"You're more vulnerable looking now. Sort of rugged looking and pale. Kind of like a vampire." She laughed again and I couldn't help but laugh with her.

"So now I'm a vampire?" Mackaela bit her lip and nodded. I smiled. "I missed you, sweetheart."

"I missed you, too." Her voice was meek.

"Can we still be friends?" I asked.

I needed to put it out there, make sure she wanted to be here and wouldn't push me away. It wasn't exactly what I wanted but it was better than nothing.

"I'd like that."

"Good, so tell me what you've been up to lately."

"I've been helping Mickey out. You know collecting, making deliveries, and all that. He needed someone to help take calls for him. Shelly's been busy with the hybrid merchandise and his latest girl toy left."

"She did?" I asked in astonishment.

The girl she was referring to was the little thing I'd encountered that night I met Mackaela. I still didn't know her name, not that it mattered.

"Yeah, she tried to tell Mickey that if I was staying at the house, she wouldn't be, and it was either her or me. She moved back home to her parents in Bellevue."

"Wow. Mick didn't even say anything about it."

Mackaela shrugged. "That's typical. He really doesn't talk about his relationships if that's even what you call them. I've yet to see a girl that can handle him and be his complete equal."

"Do you think there's someone out there for him, for anyone?"

Mackaela seemed to think about it for a moment. She stepped over and grabbed the chair from the corner and slid it over beside my bed. After making herself comfortable, she spoke.

"I think that everybody has a counterpart, not necessarily a soul mate, but that one person who just understands and gets them completely without having to question or second guess it. It's sort of like you're drifting your entire life. Just skating by, seeing millions of faces and meeting all sorts of people. And then when you least expect it, that one, the one shows up."

"You really believe that?" I was surprised by her admission. I didn't expect her to have such a profound theory about love.

"I do. Coming from someone like me, it might seem silly. But I believe it ... for other people."

"Why do you say that?"

Her eyes met mine.

"Why do I say what?"

"That you believe it for others. Why don't you believe it for yourself?"

She was silent for a minute and then responded carefully.

"I do believe it for myself, or at least I want to believe it. I just have a long way to go yet. I need to figure life out first. It might be a while before that happens for me."

"So tell me, Mackaela, what exactly are you trying to figure out?"

"Well ... " she said slowly. "You know what happened with my mom. There's that and my dad skipping out and ... other issues. I need to fix my outlook on life, on people. I've been doing that for the past month, but I'm afraid it'll all come crashing down again."

"How do you plan on stopping that from happening?"

"Sadie gave me the name of a counselor. I called her on my way here and made an appointment for next Tuesday. I think I just need to talk things out and see if a professional perspective can help me figure out the right thing to do to cope."

"That could be really good for you," I said.

I genuinely meant it, too. She needed something and having dealt with a therapist myself in jail, I knew how helpful it could be.

"Yeah?" She raised a brow as if unsure if I was being serious.

"Definitely. I had a counselor when I was locked up. I tried to ... kill myself," I admitted.

I bit down on my lip and squeezed my eyes shut. *Shit! Why did I say that?* I took a deep breath and let it out slowly before opening my eyes. When I did, she was gazing at me. Not with the horror or shock that I suspected, but with curiosity and maybe a bit of understanding.

Chapter 19

Mackaela

Simon seemed so carefree and easy going. I was surprised to hear he'd attempted suicide. I knew he struggled with losing his mom and he was wrongfully accused of a crime he didn't commit. I guess it would make sense for him to need an escape. I personally hadn't ever really considered killing myself. I think it was due to the fact that my own mother had already tried to take my life away from me and I refused to give in to what she wanted. I felt that going on living was a way to spite her.

"Did counseling help?" I asked.

I could use some insight from more than just one person on the pros and cons of seeing a therapist.

"I think it did in some ways, but it also brought out a lot in me emotionally. I was forced to look at myself and face what I was doing wrong. I had to change."

"I'm sure it wasn't all you though," I said as a way to reassure him.

Simon smiled slightly. "It wasn't all me, no. Having an addict for a mom and an abusive step-dad kind of set me in bad ways. I'm better now, but there's still days I struggle."

"What do you struggle with?" I asked quietly.

"Aggression is a big one. I tend to get riled up pretty easy. I'm always on the defensive, wanting to protect myself and others. Sometimes I have nightmares." He shrugged.

"Do you dream about the abuse?"

Simon looked away from me and narrowed his eyes at the wall. He took a deep breath, letting it out slowly before nodding.

"My step-dad would lock me in my room for hours. I'd get so hungry that I'd scream through the door until I lost my voice. I just wanted to get out of there. If I yelled loud enough, he would come in and beat me. After that, I'd run down to the kitchen and snag fruit or bread and then take off outside."

Mickey and Jack were so wrong about how he lived. There was nothing good about the way he grew up. My heart ached for him. I was grateful I hadn't experienced constant abuse like that. It made my problems seem so much smaller.

I couldn't help the tears that welled in my eyes. I had the sudden urge to comfort him like he had me so many times before. There was more to him than I originally thought. Simon swallowed hard. His gaze came back to me, looking guarded and wary.

"Once my mom died, I ended up crashing with friends. Then I rented a shitty apartment while I drank myself to oblivion. I'd get lost in girls and fights and working on cars."

"What made you decide to find Mickey?"

"I'd learned through my cell mate, who was a dealer, that Mickey was the top guy in Seattle for running drugs. I wanted to see him. I'd always thought about him growing up. When I was a kid, sometimes I'd lay awake at night and pray that Jack would come get me." Simon shook his head, clearing his throat. "I tracked him down after I got out."

"And now you're here," I said wistfully. Simon chuckled lightly.

"I'd rather be here than anywhere else right now. You and Mick are the only ones who really know the extent of what I went through. It's not something I like to talk about. It's hard to control myself around you."

I felt the same way, but I wasn't ready to admit it. Instead, I said, "Thanks, by the way."

"What are you thanking me for?"

"For sharing your story with me. I want to hide all the things about me. But I know there are good people out there with good intentions. You've shown me that."

He nodded, scratching at the hair on his jawline.

"I just want you to trust me. We have this connection. And whatever it is, whatever happens between us, I just don't want to lose you."

I sat up straighter in my chair, stretching my hand out to cover Simon's. "I'm starting to realize having people in your life isn't a bad thing. I might have trust issues for the rest of my life, but if I don't put myself out there, I'll be stuck in the hell I've created for myself. I don't want to be that girl anymore."

Simon flipped his hand over so that he could interlock his fingers with mine and he smiled at me. "I'm glad I met you, Mackaela." It was the simplest, purest phrase and yet held so much meaning.

"Me too," I whispered.

*

I went to see Simon every day after that. Mickey and I would swap shifts, me usually arriving in the morning and Mickey visiting at night. I brought playing cards and music for Simon so that he wouldn't get overly bored. It had to be rough, being stuck in a place with strict hours of visitation and nothing to do but lie there and watch TV.

It felt so natural spending time with him. Sometimes we would talk about mundane things like my plans for the day or he'd tell me jokes. I'd laugh at some of them and then laugh at how stupid the other ones were. He'd comment on my taste of music or lack of it in some cases. He said my playlist was a scattered assortment of great music and plain crap. I defended my Britney Spears albums. You never knew when you'd need a little Britney to get through the day. I wasn't ashamed of it.

Simon was my friend again, and for the first time in a few weeks, I was smiling more often than not. Almost happy, like I'd started to feel when we'd first spent time together. When I wasn't with Simon, I was doing light work for Mickey. He didn't want me in the business any more than I did. I even enrolled in some courses online in order to get my high school diploma. Sadie came over every night to keep me company.

I was beginning to notice a change in me. I wasn't really having nightmares anymore. Occasionally one would slip in, but even those seemed less intense somehow.

Mickey's meeting with his father was to discuss the new changes that Mickey wanted to make on his end of things. He explained to Jack about Hawks and what he could offer them. Jack seemed on board with Mickey's decision and wanted to come back to Seattle in a month to meet Hawks and see how things were going. Simon didn't speak to Jack again after their last encounter. I didn't blame him.

It was the following Saturday, and Simon had been in the hospital just a day shy of two weeks. The doctors and nurses all said he was healing faster than expected and gave him the go ahead to be released. I spent the entire morning cleaning his bedroom and washing the sheets since I'd slept there while he was gone. He was to remain on bed rest for another two weeks before considering any strenuous activity. He was mad about it but he didn't have much choice unless he wanted to end up back in the hospital. Mickey was picking up Simon and bringing him home, so once my cleaning was done, I decided to make a late lunch for everyone.

It was the first time in weeks that I'd actually been truly alone. Mickey still hadn't heard anything new on Ricky's whereabouts, but there was a pretty informative rumor that he'd run down to Portland and they were trying to get eyes on him. That meant I no longer needed Dom as a bodyguard.

I decided on vegetable beef soup and grilled cheese sandwiches for lunch. I knew that Simon had been eating minimal amounts of hospital food, so I wasn't sure what his stomach could handle. Soup seemed like the best way to go.

I was just plating the sandwiches when I heard the front door open. I turned down the burner with the soup atop it and set the plate of sandwiches on the table before heading for the entryway.

Mickey was holding Simon up around the waist and huffed a "Hey," as he navigated toward the living room.

I closed the door for him and tried really hard not to stare at a shirtless Simon with a pair of faded blue jeans hanging low on his hips. Even with a large bandage on his abdomen, he still looked good. His hair had grown out a little but he'd been able to finally shave a few days ago, so there was minimal stubble along his square jaw, circling his lips. Even after what he'd been through, I couldn't help the way my body responded to him. I still wanted him.

Mickey set him in the recliner and then straightened. "God, you're heavy!" He turned to face me. "It smells good in here. What are you making?"

"Soup and grilled cheese sandwiches, no biggie." I shrugged, looking in Simon's direction. "I think only soup for you though, you hungry?"

His emerald eyes looked brighter than they had in a long time. They sparkled up at me as a slow grin spread across his face. "I'm starving."

Nodding, I went to get him a bowl of soup. When I came back out, Mickey had taken the entire plate of grilled cheese and made himself comfortable on the couch. His legs were up on the coffee table, his mouth full as he balanced the plate on his lap and channel surfed. I handed Simon his bowl.

"Careful, it's hot," I warned.

"Thanks." He grinned at me. "I could get used to this," he added as I backed away from him.

"They spoiled you. I guess you think I need to be your nurse now?" I teased.

"Would you?" His brows rose, that grin turning mischievous.

I couldn't help the slow blush that surfaced at the way he was looking at me, especially right in front of Mickey.

Rolling my eyes, I said, "No." Simon shrugged.

"Can't blame a guy for trying, who wouldn't want a gorgeous nurse to tend to them?"

Mick snorted. "I know I would. That's like a guy's ultimate fantasy. Sponge bath, sexy little nurse outfit, maybe a little oral medication." He waggled his eyebrows and my nose wrinkled.

"God, that's awful!" I said.

Simon shrugged slightly, slurping some of the soup. "He's not wrong."

Shaking my head, I decided to leave them to their dumb ideas and eat my lunch in the kitchen. The last thing I needed to be thinking about was playing doctor with Simon Silver.

Simon

It felt amazing to be out of the hospital and back at Mick's place. I'd only been joking about the nurse thing with Mackaela, though it seemed she was extra attentive to me without noticing it. She kept asking how I was feeling or if I needed anything.

I wasn't used to being taken care of. It was a side of her I hadn't really expected but I was enjoying it. Our friendship as it was now was growing more with each passing day. She'd visited me in the hospital and was still living at Mick's. I liked having her around. It felt ... right.

There were a few times I would catch her gazing at me, her eyes slightly hooded as she chewed on her bottom lip. It was a good thing I couldn't move extremely fast or far yet, because I really wanted to grab her and kiss her every time I caught her with that look on her face.

It'd been two and a half days since I was home, and today would be the first time I was left alone for a few hours. Mick was busy working on new developments with Hawks and our father while Mackaela had her first counseling appointment. At the moment, I was propped up with some pillows, lying in my bed while she fluttered around the room, tidying up. She was rambling on about how everything I needed would be in reach and if I had any problems to call her right away. I smiled and nodded, my hands resting behind my head.

I wasn't paying too much attention to be honest. Her cute little ass shuffling around was a happy distraction. She was wearing these cutoff denim shorts that showcased her long legs. Suddenly she sighed and plopped down on the bed next to me.

"I don't want to go," she said quietly. Her thin fingers were picking at the lint of my comforter.

"It's going to be good for you," I said. "I mean, just think of how nice it'll be to get things off your chest. I hated counseling because it felt forced, but it was nice to have someone to talk to."

Mackaela pursed those full lips of hers and narrowed her eyes at me. "I've never talked about everything before. I've told Sadie a few things and you and Mickey, but I've never gone into great detail. What if I break down? What happens if it becomes too much?" Her eyes were searching mine, trying to find a definitive answer to her very reasonable questions.

Unfortunately, I had no answer for her. Everyone handled things differently and I didn't know enough about her issues to say one way or another.

I lowered my hands from my head and placed one of them on her shoulder, tangling my fingers in the hair there. "I can't answer that for you."

Her brow furrowed and those golden eyes turned down in sadness. She nodded slowly. I ran my fingers across her jaw, cupping her chin lightly, guiding her face up so that she would meet my eyes. "This is good for you, okay? I'm here for you if you need me."

"I know, thank you, Simon." She blew out a breath and started to move away. "I better go."

"Hold on," I ordered, startling her briefly.

She caught my eyes again and gave me a questioning look. I reached for the chain around my neck, pulling it over my head. I held it out to her.

"What are you doing?"

"Take this," I said with a half-smile. "If you start to get overwhelmed or something, just know I'm with you. Well, a part of me is with you. Maybe it'll help you calm down."

"I can't take this, Simon. It's special to you."

I flipped her hand over, lying the chain in her palm, closing her fingers around it in a fist and shaking my head.

"You're special to me. Take it."

She relented and stood from the bed.

"Thanks," she mumbled, placing it around her neck.

As she made her way to the door, she said, "Call me if you need anything. I should be back in a few hours."

"I'll be fine," I assured her. She gave me a short smile before leaving the room.

I sighed and placed my hands back behind my head. I hoped she'd be okay and gain some clarity. I was able to see a spark in her that I hadn't seen before and if I could notice that after a short time of knowing her, then I'm sure everyone else noticed, too. Mick had commented yesterday that he didn't worry about her as much. He also said that my being here helped. Sometimes I wondered if he'd picked up on our innocent flirting, but he never seemed to mention it. He trusted me, which was great, but if he knew what went on inside my head, he might change his mind.

Part of me wanted to talk to Mick about it, about her. I knew he wanted the best for her. Though I wasn't sure he'd think me a good choice for his best friend. Not when he put her on a pedestal and knew her better than anyone. I was afraid to break his trust, and I didn't want to break her heart. We were friends and if that's all we could ever be, I'd take it. I felt blessed just knowing her, having the chance to kiss those beautiful lips that no man had touched before. To be able to hold her against me, her warm soft body in my arms.

I wanted to protect her and comfort her and take away all her pain and sadness. I wanted to give her my heart and cherish her and worship her. God help me I wanted her: Mind, body and soul.

The problem with having nothing but time on your hands was your mind's ability to wander. I wished I could shut my brain off right about now. I glanced at the nightstand and saw a glass of water and two pills sitting there. *Ah, something to knock me out for a bit, perfect.* I grabbed the pills and shoved them into my mouth as I gulped down the entire glass of water.

I gingerly lowered myself further under my blankets. Within minutes, my mind was a steady buzz of nothingness and I drifted off to sleep.

Chapter 20

Mackaela

My stomach was in knots, my palms sweaty as I sat in the well-lit waiting area of Holly Pearson's quaint office. It didn't look at all how I expected because it wasn't technically an office but an old historical house that had been converted.

I entered through the glass door which had a little bell announcing my presence and was instantly greeted by a woman who appeared to be in her mid-thirties. She was seated behind a large desk that held a computer and a large desk calendar. She smiled warmly at me with kind blue eyes behind small framed, black glasses.

"Hello there. How can I help you?"

"I'm Mackaela Stone. I'm here to see Holly." My trembling fingers were firmly knotted together against the edge of my jacket.

She looked down at the calendar and then to the computer. "You're right on time, Mackaela. Have a seat. I'll let Holly know you're here." She extended her arm to motion to a sitting area that held two antique looking chairs and a small sofa.

"Thank you," I said softly.

I was trying not to show how incredibly nervous I was. My hand came up to the long chain around my neck. I began twirling the ring with my fingers to distract myself. I thought of Simon and how he told me not to worry. This was a good thing for me, I knew that, but I was afraid, too.

I wasn't waiting long, maybe five minutes, when I heard a women's voice down the narrow hall. When I saw her, I calmed a little, now having a face to put to the name. I was always on edge meeting new people. Holly was tall with chestnut colored hair that she had slicked back in a sleek ponytail. She was wearing a burgundy blazer with a fashionable scarf and jeans. She appeared to be casual and not at all the mean librarian type that I for some reason imagined. She didn't even wear glasses.

Holly said something in a hushed tone to the gal at the desk and then turned to me with a smile. I offered her a meek smile in return.

"Hi, Mackaela, how are you?" she asked with a warm tone. I stood slowly.

"I'm good, thank you."

"Come with me," she said and began walking down the hall.

She led me through a dark, wooden door, into her vast office. It was bright in this room, the large window letting in the natural sunlight of the day.

"Take a seat," she said. I stiffly settled myself onto the beige sofa and set my purse beside me. Holly had a small desk with a laptop on it and a phone, but she sat in a comfortable looking chair that matched the sofa directly across from me. "Are you nervous?"

I reluctantly nodded but said nothing. She smiled at me. "It's okay to be nervous. Have you ever been to counseling before?"

"No, I never wanted to ... talk about things before."

"That's okay. It can be hard to express yourself, especially if you aren't sure what you're feeling. So what made you come today?"

"I wanted to see if it would help to talk to a professional. I have a lot of stuff I've been struggling with for a long time. I'm trying to start fresh, learn to cope. Turn over a new leaf so to speak," I explained.

"Okay, that's great. How about we start slow before moving up to the deeper stuff," Holly said, winking at me.

Her casual demeanor and no pressure attitude caused me to smile involuntarily. I released a breath and relaxed.

"That sounds great."

"Good. So how old are you, Mackaela?"

"I'm twenty-one. I'll be twenty-two in October."

"And do you work or go to school?"

I chewed on my bottom lip, trying to think of how to answer that. "Well, I just started some online schooling to get my diploma."

"That's great! Is that all you're doing right now?"

I shook my head.

"I also work … for my best friend. I guess I'm sort of his office assistant and customer service person." *Yeah, let's go with that.*

"Okay. Do you like what you do?"

Not all of it.

"It has its perks; you know, working for a friend and all. But I want to do something else eventually. Maybe have a real career," I answered as honestly as I could.

"That's responsible of you. So tell me, why did you not graduate high school?"

And there it was. The first question that would lead to a series of others, to bring up my past and force me to face it head on. My hand, having a mind of its own, lifted to the chain again and I twisted it nervously.

"I started having problems at home when I was sixteen. I ended up moving out and school didn't seem like a priority at the time."

"What kind of problems?"

I swallowed the lump that was starting to form in my throat. There was no conversation that wasn't deep. Everything led to the demons that chased me my whole life.

"My mother and I didn't get along," I said quietly.

"That's quite common for teenagers. If you don't mind me asking, was it just a case of rebellion?" Holly asked.

I swallowed three more times before gaining the courage to speak. I let out a slow breath. "No offense, but this is already getting deep. To be completely honest, I'm not sure if I'm ready to talk about it yet." I clutched the chain tighter and blinked a few times.

Please don't cry, please don't cry.

Holly leaned forward in her chair and placed a hand on my knee. "It's okay, Mackaela. Whenever you're ready to talk is fine. I'm not going to pressure you into speaking."

"Okay." I breathed.

"You seem to be favoring that necklace. The ring is pretty. Is it yours?" she asked, changing the subject for the moment.

I was grateful for the change and began shaking my head. "No, it belongs to a friend. The ring was his mother's and he usually wears it. He lent it to me so that a piece of him would be here."

The entire exchange of the necklace between Simon and I hadn't seemed like a big deal but explaining it to a stranger made it seem more sentimental. Holly smiled.

"That's extremely sweet. He seems like a good friend. Is this the one you work for?" she asked.

"No, my best friend Mickey is who I work for. His brother, Simon, gave me the necklace."

Holly raised a brow at me. "Did you guys grow up together?"

"I grew up with Mickey. Well, I met him when I was a teenager. Simon didn't live with him."

"How long have you known Simon?"

"It's been about two months now, we're uncommonly close for not knowing each other that long."

"It's completely normal to have a deeper connection with someone even if you've only known them a short time, Mackaela. He seems to care about you an awful lot to trust you with his mother's ring."

It was a huge deal that Simon allowed me to have the ring. It made me feel comforted and yet somehow also afraid.

"Are you all right?" Holly must have read the look of contemplation on my face.

"Yes, I just ... I'm not sure how to handle having new friends. It's part of my other issues. I'm trying really hard lately to let people in, but I'm sort of confused."

"Confused how?" she probed.

I looked down at my lap and furrowed my brow. I needed to think of how to say this without sounding like a pessimist. "I guess I just don't understand why anyone would want to get to know me. I'm not used to being ... cared for," I admitted quietly.

"You weren't treated well growing up?" Holly guessed.

I let out a long breath and closed my eyes. "I was until my father left."

"And when did your father leave?"

"When I was fourteen. He left my mother and me for another woman."

"You sound ashamed," Holly noted. I lifted my head and met her eyes.

"I guess sometimes I feel like it's my fault that he left. Maybe I wasn't a good enough child or my mother wasn't good enough."

"Did he ever say anything like that to you?"

"No, he just said that people change and love is something you can fall out of overtime." I shrugged.

"Do you believe that?" Holly asked.

"No, I don't. I think that love is unconditional when it's right."

"What do you mean 'right?'"

"Meaning that you're with someone for all of the right reasons," I explained. "You truly know that deep down you would die without them in your life. I think the word love is overrated and people will lie to you just to get what they want from you. Love, the emotion not the word, is a powerful moving force and it's worth everything if you find it."

Holly smiled at me and nodded. "That's pretty powerful, Mackaela." I half-smiled.

"I'm really not that bothered by what my dad did as far as leaving. It's more how it affected my mother and me. That's what hurts."

"How did it affect you?"

"Honestly, it didn't really mean anything to me for a while. It wasn't until my mother started to become depressed and withdraw. She had to work and provide for me on her own which was something she wasn't used to. And she started to spend more time with men."

I couldn't believe I was willingly talking about this with Holly. I was surprised at the fact that it just seemed to flow from me without reluctance. I was no longer nervous.

"Did she see a lot of men?"

"She never brought them home at first. There were times when she would just go straight out after work with whomever and not come in until after I was in bed. I hated that she was acting that way, but I couldn't really say anything. She was the adult. I was afraid after my father left that she wouldn't ever smile again. She seemed cheerful again, you know?"

"But it bothered you. You weren't happy?" she inquired.

"I wasn't happy, no. But I met Mickey shortly before my parents divorced. He was kind of that peace for me, a person that

I could vent to and spend time around when I didn't feel like being at home. He made me forget the drama."

"It's good to have someone like that," Holly noted.

"If I didn't have him then, I don't know what I would have done," I admitted.

"When did you stop attending school?"

I closed my eyes and took a deep breath, exhaling slowly.

"When I was sixteen, almost seventeen, and I couldn't bear the thought of facing anyone anymore."

"Why is that, Mackaela?" Holly's voice was quiet and she continued to sit, leaning forward slightly, totally engaged in our conversation.

She was actually listening to me and though I was still un-enthusiastic to bare my soul, I knew that I needed to do this. I wanted like hell to get better. I fingered the ring around my neck and took another deep breath before speaking. When I did, it all came out in a rush.

"My mother started dating this guy. He was younger than her, maybe in his late twenties or early thirties. It was nice at first. He would spend time at the house with both my mom and me. He actually seemed like a pretty nice guy and my mom was the happiest I'd seen her.

"School had just gotten out for the summer and I spent the day with Mickey. My mother called me that afternoon and said that they were having a party to celebrate the guy's job promo-tion. She asked if I would be there and I agreed. As it turned out, Mickey got a call from his father on the way to my house that evening and he had to go home." I stopped talking sud-denly as the mental images began to resurface in my brain. It was like a bad movie playing through all the details of what led up to my worst nightmare.

"Mackaela, you don't have to go on unless you're ready," Holly said reassuringly as she patted my knee again.

I nodded as my eyes met hers. "I feel like I need to talk about this. Maybe it won't haunt me so much."

"Sometimes that can help, but if you aren't ready ... " She trailed off.

I decided that it was worth everything to take the risk. I didn't want the heaviness anymore. It was time to let it go.

"As soon as Mickey dropped me off, I had this unsettling feeling like something bad was about to happen. I wish I would have listened to my gut and stayed outside or called Mickey to come back for me. Knowing my mother was there, I decided to let go of the feeling and join the party.

"As soon as I walked into the house, I could smell alcohol and cigarette smoke. The music was playing incredibly loud. I didn't see my mother right away or her boyfriend, Jason. There was a man there, I think his name was Gary and he was one of Jason's friends. He came up to me, so I asked him where my mother was. He told me that she'd gone upstairs a few minutes before." I could feel the tears welling in my eyes as my voice started to waiver.

Holly reached out and placed her hand over mine, squeezing gently to let me know that she was here for me. I swallowed the lump in my throat and continued.

"I should have gone upstairs to find her but I didn't. Instead, I went to the kitchen where Jason was. As soon as I entered the room, he saw me and immediately came up to me, placing an arm around my shoulder." Holly handed me a tissue from the side table as the tears began to fall.

"He used to call me '"beautiful."' Initially, I'd taken it as a term of endearment. Looking back, he never said it in front of my mom and now I know why." A sob broke free from my throat as I dabbed at my eyes once more.

"So when he put his arm around me, I could smell the alcohol on him and his eyes were glassy. He was definitely drunk. He had said, '"Hey, beautiful, care for a drink?"' I, of course, being used to hanging out with Mickey and his friends, had drank before and my mother knew about it. She didn't care so I didn't hesitate to accept it.

"I know now that you should never ever accept a drink from someone. I should have just taken a beer or made my own or not had anything at all. He claimed he made me whisky and coke. I'd never had one before, so when he handed it to me and I took a drink, I assumed it tasted fine. Everything was okay for a while until I was about halfway done with my drink. This is where it starts to get hazy," I explained. Holly, who was still holding my hand, softly nodded.

"Take your time, honey."

I looked down at the tissue in my hands. I was ringing it around and around anxiously, trying for the millionth time to piece everything together and describe what happened. The part that haunted me the most was not remembering a lot of what actually happened. Just bits and pieces. My nightmares filled in the rest.

"He led the way out the back door toward the garage. I remember him clutching my hand tightly. As soon as we went in, he shut the door and turned to me. It was dark in there but I could sort of make out his face and those dark eyes that he had. They were darker than normal somehow. Then he grabbed me by the shoulders. I remember asking him what he was doing, but he ignored me and turned me around so that my back was to the door and he pressed me up against it.

"I remember telling him to stop. I can almost recall begging him to stop and saying that I wasn't ready for this. It was like a dream, an out of body experience. I couldn't really feel it. I was there but not there and in my head I was screaming for him to stop!" More tears began to fall relentlessly as I told my story.

"The next thing that I recall is waking up in my own bed alone." My voice was strained and another sob rocked through me. I gave in to the sorrow and let myself cry, not caring where I was or who I was in front of.

Holly remained quiet, holding my hand with hers and consoling me with soft murmurs. I let years of pent up fear and sadness release from my system, and when the last tears fell, I felt cleansed somehow.

Chapter 21

Mackaela

Holly talked to me about being the victim of rape and some of the coping mechanisms that could help. I was scheduled to meet up with her again next week at the same time and was actually looking forward to it. Years of pent up fear and confusion had been released during my first session with her. If I kept at it, who knows how much better I'd feel.

I pulled into the driveway beside Simon's Range Rover which had sat untouched since the shooting incident. I hoped that he was able to rest. I knew he was bored with having to be stuck in bed day in and day out, but the more he rested the sooner he could heal. I wanted to do everything in my power to make sure he was comfortable and taken care of. It wasn't that I felt guilty about him saving me, even though I'd often think about the fact that he actually took a bullet for me. He literally risked his life for a girl he hardly knew. It spoke volumes about who he was as a person and made it easier to find a way to trust him.

I tossed my keys and purse on the bench in the entryway and made my way up to Simon's room to check on him. He was lying on his back, his brow furrowed. He mumbled something and then sucked in a sharp breath. He let out a loud moan as if in pain. I darted to the bed, kneeling beside him. His forehead was damp, his cheeks pale.

"Simon, wake up," I murmured, curling my hand on his bicep.

His head moved side to side before he spoke in a whisper., "Just leave me alone."

"Hey, you're dreaming. Wake up.," I said a little louder, shaking him slightly.

Before I could say anything further, his right hand covered mine, gripping my wrist tightly. His eyes flew open as he heaved a breath.

Blinking up at me, his brow crumpled. "Mackaela?" he murmured, releasing me.

I nodded. "Yeah, I'm here."

"You're real, you're here." He blinked at me as realization sunk in. "It was a dream." His voice wavered slightly.

"Are you okay? I thought you were hurt," I said tentatively, gliding my finger below his eye.

He'd been crying. My gaze lowered to his parted lips. He was so vulnerable, so much like me. He lifted his hand, brushing the hair back from my face, tucking it behind my ear. My eyes drifted closed at the contact.

Before I could make sense of what was happening, my head lowered toward his. It was as if I had the sudden urge to comfort him the only way I knew how. Maybe I was seeking my own comfort after ripping myself open earlier.

The moment my lips pressed against his, he groaned, parting his lips and tasting me with an intensity that ignited a fire within me. I gave as much as I was getting, shifting myself closer to him but trying not to hurt him or his wound. He ran his tongue against my bottom lip, making me moan as he ran his fingers through my hair, over my neck, my cheek. Before it could go too far, I pulled away from him.

"Simon ... " My breath was erratic, heart pounding mercilessly in my chest. "You're still healing."

His eyes opened slowly, giving me a short nod as he removed his hands from me. "I'm sorry, I wasn't thinking clearly. I had this dream and it ... was pretty intense. I just needed to forget." He ran a hand through his hair.

"Do you want to talk about it?" I asked, shifting so that I was sitting up fully beside him.

He let out a breath, straightening the covers over the lower half of his body. "My mother was in it. She spoke to me."

"She did?"

Simon began to lift himself slowly so that his back was now propped against his pillows.

He gazed across the room, staring at the dresser on the far wall. "It was so strange. It felt so real. I was in this meadow and the sun was shining and there were flowers everywhere. Daisies mostly, those were my mother's favorite." He glanced at me and smiled. "I saw her there, so I went to her. The way she touched me, her voice and how she looked, it was all so real."

"No wonder you were so shaken," I said quietly.

I had the urge to hold his hand or put an arm around his shoulders. I just wanted him to know that I was here, that I would try to be here for him as best I could. But I was afraid if I touched him again, I'd kiss him again.

"I didn't want her to leave. I feel like I never really got the chance to grieve when she died. So much had happened before and after her death."

"I'm so sorry, Simon." It was all I could think to say.

He gazed at me, smiling slightly. "I'm sorry. I shouldn't be unloading on you. Not when you just got back from the counselor."

I shook my head.

"Don't worry about that now. What did your mother say in your dream?"

His jaw muscle flexed as he glanced up at the ceiling before dropping his gaze to his hands clasped against his stomach. "She said she was proud of me."

His shoulder lifted slightly in a shrug before he closed his eyes and exhaled soundly. When his eyes opened again, they were brimming with tears. "She saved me. I thought about her a lot after being shot. She said I had so much left to live for and people who needed me. Like Mick. I feel like maybe I can help him realize he doesn't need to be in the business. He deserves better. We all do."

"He's definitely changed since you've come back into his life," I admitted. "He seems to think more about those around him, not just me. I honestly don't know what he'd do without you now."

"What about you?" he asked in a soft voice.

My eyes searched his and I bit down on my bottom lip. "Me?"

"Have you changed since knowing me?"

"You know that I have," I said softly.

I wound my hands together nervously as I stared at the comforter beneath me. I wasn't sure how to respond. I wanted to tell Simon exactly what he made me feel, but I was scared. I thought about how much better I felt just a short while ago after opening up to Holly. Couldn't I do the same with Simon? Risking a glance at him, I licked my lips.

"Simon, when you showed up, I was in a dark place. I was stuck in this never ending cycle of just getting by day to day. I wasn't worried about living as long as I was simply surviving. I had nightmares, I still do occasionally, of being raped or burned."

His eyes remained locked on mine intently but his expression was unreadable. Shaking my head, I continued. "There's something about you, like a light to my darkness, and you were able to open me up in a way I've never experienced. It's terrifying because I don't know what this pull is between us, but I feel it. I feel. You make me ... feel again." My voice trailed off in a whisper and I let my gaze fall back to the comforter.

My confession hung in the air between us. I felt his body shift toward me, his warm fingers intertwined with mine. I cautiously lifted my gaze to his. He swallowed and drew in a shaky breath.

"I know." He spoke so low I barely heard him.

My face crumpled in confusion. Simon's lips tilted up slightly, his thumb tracing circles inside my trembling palm.

"We were meant to know each other. For some crazy reason I can't comprehend, I'm lucky enough to know you."

I felt the tears welling yet again and I swallowed my heart as it beat faster, crawling up my chest and into my throat.

"I want to hide the truth from you, Simon. It's so dark inside me sometimes that I'm scared if I become too attached to you, I'll only let you down." A tear rolled down my cheek and I quickly swiped it away.

Simon shook his head and took his hand away from mine, moving it up to my chin, gently curling his fingers against it.

"Nothing you say or do will ever let me down sweetheart. Look at how far you've come just in a matter of months. You're already rising from the ashes of your past. You just have to keep fighting. You have to fight, gorgeous girl, and you can do anything, be anything. I believe that when I look at you."

"I care about you, Simon. I don't know what you did or why I deserve a person like you in my life, but it's true. I do care about you."

His thumb slid across my cheek, wiping my tears away.

"I care about you too, sweetheart. More than I should, more than I thought I ever could. You've gotten under my skin."

Simon

Mackaela had just opened up to me more than she ever had and it felt like a piece of my cracked heart had fused together. I wished I could take away every bad nightmare from her. When she told me about the nightmares, a mixture of emotions went through me. I was angry that someone had power over her to make her feel helpless. I was sad that she'd been dealt such a shitty hand at a young age.

We sat in silence for a while. Both of us soaking in this new admission between us. The medication must have still been in my system because I began to feel sleep pulling me in again. I lowered myself further down on the pillows and let out a yawn.

"You should get some rest," Mackaela said. "I don't want to keep you awake."

I rolled my head to the side, glancing up at her. "Will you lay with me?"

I wasn't ready to let her go yet, to have her away from me. Maybe it made me a chump, I didn't care. This girl had a massive effect on me and I was totally tangled up in her. She chewed on her bottom lip, deliberating for a moment.

"Please?" I said quietly.

Mackaela's gaze drifted to mine and an unreadable expression filled her eyes. She nodded, sinking down next to my side carefully. We both lay there on our backs, my arms bent with my fingers interlocked on my stomach, her arms loosely at her sides.

After a few minutes, I let the arm nearest her glide down to the mattress, my fingers lightly brushing her forearm and wrist. When she didn't move away, I hooked my fingers with hers. I couldn't think of a single better way to embrace darkness than feeling her warm soft skin against me.

*

I awoke a few hours later to the sound of the front door slamming downstairs. My eyes shot open and I immediately rolled my head to my left, seeing Mackaela sound asleep. Those long dark lashes rested on her cheekbones and her full, pink lips were slightly parted. She looked so peaceful, so innocent right now. Her face smoothed of any worry lines. Her eyelids fluttered when I tucked her hair behind her ear.

"Wake up, sweetheart," I said softly.

I ran my hand down her shoulder, dragging my fingers up and down. She began stirring, her golden eyes opening slowly.

"Simon?" she breathed.

I couldn't help but smile at the way she lifted her head and took in her surroundings. Once she seemed confident of where she was and why, she sat up straighter. Clearing my throat, I sat up a little.

"I think Mick's home."

Mackaela ran a hand through her long brown hair.

"I must have been more exhausted than I thought," she mumbled.

Mick called out for her, and I heard him ascend the stairs. She immediately jumped up from the bed, smoothing her clothes and dragging a hand through her hair again.

"I'm in here," she said, moving toward the door. Mick entered my room, his brows raised.

"I tried calling you."

"Yeah, my phone must be downstairs. I guess I didn't hear it," she explained.

Mick shifted his gaze to me.

"I'm actually glad you're home," I said, pushing the blankets off. "I need help getting to the bathroom. I'm sure Mackaela doesn't want to accompany me." I smirked at her, seeing her cheeks darken. I chuckled. "Didn't think so."

"Sure, man, no problem. I need to talk to you anyway. Sounds like we're ready to bring Ricky down."

I glanced over at Mackaela, catching her staring at me, specifically my stomach and the black boxer briefs I was wearing as Mickey helped me out of bed. As soon as she noticed, she shifted her gaze to the door.

"I'm going to look for something for dinner," she said to no one in particular as she left the room.

Mick chuckled, rolling his eyes as I hobbled toward the bathroom.

"What?"

"Did you see her blushing? I've never seen her like that before. Wonder why she's like that with you?"

I shrugged. "Beats me. It's probably because I'm hot."

He stopped suddenly, loosening his hold on me. I braced myself against the door frame.

"You didn't make a pass at her, did you?"

I froze momentarily.

Fuck, where the hell did that come from? "No, man. She isn't the type of girl you just mess around with." It was the truth. I didn't want one part of Mackaela. I wanted all of her.

"Good. I don't want her getting wrapped up in something she isn't ready for."

And that right there told me everything I needed to know about my brother and how he'd react if he knew just how invested I was in his best friend. I'm glad we hadn't said anything to him. Although, I couldn't lie forever, and I didn't want to. The truth would come out eventually because there was no way in hell I was leaving her alone. Even if that meant pissing off my brother.

"Anyway, I sent Hawks down to Portland to snag Ricky. He's being held at a warehouse down there by one of his men. He should be transported back to Seattle in the next couple of days. I'll handle it from there."

There was a darkness in his eyes as they held mine. A promise that Ricky Delgado would suffer for trying to take my life, for attempting to kidnap Mackaela. I nodded at my brother. Maybe I was more cut out for this business than I wanted to admit because I didn't feel the least bit sorry for Ricky and what Mick would do to teach him a lesson. I'd only wish that I were healed enough to offer a few punishing blows as well.

Chapter 22

Mackaela

Once downstairs, I took a seat in one of the bar stools at the island and let my head fall into my hands. I'd woken up to Simon's beautiful eyes staring back at me. My heart was still beating irregularly at the way he looked at me. Like I was special, like he wanted me. It was out there now, how we felt about each other, and I wasn't sure if I could shake him anymore. I didn't want to. Simon Silver had crept into me, gotten under my skin, and took up residence in my heart. There was no denying we had something special. That we connected in a way that for the first time in my life made me feel understood, made me feel okay.

I didn't hear Mickey enter the kitchen. He startled me when he spoke.

"You okay there?" he asked as he backed against the counter, leaning against it with his hands propped on either side.

My head snapped up. Mickey of all people would know something was up. I didn't want to talk to him about it, at least not until I could get my bearings.

"Sure, I'm fine. I just have a lot on my mind. The counseling appointment was pretty intense."

He nodded, crossing his arms over his chest. "Did you talk about the past?"

"Yeah. At first, it was hard to open up, but once I started talking it all just kind of fell out. Well, some of it anyway."

I didn't like being under his scrutiny, so I got up and started rummaging through the fridge. I was getting hungry and cooking would be a welcomed distraction.

"What did you talk about?"

I closed my eyes and let out a slow breath before righting myself and closing the door to the refrigerator.

I turned around and met Mickey's concerned gaze. "I told her about what happened with my mom's boyfriend. I spilled every last detail about how he did what he did."

We stood there in silence for a few moments before I turned back around, looking through the cupboards. I decided to make spaghetti because I knew Simon liked it and I wanted to thank him for being there for me, for understanding me. The way to a man's heart was his stomach, right?

"I'm going to make spaghetti for dinner, you all right with that?" I asked over my shoulder as I grabbed the noodles.

"Sure thing." Mickey started to walk out of the kitchen but stopped short at the entryway.

I clutched the box of noodles, blinking at him. I watched his eyes lower to my neck and then my chest. His brow crumpled, his gaze shooting back to mine, piercing me with a heated look.

"Why are you wearing Simon's necklace?" Mickey's head cocked to one side, his eyes never leaving mine.

My throat went dry. I couldn't tell if he was simply curious or if he was upset. The truth was the only thing that came to mind and so I told him.

"Simon let me wear it for my session. He said it might bring me some comfort. I was pretty nervous before I left here." Mickey crossed his arms again and narrowed his eyes at me.

"What were you two doing before I got here?"

"Talking, we were just talking. I was telling him about the counselor and he had a dream and—" I was rambling, answering too quickly and I knew that Mickey knew.

The realization of just how close Simon and I had gotten was coming to him little by little.

"You two seem to have bonded more. Especially in the last week," he spoke carefully.

I licked my lips, shaking my head. "You wanted me to trust him, Mickey. He comforted me when my mother died, he ... saved my life. I care about him." My voice was unsteady, meek.

I wasn't at all sure what his reaction would be. I was crushing the damn box of noodles, but I couldn't loosen my grip. Mickey's eyes widened as he marched toward me, stopping once we were toe to toe.

"You care about him?" he asked incredulously.

I swallowed and nodded, my eyes falling to the tile floor.

"Did he touch you?" He growled.

My head snapped up, eyes narrowing to slits. "No! Well not in any way you should be worried about."

Mickey's eyes darkened, his jaw tightening as he clenched his fists at his side. "What the fuck is that supposed to mean?" He was upset, I knew that much.

My irritation rose as he looked at me accusingly. Mickey wasn't my dad, he wasn't my older brother, though he sort of felt like one at times. I always appreciated his protectiveness toward me, but there were some things, personal things, that he had no business knowing. Mine and Simon's whatever it was, was not something I cared to discuss with him.

My glare matched his as I stood straighter and looked him in the eyes. This was exactly what Simon was worried would happen. I hadn't thought it would be that big of a deal. Apparently, I was wrong. I didn't like that he would think Simon would do anything to hurt me.

"It means exactly what I said, Mickey," I spat out.

"Did you two have sex? Because I've got to tell you, Mackaela, that guy is nothing but trouble."

I scoffed. "Are you serious? Simon is your brother. You've been singing his praises and pretty much pushing him on me since day one!"

"Not in that way!" Mickey yelled, stepping even closer to me.

If it was any other man, any other person, I may have cowered and let my head fall. Not with Mickey Silver. I wasn't afraid of him.

"We didn't have sex! God, Mickey, do you really think that low of me, of him?" His face fell slightly and he loosened a breath, dragging a hand through his sandy hair.

"I'm sorry, that was out of line. I just don't think it's a good idea for you to go and get all hung up on my brother. I'm sure it's just a phase, you've been vulnerable and emotional."

Mickey seemed like he was talking more to himself, trying to work it out in his mind. I shook my head in exasperation. What I felt for Simon wasn't a phase. If it was, then walking away from him would have been a success. It wasn't. Even after he got shot, I'd thought I could live without him but only ended up miserable. He was more than just a distraction, more than a crutch.

"It has nothing to do with my mom's death or the shooting. I mean in some ways, I guess it does, but I'm not using him as a distraction to mask my feelings. If anything, he makes me want to bring my feelings out. I'm drawn to him, Mickey." My voice grew quiet.

Mickey rubbed his forehead with his fingers and then threw his arms out to his side. "Are you aware of the fact that Simon has a reputation for messing around?" Mickey shot me an outraged look. "Come on, Mackaela, he isn't the keeping kind. He's never cared about anyone but himself up until recently, but maybe it's an act. We don't know."

"You really think he's lying to you? Not being genuine? He took a bullet for me!" I argued.

He ignored me.

"Besides, once he gets better and has enough money, he'll be leaving. What are you going to do then?"

I shook my head. "I don't know yet, okay? I don't know what will happen or what I'm going to do. I can't even tell you what tomorrow will bring at this point, because God knows it's been one shit storm after another. I find solace in him, Mickey. Simon gives me a sense of peace that I've never felt before. I feel things that I've never felt before."

Stupid tears began to fall, giving away my tough façade. I sniffed and wiped at the liquid running down my cheeks. Mickey sighed, bringing his arms around me, pulling me into a tight hug. He squeezed gently and kissed the top of my hair.

"I'm sorry, Mackaela," he said softly.

"Do you want me to be unhappy? I just want to be normal again, Mickey. I want something that I've never had before. I want him," I cried.

Mickey gripped me tighter and I felt him nod against my head. I continued to cry, surprised at myself for admitting what I felt about Simon not only to Mickey but to myself. There was no way I could live without Simon Silver.

Simon

I tried to sit up a little more and brace for whatever rant Mick was about to instill on me. I heard him and Mackaela arguing downstairs and while I considered hobbling down there, I figured they needed the time and I needed my strength for when he came up here.

Mick glided into the room with his arms crossed. She entered behind him with fresh tears in her eyes and wet cheeks. He made her cry, and that made me angry. I let my gaze slide over to Mick and I gave him a pointed glare. His expression matched my own. I didn't give a shit if I was laid up, nursing a gunshot wound. I would pound his face in for making her cry.

"Mackaela has enlightened me to the state of affairs you two have going on." His voice was cold.

"I'm not denying anything, Mick," I said with just as much disdain.

"You lied to me, Simon. I asked you more than once if something was going on between the two of you. You blatantly lied over and over."

He wasn't wrong. I did lie, and I felt like shit about it. I felt bad that I caused him to rethink his trust in me. But I wasn't sorry for caring about Mackaela.

"I wasn't sure what any of it was yet. We have a connection, it just happened. It wasn't my intention to pursue her the second I met her. She was grieving the death of her mother, I'm not heartless. I knew that she was vulnerable. She still is. I'm not taking advantage of her, Mick." My gaze shifted to the girl in the doorway. She was looking at me. "I would never hurt her," I added quietly.

"How can you be so sure about that, Simon?" Mick countered. I met his eyes again. "You lied to me, you hurt me, and I'm your brother. I'm blood."

"I should have told you how I felt about her. I'm sorry. I just wasn't sure how you would react and to be honest, I'm not in much of a state to defend myself." I let my hand sweep over my injured form.

Mick relaxed slightly. "I understand that. But Mackaela's my best friend, my sister, and there is so much about her that you don't know. It takes a strong person to be there for her. To love her unconditionally. Do you think you can handle that?" he asked. "That you'll stay by her side through thick and thin even on the bad days?"

I narrowed my eyes at Mick. "Would I even offer to admit I care about her if I couldn't?" I gritted out.

Mick shrugged. "I don't know. At one time, I'd trust your word, but you lied to me."

I shook my head.

"I wasn't lying to hurt you. It was to protect her! I told you I wasn't sure what I was feeling yet, what she was feeling."

"It's true," Mackaela spoke up and Mick shifted his gaze to her, which softened. "He told me he was worried what you'd think. When I kissed him, he was the one to stop it."

Mick's eyes widened and he turned an icy glare on me. I swallowed and nodded in agreement. "She kissed you?" he bit out.

I let out a breath. "Yeah, bro, she did. I told her we had to stop."

"How commendable," Mick said in a snide tone. He let out a frustrated breath. "I just don't know what to think right now. I'm not sure what to make of this. I need to take a walk or something." Mick turned abruptly and left the room.

Mackaela and I remained silent, gazing at each other as we listened to Mick's retreating footsteps. There was a loud bang as he opened and slammed the front door. She exhaled, shaking her head.

"Hey, come here," I said softly. She hesitated for a moment, then crawled up carefully from the foot of the bed to my side. I held my arm out and she sank into me, her head resting against my shoulder as I held her against me.

"I'm glad I told him. Sorry for throwing you under the bus with me," she spoke quietly.

"He had to find out eventually. I'm sort of relieved," I admitted.

I squeezed her gently and let out a sigh. I turned my head toward hers and kissed the top of her head. "I meant what I said to Mick." She tilted her head up to look in my eyes.

Her brow crumpled in confusion. "What part?"

I brought my other hand up to rest against her cheek and pressed my forehead to hers. I felt her shiver lightly. "I could love you unconditionally." Her lips parted in a gasp. "Can I kiss you?"

She didn't respond right way. She swallowed and licked her lips as her head tilted up toward me. I had to convey everything I felt, exactly what she made me feel. Slowly, I ran the pad of my thumb across her cheek and lowered my lips to hers. I pressed against her mouth gently at first, savoring the feeling of those prefect full lips, the ones that I dreamed about.

Her mouth parted for me and I deepened the kiss just a little, still keeping a clear head. I wanted to put her flavor, her scent, to memory. I needed something to think about when we weren't together. Her hand traveled tentatively up my arm to my shoulder, sliding behind my head where she curled her fingers against my scalp.

A surge of warmth rushed through me, causing my spine to tingle. I could sit here for hours, days, weeks, with my arms wrapped around Mackaela and my lips against her skin. It felt like that much time passed, but all too soon, the voice of reason sounded in my mind and I knew we had to stop. I let my lips wander down her chin to her neck, smiling against her skin before pulling back.

"You're amazing," I whispered, kissing her lips one more time. She smiled shyly.

"I could say the same about you."

"I wish we could stay like this forever. I love the way you feel in my arms." I tucked a loose strand of hair behind her ear.

"Simon, I need to tell you something." She pulled back further and I reluctantly let her go. My body was hit with a rush of cold as she drifted out of my arms to put some space between us.

Her gaze faltered from mine and she looked down at her hands in her lap. I knew whatever she was about to tell me was substantial. She let out a long sigh, lifting her eyes to mine once again.

"I was raped when I was sixteen. The only men I've ever been with haven't been my choice. All of them were clients and not once did I feel anything that you make me feel just by kissing me," she said.

I bit the inside of my cheek. It made me sick to think that she let herself be used for so long. That she didn't know how positive intimacy could be. I could understand her demeanor a little better now. How could you open up to anyone, especially a guy, if all you thought they wanted from you was your body? I didn't know what to say to her. There were so many words that came to mind, but nothing felt right. Not even an apology.

"I talked to Holly, my counselor, about it. It helped. I don't want to be a cold, untrusting, scared girl anymore. I want to be bigger than the things that haunt me. More than the sum of my past mistakes. You said you could love me unconditionally. If that's true, then you have to know all of me. You have to know there may be days that I fall."

"Then I'll pick you up. If you need to vent, vent to me. If you need to cry, cry on my shoulder. If you just want to be held, I can do that. Just please, please don't ever think that you can't talk to me. Don't shut me out," I all but begged.

I wasn't used to being this vulnerable, but she needed to know that I was a man of my word. No matter what, I'd accept her. A slow smile crept up her lips.

"Why do you always know the right things to say?"

I shrugged.

"I don't. I guess it's just easy to tell you what I'm feeling. Thank you for telling me about your past. I'm sorry for what happened to you, nobody deserves that. You especially didn't deserve any of what happened to you." I reached my hand out and rested it on her thigh, squeezing gently.

"I know that now," she said.

Chapter 23

Mackaela

There's something that happens to your heart when you find out just how deeply someone cares for you. It expands and a weight is lifted. It's like you can breathe again or maybe for the first time. It's remarkable and commanding and frightening all at once. I wouldn't trade this feeling for anything in the world.

It felt good to be open with Simon and share more with him about my past. It amazed me how much easier it was to tell him about the things that I'd been through. He never condemned me or blamed me. He simply listened, and in return, I listened to him. The similarities of our circumstances astonished me. If I hadn't believed in fate or destiny or faith before, I was starting to become a believer now. How could you not think about miracles when it was staring you right in the face in the form of a six-foot-two, emerald-eyed, beautiful man? It was like he was made for me to help me get through life. To keep me from being alone.

After a while, I decided to start the dinner I'd been preparing.

I was down in the kitchen while Simon rested in his room when I heard the sound of the front door open and close.

I knew it was Mickey. I peered around the entryway of the kitchen, watching him carefully. He looked calmer than the last time I saw him. His head turned, catching me, and I shot him a genuine smile.

I wasn't mad at him for overreacting. He was protective of me. I probably would have done the same thing if roles were reversed.

"Hey, Mack." He approached me slowly.

"Hey, yourself. Where did you go?"

"To clear my head, talked to Dom a bit, too. Listen, I know that I sort of went overboard earlier."

"Just a little, don't worry about it. I get where you're coming from. I know you only want the best for me and you thought Simon betrayed you somehow."

"I'm sorry, Mackaela. I just didn't expect there to be this deep connection between the two of you. I mean you hated him when you first met him."

"That's true, I did. But, Mickey, after I found out my mom died and my world came crashing down, he was there."

"I was there, too," he said quickly, and I smiled at him, placing a hand on his shoulder.

"You were there, too, but when you had to leave and he stayed with me ... It was just ... Something about him. He helped me because he wanted to, not because he felt obligated."

"I don't feel obligated to help you," he argued.

"I know. But as a stranger, he showed so much compassion for me, it helped me grasp that not all people are bad in the world. I've been living in fear this entire time with a veil over my face. I don't want that anymore."

Mickey's hand came up to rest against my cheek. A slow smile crept up his lips into a wide grin.

"I've worried about you for years. I always wanted more for you than this life, than the pain that you had to go through.

Here you are now, changing into something better. A more confident woman." He pulled me into a severe hug, squeezing me so hard that I squealed and had to struggle to get loose.

When Mickey finally pulled away, he frowned. "I better go apologize to Simon. I feel like a real dick for overreacting, it's not like you two are in love or anything yet."

Something between a laugh and gasp came out of my mouth and I coughed to cover it up. Mickey beamed at me and then headed up the stairs to Simon's room. I went back to putting the noodles in water and preparing the vegetables for the sauce.

I wasn't in love with Simon. We hadn't known each other that long. He was just someone that I connected with on a different level than anyone else. Albeit a deeper level than most. Simon was one of few people that really understood me, who I could bare my soul to. He was the guy I had dreams about. Scorching dreams that left me reeling when I woke up. I mean if I were looking for a damn near perfect "boyfriend," I guess Simon would be in the running.

I stopped mid chop of my tomatoes and gripped the counter top with both hands. I replayed my conversation with Holly earlier about how Simon gave me the necklace that belonged to his deceased mother. I remembered the dream that he had told me about. I thought of the fact that he literally took a bullet for me. My ears began to ring and my heart pounded in my throat.

Holy shit! Was I in love with Simon Silver? Just when I thought I was gaining some footing in life; I was thrown with yet another curve-ball. I didn't think I was ready for that kind of admission yet. If ever. That didn't mean the truth wasn't staring me in the face.

*

"Would you stop moving?" I placed a hand on Simon's bare chest, pushing him down.

"It's going to hurt, I know it," he whined with his fists clenched at his side.

I raised a brow at him and smirked. "You're a wimp."

"You try having a giant sticker attached to your ribs and then ripping it off. It fucking hurts, Mackaela." I rolled my eyes, unable to contain the chuckle that escaped.

Simon glared at me.

"I'm sorry," I said, biting down on my bottom lip. "I'm sure it does hurt. We need to see how the wound is healing though and I need to clean it."

Simon had a doctor's appointment this afternoon and wanted to get cleaned up and showered. I was helping him because Mickey had another meeting to go to.

I thought it was awfully convenient considering up until an hour ago, he had no plans. I was also fairly sure it had to do with the new girl he met last week. Her name was Claire and she was dating a new dealer Mickey had hired. The guy, Cory, seemed to bring her along to run deals sometimes. Just because she was taken, didn't mean Mickey wouldn't enjoy the eye candy anytime he wanted. I had to admit, she was stunning with long blonde hair and these unique, deep blue eyes that almost looked violet. He didn't openly talk about her, but I could tell he liked her. Last week she was at the office with Cory and Mickey kept staring at her.

It had been two weeks since Simon and I had admitted how we felt toward each other. I'd met with Holly three times so far and we talked about everything from the things in my past to the fears of my future. I laid it all out on the table for her, finally speaking about my mother's death and the regrets that I had. We talked about Simon and how he was helping me by being not only a friend, but something more. Simon and I were almost like an extension of each other. His pain was my pain and the other way around.

After Mickey found out about us, I began sleeping in Simon's bed. I found that I slept better next to him, and the nightmares were at bay when he was near me. Due to Simon's injuries, there was no way we could be together in the biblical sense yet, though the tension was growing stronger each day. We were forced to take things slow and I was okay with that. Just knowing he was beside me, touching me in some way, made me feel good.

Mickey didn't seem so happy about the new sleeping arrangements, but I brushed it off. Honestly, he was kind of acting like an old man, calling us "kids" and telling Simon to "be careful" with me. It was endearing for the most part and really kind of sweet.

Simon and Mickey were just as close as ever, which made everything easier. I couldn't actually remember much of the pre-Simon Mickey. I liked him a lot better now. It seemed that Simon Silver was good for everyone.

Mickey was working on selling his shares of the business to Hawks in Olympia. He mentioned wanting to downsize and possibly move on from the whole drug business himself. Apparently, Jack was trying to talk him into moving down to Portland. Mickey wasn't sure if that was a move he wanted to make. Simon and Jack still had yet to speak to each other and I still hadn't talked to my own father since after my mom died. He didn't try to get a hold of me and I wasn't ready to open up to him, though Holly and I were working on that in my sessions.

Simon admitted to wanting to speak with his father, but he was waiting until they were face to face again. It was just easier that way, he had said.

"Shit." Simon gripped my bare thigh that was resting on the bed beside him.

"Almost got the edge up," I murmured as my fingers pinched the corner of the tape that lay over the large gauze square.

I was trying really hard to be delicate. I finally lifted part of the tape slightly when Simon groaned. My gaze shifted to his. "I'm just going to rip it off okay?"

Simon nodded and flinched preemptively.

"It might help if you don't think about it," I offered.

"I've been trying to do that already. It isn't working," he growled.

I pursed my lips and thought about what I could use as a deterrent for the current situation. Suddenly the idea hit me, though I was a little uneasy admitting this embarrassing secret to him.

"Did I ever tell you about the dream I had of you?" I asked quietly, already feeling the heat rise in my cheeks. Simon's brow furrowed.

"You've dreamed of me?"

I nodded.

"I have. I still do occasionally. This particular one though, it was ... an intense dream. One that I don't think I could forget even if I wanted to."

A wide smile broke out across Simon's face. "Was it a sex dream?"

I nodded sheepishly. Simon bit down on his lip and his eyes darkened.

"That's hot, Mackaela. Tell me about this dream."

I made sure my fingers stayed secured to the tape on Simon's skin, but used my other hand to trace along his lips with my index finger.

"We were making out on the couch downstairs. You were kissing me and touching me all over." I kept eye contact with him while I spoke.

I had to get his mind off what I was about to do to him.

"You laid me back on the couch, I could feel every inch of you." I dropped my voice lower.

"What happened after that?" he asked huskily.

He was definitely distracted. I bit my lip to hide my smile.

"Well," I placed my hand on his chest, lowering my lips to his ear. "I woke up from a mind blowing orgasm." As soon as I finished those words, I yanked on the tape as hard as I could.

Simon yelped and then growled, shooting daggers at me with those emerald eyes. I couldn't help but smile to myself. I had taken the bandage off successfully.

"You're so mean." He glanced down at the wound, lightly running his finger over the scar.

"You've said that a lot since you met me. I think by now it shouldn't come as such a shock." I shrugged.

"Why would you do that?" he asked, glancing back up at me.

"I had to distract you to get the damn bandage off." I tapped my finger to his nose, smirking, and stood abruptly.

Simon's arm shot out and grabbed my wrist. "Were you lying about the dream?"

I began shaking my head, the blush reappearing. "No." Simon nodded.

"That's really hot, Mackaela."

I threw the bandage away and came back out with some antiseptic and a warm washcloth.

Simon's wound looked like it was healing well. He was able to move around more and get up and down the stairs as long as he was careful. I sat next to him, cleaning the area gently.

"I hate that I've been trapped inside this house for so long other than doctor's appointments," he said. I felt bad for him.

If I were him, I'd be going stir crazy, too. "I'm sure the doctors will let you have more freedom soon. Seriously, this seems to be healed."

"I feel great. It doesn't hurt much to move anymore. As soon as I'm back to normal, I want to take you out somewhere." Simon's fingers ran up my arm slowly causing goose bumps to raise. My stomach dipped. I met his gaze. "You've been really good to me and I want to repay you." His fingers moved to my shoulder then trailed along my collarbone.

My blood warmed. I couldn't help my body's response to his hands.

"Will you go out with me, Mackaela?"

I nodded instantly, not sure if I could speak.

Simon sat himself up slowly, using his other hand as support. He leaned forward until his face was mere inches from mine. My breath came out in low pants as he slid his hand over my neck gingerly, tangling his fingers in the hair at the back of my head. Simon parted his lips and slipped his tongue out, tracing along my bottom lip before sliding inside my mouth to taste me.

He groaned low in his throat and gripped my hair tighter, pulling me closer to him as I melted. I wasn't ready for him to stop yet. I let my hand glide up his uninjured side and move around to his back. Without hesitation, I pressed my hand into his shoulder blade, on top of that glorious tattoo of his. My fingers splayed and gripped his muscles in that spot before raking my nails down slowly. I felt him shudder under my touch. A growl sounded from the back of his throat. He pulled back; his eyes pinned me.

"As much as I love kissing you, sweetheart, we've got to stop."

I let out an exasperated sigh. Like I said, the tension was becoming almost unbearable between us. I was frustrated beyond belief with this man, but I also knew he'd be worth the wait.

"Why do you always tell me to stop?" I pouted. Simon shook his head and chuckled.

"Believe me. I wouldn't have stopped if it weren't for this." His hand swiped down his side. Right, his wound.

"Did I hurt you?"

"No, you didn't hurt me. When I do get the chance to really have you though, I don't want to have to be careful." His voice was low, promising, and it made my stomach coil and tighten in anticipation. My heart stuttered.

Simon went to take his shower and I used that time to tidy up the room. This wasn't really an uncommon thing for me, considering Simon had been out of commission for the last month. Lately though, I was making him fold his own clothes and put them away because I refused to let him think I would enjoy being the obedient little house wife type. I was a strong independent woman who wanted an equal partner.

Before I had the chance to contemplate my thoughts on even considering being a "wife," my phone began vibrating on top of the side table and I reached across the bed to grab it.

"Hello?"

"Hi, is this Mackaela Stone?"

"Yes." I couldn't identify the voice.

"This is Donovan Sampson from the Terrace View Cemetery. I just wanted to inform you that your mother, Lindsey Stone's urn has been placed here."

I closed my eyes and took a deep breath. "Thank you."

I don't know why the tears were coming now. Perhaps it was because it was one more part that made her death final.

I hung up the phone and sunk down on the bed. The treatment facility had called me a few weeks back and said that the arrangements for a spot in the mausoleum were taking longer than expected. I was overcome with a sense of relief and remembrance now that she was officially in her final resting place.

I had grieved my mother for the last few months, not only in private but also in my sessions with Holly. I was strong enough to move on from the negative memories. I think I could be at peace with my mother's death now that she was finally buried. It only clarified for me that I was heading in the right direction with my life.

Everything was going to be okay and the more I looked toward the future, the less I feared, the easier life would be.

Chapter 24

Mackaela

The doctor gave Simon the go ahead to start taking part in more normal activity. They were impressed at how well he was recovering. Due to his age and how well-maintained his body was, it wasn't surprising. There was no way he'd be able to run a marathon or even lift heavy weights yet, but he could move around less restricted and get out of the house.

Simon immediately begged to drive my car when we left the doctor's office. I relented, only because he gave me sad eyes and a pout that made my heart rate spike. The boy was gorgeous and he knew it.

"I'm starving. Can we go get some food?" Simon asked as he fumbled with the radio.

"Sure, what do you want?" I watched as he pursed his full lips and brought a hand up to his scruffy chin, rubbing it between his thumb and index finger.

"I want fish and chips. Do you want to go down to Pike Place?"

"Are you sure you're up to walking that much? I don't want you to over-do it."

Simon rolled his eyes and scoffed.

"I'm fine, Mackaela. Come on, I need to be out for a while." He gave me that pouty look again and I sighed.

"As long as you think you'll be fine. I'm not carrying you to the car if you get tired," I teased.

Simon chuckled. "Deal," he said and his hand moved away from the stereo to rest on my thigh.

I couldn't help the slow smile that spread across my lips. He was always touching me absently. It was as if I was a magnet for him. I didn't mind.

Simon parked my Mustang in the closest lot he could find when we got to the Pike Place area. It was a Wednesday afternoon and early enough that there wasn't an abundance of people, which was nice.

I made a point to stand closer to Simon in the event he began to tire out. I also tried to walk a little slower so that he wouldn't overexert himself, but he was on to me. He grabbed my wrist and tugged gently, telling me to relax.

We ended up at a restaurant down by the docks with the best fish and chips Seattle had to offer. Our booth was situated directly next to a large window with a view of the water and the Great Wheel on the pier.

"Do you prefer dogs or cats?" Simon asked, popping a fry into his mouth.

My brows rose. "Are you onto the elementary school questioning again?"

Simon shrugged. "It's a good way to get to know a person."

"You know more about me than most people."

"True, but that's deep stuff. I want to know everything about you."

I shook my head but answered anyway.

"I like the low maintenance of a cat, but I prefer dogs. Cats are sort of selfish."

"I agree. I like dogs much better than cats. What's your favorite food?"

"Seriously, Simon, are these pick-up lines you usually use?"

"Just answer the question, Mackaela." He narrowed his eyes at me.

"Fine, but don't make fun of me okay?" He nodded, waiting for me to proceed.

"My favorite food is peanut butter and jelly sandwiches." His lips twitched and I chucked a fry at him.

He laughed and tossed it back.

"You're making fun of me."

"No, I'm not. I just don't understand why you would choose that of all foods. I mean, you can cook really well."

"I like the simplicity of it. It's a comfort food," I replied with a shrug.

"I guess when you explain it like that, it makes sense. What about your favorite season?"

The rest of lunch was filled with more generic questions that Simon wanted to ask me. By the end of it, he knew all the useless things about me. My favorite season was fall, my biggest fear was heights, I'd never broken a bone in my life, and so on.

I decided to turn the interrogation around on him, which he didn't mind at all. His favorite season was summer and supposedly he didn't have any fears. I didn't believe him but wouldn't press it yet. Simon had broken fingers from fighting and his leg when he was about eight years old. He said that he was climbing a tree and fell out of it. To top it all off, when I asked him what his favorite food was he swore it was my spaghetti. I couldn't help but feel a little proud of myself and flattered with his compliment.

We were wandering around Pike Place Market now. I asked Simon if he needed to rest and he brushed me off, claiming that he felt better than ever. He didn't seem to be favoring his side or wincing in pain, so I believed him. As we roamed through the throngs of vendors and merchandise, Simon slipped his hand in mine. His touch was warm and he ran his thumb against my palm absently as he talked about remembering coming here as a kid once with his mother.

Somehow the topic of candy was brought up and that led to saltwater taffy. He ended up buying a huge bag of the assorted flavors. After a few hours, we wandered down toward the water and found a bench to sit at. It was pleasantly sunny today, no rain and minimal clouds.

We sat side by side quietly, Simon still holding my hand. I took in the waterfront and watched as a seagull flew high up into the sky before swooping down toward a cluster of rocks. It reminded me of the times I was younger and would come here with my mother. I could imagine myself chasing after the seagulls and begging her to get us a boat so that we could go whale watching. I was lost in my thoughts of childhood and innocent times when Simon's voice broke through.

"What are you thinking about?" he asked quietly. I slowly turned my head toward him, meeting his eyes.

"I miss certain things about her. We used to come here when I was younger, before everything changed." My gaze shifted back out to the Sound.

I could feel tears beginning to form behind my eyes. I chewed on my lower lip, feeling Simon squeeze my hand reassuringly.

"I got a call earlier when you were in the shower," I said.

"What about?"

"They placed her at the cemetery finally. They wanted to let me know she was there if I wanted to see the niche they'd assigned. It's weird. I feel a sense of peace now in knowing she's finally laid to rest. But a part of me feels like it's the end somehow. I've moved beyond the grief, but I still miss her." A tear escaped and rolled slowly down my cheek. I quickly wiped it away.

Simon loosened his hold of my hand and wrapped an arm around me, drawing me into his body, his warmth, and comfort. More tears fell then and I threw my arms around him, my head resting against his chest.

"I miss her so damn much, Simon." I sobbed. "I hate that I lost her before I could tell her that I loved her. I do love her."

Simon rubbed small circles on my back and I felt him kiss the top of my head. "I know you do, sweetheart; she knows you do."

I nodded against his shirt, letting him hold me for a while longer. Once the tears subsided, I lifted my head and took in the emerald eyes sparkling down at me.

Simon brought a hand up to stroke my cheek and pressed his forehead against mine.

"Thank you," I whispered.

"You don't have to thank me. Whenever you're hurting I'll always be here to hold you, no matter what." His lips gently pressed against mine softly.

I was still trying to figure out how I got so lucky meeting Simon. His comfort, his words, everything about him was perfect.

Simon

Being cooped up for over a month, lying in bed for hours on end, gave me a new appreciation for the little things. I was a different person now. Not knowing whether you might live or die will do that to you. I've been on the brink of death more times than should be possible in one lifetime.

The first time, when my mom died, I was sure my life was over. Todd was either going to beat me to death or throw me out on the streets. As a teenager, I didn't know the first thing about responsibility and taking care of myself. Thinking back on all the times I drank to oblivion or picked fights with dangerous people, made me cringe now. I'd been young and so very stupid.

After I was sentenced and thrown in jail, my mind was wrecked. I recalled sitting in a cold, dark cell and seething with anger greater than I'd ever felt before. I didn't understand how I could be charged so harshly for something that was similar to what I'd been through nearly my entire life. Todd was the one that should have been in prison.

I began taking my aggression out on other convicts in the yard or the cafeteria. One wrong look from any person, and my fists were flying. After a while, my anger turned to sorrow at how lonely and abandoned I felt. My real father hadn't come to save me, my mother was dead, and I had no one to talk to.

The night I tried to kill myself was a turning point. I sat at the end of my hard cot with a broken piece of glass to my upper arm. My intention was the Brachial artery as it was further up and closer to my heart. The thought was that I'd bleed out quicker if I hit it. I thought about who might miss me if I were gone and came up empty. That was when I put the glass to my skin and began cutting it open over and over again. I had to bite down on the flimsy wool blanket to silence my screams. I didn't want to give myself away.

The next morning, I was awoken by two guards and a nurse who found me unconscious in the middle of the night. I remember begging them to leave me alone and let me die. Of course, they wouldn't and I was put in a mandatory counseling session for the remainder of my stay. Not only that, but I was also on suicide watch for a few weeks until I finally opened up to the counselor. I changed for the better and grew as time went on after each incident. I came to realize that sometimes you have to just keep fighting. I initially had the large, winged tattoo done to cover up the scars of my moment of weakness. It was now a reminder of how and why I was saved.

When I found my brother again, everything transformed for me. Meeting Mackaela, being around her and knowing her, further helped in justifying my reason for living. My goals and dreams were now tangible. I wasn't going to let anything get in the way of a promising future. I no longer wanted to hold regret in my heart for words left unsaid or broken promises. I wanted to give my all and be everything I could be, not just for myself, but for her.

I lay in my bed, one arm tucked behind my head and the other securely around Mackaela's shoulders, absently running my fingers along her arm, through her hair. She'd fallen asleep a little while ago and I could hear her low, steady breaths. I hugged her close to my side, kissing her temple. I was falling for her. I think I already had but having her next to me now solidified the feeling.

For the first time in my life, I wanted to be a good man. I wanted the house, the picket fence, the suburbs, the kids. I saw a future with her. I didn't want to freak her out and admit it too quickly though. We were taking things slow and that was okay with me because I wanted to do things right. I wanted to make sure that Mackaela was ready for the amount of love I had to give her. And I planned to spend the rest of my life doing that.

Chapter 25

Mackaela

I'd officially graduated high school, completing my online courses this week. I was one step closer to a new future, a better one. Mickey took it upon himself to throw a congratulatory party at the house tonight. I was still working up to not being so socially anxious. He promised it would only be a few of us, a small barbecue.

I was still staying at his house but had been back to my own apartment a few times to get clothes and other things I needed. I found myself escaping there occasionally for moments of solitude as well. I missed painting and Holly actually recommended that I do it as a form of therapy. I found it helped a lot. Though it was nice to have the time to myself, I much preferred being with Simon.

The sound of the shower running in the connected bathroom echoed through the room as I woke up. There was a knock on the door and I opened it to find Mickey leaning against the door frame, watching me carefully.

"Morning, Mickey, what's up?"

He narrowed his eyes and then a slow smile crept across his lips. "Am I interrupting anything?"

I rolled my eyes. He did this a lot; assuming he'd catch us in the act. He went from best friend to overbearing parent in the last few weeks.

"Not at all. Simon's in the shower. I'm just waking up."

"I wanted to talk to you about this afternoon. Sadie and Dom are coming early, she just called me. She tried your cell but it went to voicemail."

"Yeah, it's on the charger. I silenced it last night."

"Well anyway, call her back. I think she wants to go shopping with you for the food and stuff."

"You know you don't have to do this," I started to say, but Mickey put a finger to my lips to silence me.

"I want to, Mack. You deserve it and I'm so incredibly proud of you. Besides, we're due for another celebratory party. There's been a lot of great new things recently."

"What great new things?" I asked. I could tell by the look in his eyes there was more he hadn't told me. A Cheshire cat-like grin grew on his face and his eyes sparkled.

"I got a call from Hawks last night after you two went to bed."

My brow crumpled in confusion.

"So?"

Mickey rolled his eyes and sighed. "So ... I just sold part of the business to him for a good amount of money."

"Are you serious? Jack was okay with it?"

I knew that Mickey wanted to start cutting away from the business and he'd mentioned selling to Hawks, but I didn't realize it would happen so soon. What would this mean for him now, for me? What about Simon?

"You okay?" he asked, brows inching up.

"Uh yeah, sure, I'm okay."

"Liar," he muttered. I sighed.

"I knew this was coming. I guess I just didn't realize how soon."

Mickey squeezed my shoulder and offered a small smile. "I wasn't expecting things to move so quickly either to tell you the truth, but apparently Jack was eager to get Hawks in and me out. When I talked to him last, I told him I wanted out sooner rather than later."

It was my turn to look at him questioningly. He continued to explain. "I guess I've just lost the passion for hustling. With everything that happened with you and your mom dying and Simon coming back after all this time, it makes me think about my priorities. Family, friends, all these things are so much more important than running drugs and pimping out girls for money. I don't want to be like that anymore. Apart from getting my revenge on Ricky Delgado, I'm going to push more responsibility on Hawks."

It had been weeks and they still hadn't caught Ricky. He was said to have been in Portland and held, but by the time Mickey got there, he was gone again. It was unnerving, but he hadn't retaliated yet and Mickey was certain he'd lay low for a while.

I began shaking my head, unable to stop the smile that drew up at the corners of my mouth.

"Why are you looking at me like that?" He pinned me with a glare and crossed his arms.

"You're going soft, Mickey Silver. I knew you'd eventually want out, but you've been pretty driven since the day I met you." I smirked at him. "Is this because of a girl?"

"Of course not," he scoffed. "I'm just growing up, everyone is. I want more for my life." He spoke quickly, too quickly, and I bit my lip to stifle a laugh.

He was so cute when he was all flustered. I shrugged.

"Whatever you say, buddy." I clapped him on the shoulder.

Mickey rolled his eyes and then pinched my waist.

"Ouch!" I said with a giggle as I stepped back.

Mickey laughed, too. It was then that my attention was drawn to the sound of the bathroom door opening. Simon appeared, his hair wet and disheveled, that tattoo on his chest gleaming. He was in nothing but a blue towel knotted just below that delectable V of his hips. I bit my lip and let my gaze wander up to his eyes. He winked at me before turning his attention to his brother. I nearly forgot Mickey was still here, standing next to me.

"What's up?" Simon asked, standing beside me.

I could smell the body wash he used and it made my stomach flutter. Mickey's gaze darted between the two of us.

"I was just telling Mackaela the good news. Hawks bought part of the business."

"That's great, Mick. Jack's okay with that?"

"More than okay actually. You know how our father is. It's all about business."

"Right. So what are you going to do now?" Simon asked.

Mickey uncrossed his arms and shoved his hands in his pockets. He looked between Simon and me again with a wary expression. Letting out a long breath, he met Simon's eyes.

"Well, the amount of money I got is pretty substantial. I know you have other goals, so I figured I would give you the rest of whatever you need to get that garage running."

"No shit? Just like that, you're going to gift me the cash?"

Mickey nodded.

"Yeah, bro, you've done more than enough for me." Mickey glanced at me then. "You pretty much single-handedly fixed my best friend. I owe you."

The look Mickey gave me was mixed with love and adoration. My throat swelled.

"Mick, I don't know what to say. I mean, I appreciate what you want to do but I can't just take your money." Simon's voice was quiet.

Mickey turned his gaze back to him and smiled, slapping him in the stomach. "Don't worry about it, Simon. I'm giving you the money and if you don't take it, you're going to have to fight me." Mickey playfully put up his fists, dancing around in front of Simon as if they would start boxing. Simon shook his head and let out short laugh.

"Seriously, Mick, I thought it would be a while longer. I'm not even sure where I want to go or what I want to do yet."

Mickey stopped moving around and shrugged.

"I'm not kicking you out or anything. Take your time. I just don't need you running errands or kicking people's ass for me anymore. Besides, you've been out of commission for a while now anyway."

Simon furrowed his brow, eyes falling to the floor. He seemed to be lost in thought and didn't speak for a while. When he finally met Mickey's eyes again, his lips tipped up on one side.

"I guess all I can say is thank you. Really, Mick, it means a lot to me." His voice was thick with emotion and I took that as my cue to grab a shower.

The Silver boys needed a brother moment. I didn't want to stand in the way of bonding.

"I'm going to go shower and then call Sadie," I said as I stepped around Simon toward the bathroom.

Simon

I couldn't believe Mick had sold a piece of the business that my father created and wanted to give me some of the money from it. There was a small part of me that felt like I deserved something monetary for the shit I had to endure growing up, just to spite my father. I hated Jack Silver for abandoning me with my mother and Todd. It was apparent to me that he never once had any concern for where I was or what I might be going through even if he told me differently.

A bigger part of me though, the most important part of me, wanted nothing more than to just be around my brother and work whatever job I had to. Now that I had him in my life again, I couldn't imagine not having him around all the time. I would miss him if I left. There was no doubt in my mind that Mick was no more like our father than I was. I loved my brother and was grateful for everything he'd done for me these last few months.

Not only that, but Mackaela was slowly becoming my world. I knew I couldn't give up my brother and I definitely wasn't about to walk away from her. I actually felt like I belonged in Seattle for the first time ever.

Mick left the room after giving me a heads up that he wanted me to go with him to run for alcohol. I closed the bedroom door and began to get dressed. I had yet to put on a shirt and my jeans were hanging low on my hips, unbuttoned, when Mackaela came out of the bathroom.

My mouth went dry at the sight of her long hair hanging down in loose, wet waves. The only thing she wore was a towel that stopped in the middle of her thighs. Fuck, it was getting harder and harder to resist her. Pun intended. I was going crazy taking things slow with her. To the point that I was afraid our first time would end too quickly. She was so damn gorgeous.

Smirking, she took a few steps toward me. I wasn't entirely sure what she was going to do, but I was suddenly very aware that the flimsy cotton towel didn't leave much to the imagination. I licked my lips slowly as her gaze locked with mine and she stopped directly in front of me.

"How are you doing?" Her eyes shifted from fire to concern in an instant.

"I'm all right," I murmured.

Mackaela nodded and her gaze shifted to her hands that were curled together in front of her.

"Simon, can I ask you something?"

"Sure." I was trying really hard to keep my voice even.

I didn't think she realized how damn sexy she looked right now. Still looking at her hands, she spoke in a weak whisper.

"When you leave ... I mean once you're gone, will we still be ... you know, friends?" Her head lifted and those golden eyes were watery.

Damn, she thought I'd leave her? After the time we spent together, the conversations we had? That hurt. There was no way I'd ever let her get away from me. She needed to know that. I raised my hand to her damp hair, running my fingers through the ends, meeting her eyes.

"Sweetheart, I'm not leaving you." I cupped her face in both my hands, resting my forehead against hers. She let out a small sigh and closed her eyes. "I don't think you understand just how much I care about you." I withdrew and placed a kiss on her cheek and then the corner of her mouth. "I wouldn't leave you, I couldn't." I touched my lips to hers softly.

"Simon, I wouldn't ask you to stay. I don't want to hold you back. You have your own plans and I won't stand in the way of them. I don't know what I want yet. You can't wait around for me to figure my shit out."

I immediately began shaking my head and pulled further away from her. I gripped her chin gently and forced her gaze to meet mine.

"You're my plan. I can't have anything or be anything if I don't have you. You're a part of me. We have a bond that can't be broken. You know this." I watched as her eyes filled with tears and a small sob broke free.

So quickly, before she could shed another tear, I angled my head and smashed my lips against hers. Her mouth parted in a gasp and I took the opportunity to deepen the kiss, conveying everything I was feeling toward her. My hands lowered to her waist and I drew her closer to my body. I could feel her chest against mine, her hips against me, pressing closer still.

I groaned and clutched at her, trying not to remove the flimsy barrier that kept me from seeing and feeling her skin. I let my lips wander across her now flush cheeks to her jaw and up to the hollow below her ear that I knew drove her crazy.

"You have my heart," I whispered. "I can't leave that behind. Ever." I cradled her head in my hands. "Do you understand?"

She nodded and a small smile formed on those incredible lips. "Good, now I think you better get dressed before I lose all of my sanity." She giggled, stepping away from me.

"It's good to know I have the same effect on you as you do on me," she said as she turned around and grabbed her clothes from the dresser.

As she walked back to the bathroom, my eyes roamed over her retreating form. I blew out a breath, dragging a hand through my damp hair. I was going to explode if I couldn't have her soon.

Chapter 26

Mackaela

"So you two are officially like a couple now?" Sadie asked with so much excitement in her voice, you'd think she was in the relationship.

"Wow, you go right in for the kill don't you?" I grabbed a bag of chips off the shelf. "How many different kinds should we get?" I asked, placing my hands on my hips and perusing the enormous selection.

"I don't know and I don't care as long as we have these!" She nearly pushed me over to snag a bag of Cheetos.

"Chill out, chick. It's only Cheetos," I muttered.

Sadie narrowed her eyes at me and then pointed to her expanding belly. She had quite the cute bump now. "This kid is a Cheetos freak, well at least right now. I crave nothing but junk food lately. Sorry for shoving you, Mackaela." I laughed.

"No biggie, now I know not to get between a pregnant woman and her snacks."

"Back to the subject, what's up with you and Simon?"

I groaned, grabbing a few other kinds of chips and throwing them into the cart.

I loved her, but I wasn't even sure what to label me and Simon right now. Where should I start?

"We're together, I guess. I care about him and he cares about me." I shrugged.

I wandered down the aisle toward the other snacks. Sadie caught up beside me, pushing the cart.

"You've never dated anyone that I've known about before," she said with a look that let me know she had thousands of questions running through her head.

"I haven't dated anyone ever," I replied. "I don't know how to explain it, Sadie. We just have this ... bond."

"Like you two were made for each other," she said with a sly grin.

"Such a romantic, does Dom know about this?" I quipped.

"Of course he does. He's a hopeless romantic himself." I knew Dom was a lot softer than he looked, but I couldn't imagine him doing the whole hearts and flowers thing.

"Really?" Sadie nodded. "Hmm, I may have to give him shit for that later."

She laughed and we headed to the meat area to get the chicken and steaks that Mickey was going to grill.

"So are you in love with him? Did he tell you that he loves you yet?" she pressed.

"Good Lord, Sadie!" I said, exasperated. "No, we haven't said that yet, but I don't know. I think I could love him ... eventually."

Sadie put an arm around my shoulder. "I'm really happy for you, Mackaela. Honestly, I don't know all the sordid details of what happened to you in the past, but I like seeing you cheerful now."

I couldn't help but smile at her words. There was so much I missed out on before. I now cherished the girl talk with Sadie just as much as the time with Simon. I was enjoying the perks of who I was becoming.

We finished our grocery shopping with more than enough food to throw a party. I'm sure we could feed an army with the amount of stuff we got, but Mickey had said it was better to have too much food than not enough.

After we got back to the house, Sadie and I began prepping the food, placing chips in bowls and cutting fruits and vegetables to set out with different dips. When the guys came back from the liquor store, they each carried a paper bag full of different bottles of alcohol. Simon walked in first, setting his bag on the counter next to me. I peered into it and shot him a questioning look.

"What?" he asked with a lazy smile.

"Should you be carrying something so heavy?"

Simon furrowed his brow.

"I'm fine, Mackaela. It's not like I was bench pressing it."

Mickey began taking bottles out and arranging them on the counter.

"How thirsty do you think people will be?" Sadie joked and slapped him on the shoulder.

Mickey grinned. "Pretty thirsty, I imagine. It's hot out there."

"How many people are coming again?" I asked.

Mickey shrugged. "I don't know, maybe twenty. You know how it goes though, Mackaela." I nodded.

I knew exactly what happened when Mickey threw parties. It always started with a few familiar faces and ended up with random invites after the drinks started flowing. This would be no different than the last party he had.

"Lighten up," Mickey said as he placed an arm around my shoulder. "We have a lot to celebrate and I want you to have a great time." He gave me that wide smile that always made me melt.

He was right after all. Things were going really great right now and I was finally at a place where I was genuinely happy. I would try to let loose, relax, and be like a normal twenty-one year old girl.

"It's cool, Mickey, just don't get too hammered. I'm not taking care of you if you puke."

Mickey laughed and squeezed my shoulders.

"I promise," he said.

*

I sat in a lawn chair, watching Simon and Mickey grill up the food. The way they communicated with each other put a smile on my face and warmed my heart. I didn't think I'd ever seen Mickey as happy as he was having his brother by his side. I was glad they were able to be together again and forgive each other for what Jack put them through in the past.

At times, it was sort of eerie watching them because their mannerisms were strikingly similar. The way they ran a hand through their hair or how they'd smile. Other than the difference in hair and eye color, you might think they were twins. Without a doubt, they were related.

The backyard was already full of people talking and drinking. I brought the bottle of beer I was drinking to my lips, taking a sip. Pulled out of my people watching and thoughts, I heard the chair next to me move and turned to see Simon taking a seat. He shot me a wink. He was absolutely gorgeous, there was no denying it. He tilted his own beer to his lips and I couldn't help but watch his throat muscles move as he swallowed.

"Hey," he said in a gruff whisper. My eyes wandered back up to his. "Don't look at me like that." He smiled and I saw the playfulness in his eyes.

"Like what?" I asked innocently.

Simon shook his head. "Like you really want a taste of me right now." He trailed his fingers up and down my arm, giving me goose bumps.

"I do want a taste of you," I said, matching his low tone.

I couldn't help but express how much I wanted him. He was driving me crazy. I'd never felt such a deep desire for anyone in my entire life.

Simon's eyes darkened and he leaned his face closer to mine. His lips brushed over my ear. "Careful, sweetheart, or I'll take you up to my room right now."

An involuntary shiver of pleasure rolled through me from my head to my toes. I gasped softly at his threat. I let my fingers run from his square jaw, down his neck slowly. I felt him shudder at my touch and a small smile spread across my lips.

"Do you promise?" I breathed.

Clearly I caught him off guard. He pulled back from me slightly and his eyes widened.

"Hey, man, how you feeling?" A tall red-headed guy that I remembered as Adam suddenly appeared beside Simon and clapped him on the back.

Simon shook his head as if to clear his thoughts and slowly turned his attention to the guy who was taking a seat across from him.

"Hey, Adam, I'm doing great."

Swigging the last of my beer, I stood and lowered my head to kiss Simon's cheek. Before he could say anything, I straightened and made my way to the house to grab another drink and talk to Sadie.

I knew I was one hundred percent ready to be with Simon now. But I had never been with anyone where it actually meant something. Maybe a little pep talk with my best girlfriend would help squash that fear.

Simon

"I heard Jack let Ricky slip in Portland," Adam said.

I nodded and took another swig of my beer. It was either my father or Hawks. Either way, the whole situation pissed me off. "That's the rumor."

I really wasn't in the mood to shoot the shit with him at the moment and I didn't want to get into how frustrating it was that the man who tried to kill me was still free. My brother assured me he'd handle it and I believed him. Supposedly Randall Hawks had more people than Mick originally thought working for him and had eyes in every city from here to the Canadian border.

I had other things on my mind now anyway that involved the stunning woman who'd sauntered away. That girl was definitely something else. I wanted to protect her and own her at the same time. She had a fragile and broken heart, but I was certain I could heal it for her.

The way she so easily placed a kiss on my cheek as she walked away left my head spinning. It was a simple gesture, but somehow I knew it held a deeper meaning. I knew without a doubt that she was home to me. She and Mick were the family I'd always wanted.

I thought about living in a house with her, watching her paint in a room with floor to ceiling windows. I pictured her looking similar to how Sadie did now, a small round belly carrying my child. It was in that moment that I knew it didn't matter what I was doing or where I was, as long as she was with me. I needed her. We were made for each other.

Adam continued talking to me and another guy that came over. I tossed in a few words here and there but I really wasn't interested in the conversation. Mick sat down next to me, swirling a glass of scotch in his hand.

"So, what are you thinking about doing with your life now?" he asked.

I'd been mulling over what I wanted now that he was generously giving me money. I still couldn't believe he'd offered.

"Well first of all, I really hate that you just want to hand me money," I began.

Mick shook his head dismissively. "It's happening, Simon, so deal with it."

"I know it is, and I appreciate it, Mick. I really do." I shifted my body toward him and looked him directly in the eye. "I don't know what I want to do now. I mean, I thought I wanted to settle in some quiet town and set up shop. Things have changed a lot in the last few months." Mick nodded.

"Yeah, tell me about it. My priorities are way different now," he admitted.

"I was thinking maybe I want to stay in Seattle, you know, so we can hang out." I shrugged. Mick smiled.

"Me and you hang out, or you and Mackaela?" He smirked and raised a brow.

"Come on, bro, I told you how I feel about her. Of course I want to be where she is, but that isn't my only reason for staying. I like having you in my life again. I missed you." I gave him a swift punch to the shoulder.

Mick swung back and got me in the same spot. "That'd be cool, Simon. I like having you around, too."

"I was thinking we could get into opening a shop together. You're damn good at the networking end of shit and I have no clue what to do. I'm better with the labor end."

"You want to go into business with me?" he asked, looking genuinely surprised.

"Yeah, as long as it's legit, no drugs or fights." I studied him carefully as he sat there, weighing my proposal.

Clapping me on the shoulder, he said, "Let's do it, I think it'd be great."

It was settled. After a few hours and another few beers, Mick and I decided that we would start a business together and began discussing plans to get started. He couldn't walk away from the family business entirely yet, but he was working on a clean break and had more time to help with the startup. I was going to look into places around town to get the garage up and running and he'd talk to some of his contacts about all the legalities and other information.

Strangely, I felt a weight lift off my shoulders. One more piece of my life was falling into place.

Later on in the evening, Mick turned up the music from his expensive sound system and drinks started flowing heavier. I was mindful not to drink too much since it'd been awhile for me and I wanted to savor every moment spent with Mackaela.

She and I sat on the lawn near a tree, tucked away from the majority of the party outside. I held her hand, making small circles on the inside of her palm with my fingertips. I watched her face as she gazed up at the sky, a small smile playing at her lips.

"You're incredibly beautiful," I murmured. Her smile widened slightly and she shifted her gaze toward me. "You look content. I like seeing you this way." I ran my free hand through her long, silky hair.

"I am content, Simon. I like feeling this way."

"Did Mick tell you about our new business venture?"

Mackaela nodded.

"I'm glad you're not going anywhere."

I cupped her cheek and tilted my head closer to hers. "I told you I wouldn't leave you."

"I know."

I stroked her smooth skin with the pad of my thumb and pressed my lips against hers.

Her arms wound around my shoulders, fingers gripping my hair. She deepened the kiss, igniting my body.

Moving my lips to her ear I whispered, "From the moment I met you, you had me."

I pulled back slightly and stared into her eyes, darker now with the night sky.

Chapter 27

Mackaela

Our eyes locked in the darkness and I licked my lips slowly, running my hand along his neck, up to his face where I held his cheek, stroking gently with my thumb. I could see just how much he cared for me in those emerald eyes. I drew in a steady breath.

"You're home to me, Simon Silver. Before you, I was content with loneliness. I was afraid of seeing what love did to people. As easily as it's given, it's taken away and leaves people broken and damaged. I know my mother loved me. She was only fragile because of what my father did to her. I can see that now, because of you. You came into my life and moved something in me. You were able to help me find myself again."

I leaned in and kissed him as I felt tears fall to my cheeks. He held me tight, tasting me, nipping at my lower lip, and driving me wild. After talking to Sadie earlier, I knew I was ready to take things to the next level.

I was worried about seeming easy and was scared that the memories of times before would stop me from being able to be with Simon. I didn't know how to associate emotions with sex because I'd always detached during the act. She assured me that if we genuinely cared about each other, there would be no way that being with Simon would compare to the other times.

"Not all men want you for your body, Mackaela," she'd said. "I see the way he looks at you, the way he touches you, just to feel you for a moment. The man is smitten."

After thinking of all the times I'd fallen asleep in Simon's arms and how much time we spent talking, I knew what she said was true. And now, under the stars with him, I felt it in my heart. Every doubt, every fear, melted away as if it never existed.

"I've never wanted anything more than I want you right now," Simon spoke in a gruff whisper.

"Do you want to go back to my place?" I asked quietly, my breath coming out uneven.

His brow furrowed for a moment, registering what I was asking. He swallowed roughly and nodded. There was no way I was going to make love to him here at Mickey's house when a party was in full swing. I wanted to be completely alone with him.

Both of us stood, he held my hand, pulling me toward the house. Mickey was just inside the kitchen talking to the new dealer, Cory, and his girlfriend Claire. I offered her a brief smile and she returned it. She really was a pretty girl, but I saw sadness in her eyes that made me wonder if she too had her own secrets.

I noticed how Cory seemed to forget she was there as he drank from a red Solo cup and talked to Mickey and a few other guys around. Mickey studied her, his eyes searching her face. Simon clapped Mickey on the shoulder as he came up beside him, still keeping hold of my hand.

"We're getting out of here, bro," he said.

Mickey raised a brow, turning to look at me. He cocked his head to the side and a slow smirk spread across his face. I could feel my cheeks heating at his perusal and rolled my eyes.

"Where you going?" he asked Simon but kept his eyes on me.

"We're going back to Mackaela's place. I'm kind of partied out and it's quiet there," Simon replied easily.

Mick shot him a questioning look and then sighed, shaking his head. "I expect you back tomorrow morning to help clean this place up," he said in a fatherly way.

I couldn't help but chuckle at the tone of voice he used and the stern way he looked at Simon.

"Sure. See you tomorrow." Simon dragged me along with him toward the door.

Simon

I was incredibly nervous as I started up the Mustang. The roaring engine barely registered in my ears. My palms were sweating as they hugged the steering wheel. I fumbled with the radio as I drove. I risked a sideways glance at Mackaela. She was softly singing along to a song. A smile worked at the corner of my mouth as I reached over and placed my hand over hers.

"I'm sort of mortified by the way Mickey reacted to you telling him that we were going back to my place," she said with a chuckle.

I couldn't help but laugh thinking about the way my brother went all parental on us. He definitely had that look in his eye that if I fucked up, he'd kill me. I had no intention of doing any harm to my girl tonight. It was going to be all love.

It wasn't a far drive to the apartment complex, but it felt quicker than normal with my nerves fully engaged. As I parked the car and shut off the ignition, I realized this was the first time I was consciously having sex with a girl. It was also the first time I actually cared enough to make sure it was special. The fact that this was essentially her first time caused my stomach to twist in knots. I closed my eyes and let out a deep breath.

"Stay here," I ordered softly as I opened my door, closing it soundly behind me.

I strolled around the front of the Mustang to the passenger side and opened her door. Mackaela's smile was wide, her golden eyes sparkled as she looked up at me.

"What a gentleman," she murmured as she stepped out.

I reached for her hand, my own ridiculous smile plastered on my face. I leaned in and kissed her softly and she threw her arms around my neck, pulling me closer to her. I pressed my body against her, forcing her back against the car. She whimpered against my lips as I cradled her face in my hands, tasting those glorious lips like I would die if I broke away.

Reluctantly, I pulled back and pressed my forehead to hers. "Let's get upstairs," I whispered.

Once we were inside with the door securely locked, I pulled her into me and began kissing her again. This time there was a desperation between us and an intensity that rivaled anything I'd ever felt. My hands traveled down her arms, trailing along her ribs, before catching her hips and aligning them with mine. She clutched at my shoulders as I lifted her against me. I groaned as her slender legs wrapped around my waist.

"I want you, Simon," she breathed in my ear, sliding her body against mine.

With my hands now cupping her outer thighs, I pulled her against me tighter as I began walking toward her bedroom. It was difficult to manage in my lust-filled haze. Once I made it, I set her down gently next to the bed.

"Lay with me," I murmured against her lips.

I felt her nod before she stepped away from me, slipping off her shoes as I did the same. I wanted to make this perfect for her. Wanted to show her how incredible we'd be together in every way.

Chapter 28

Mackaela

We lay there in the middle of my bed, facing each other, getting lost in each other's eyes. My breathing had slowed down but my heart was still hammering in my chest. I wasn't scared at all now. It was the anticipation of what was to come that had my body in a frenzy. Simon's mood seemed to match mine and I noticed his breath catch as he brought a hand up to stroke my hair away from my face. His fingers left a lingering heat as they traveled down my arm.

My heart began to beat faster as he rested his hand on my hip, tugging me closer to him. I willingly went, lining my body up against his. I kept my other arm tucked under my head against the pillow. Simon's gaze moved down the length of my body excruciatingly slow as if he were taking me in and memorizing the moment.

When those emerald eyes finally found their way back to mine, they were hooded and sparkling. His fingers came up to my shoulder and he gently brushed my hair back, smoothing a hand over the side of my neck, setting my skin on fire. Simon rolled, hovering over me with a leg between mine as he kissed along the path of my scars.

I was no longer self-conscious of them. They were a part of me and I embraced it.

He looped a finger around the strap of my tank top, sliding it down my shoulder. His lips continued the descent to just above my breasts and back up. Heat flooded between my thighs as his mouth hovered over my own. As soon as his lips touched mine, I drew my hand up and fastened it to the back of his neck. Simon clutched at my hip as the kiss intensified to the point that I could hardly breathe.

I would much rather have him than fill my lungs with air at this point. He slid his tongue along my lower lip before playfully bringing it between his teeth and biting down gently. I whimpered. Simon pulled back slightly. His eyes never leaving mine, he lifted the hem of his shirt and completely removed it in one fluid motion. I bit my bottom lip at the sight of his amazing body and the tattoo on his chest that meant so much to him. He was perfect.

I brought my hands up to his smooth chest and ran them down slowly. I felt his muscles tighten beneath my touch as he groaned. My eyes remained glued to his as my curious, trembling hands ran lower. Simon bit his bottom lip, sucking in a faltering breath as I ran my hand over the bulge in his jeans. He greedily grabbed my face, kissing me roughly. I let my legs fall open so that he could position himself between them. He lowered himself gently, rocking against me to create a glorious friction.

"You feel so good, sweetheart," he murmured as he moved his mouth along my neck and jaw.

My hands wound back around his neck, my fingers sinking into his hair, lightly tugging. His head moved lower as he kissed my chin to my collarbone. He lifted the light fabric of my tank top, heating my skin with his palm. My stomach muscles coiled and tightened at the thought of what his fingers were capable of.

He traveled upward now, stopping just under my breast. I moaned against his soft lips as he pressed himself against me. He moved his other hand behind me at the small of my back and pulled my upper body closer to his bare chest. I used my elbows to prop myself up, supporting my body. Simon's head lifted. He stared down at me with fire in his eyes.

"I want to see you," he growled in desperation.

His chest rose and fell with his ragged breathing. I swallowed the nerves that came with baring myself to him and nodded. He sat back on his heels. Grasping the hem of my top in both hands, he slowly began moving it up my skin and over my head. I watched as his eyes roamed over my chest before dipping lower. I knew the exact moment he saw my other scars. His brow furrowed slightly.

Tentatively, his finger grazed along my rib cage down to my hip. I wasn't sure if I should say something or not. My heart pounded in my throat. Just as I was about to speak, Simon's head lowered to kiss along the longest scar. My body relaxed and I fell back against the bed, my hands gliding over his shoulders. After those kisses, his mouth went upward over my bra to my lips. I let my wandering hands explore the tattoo that covered his shoulders and back. My nails drug across his skin slowly and he moaned in my ear before gently tugging on the lobe. My hands slid back up his shoulders, to his chest, marveling at how strong he felt.

I felt a shiver run through him as I traced along the picture at his heart. I lifted my head and pressed my lips against it, causing him to tremble once more. My hands continued their exploration until I found the button of his jeans, quickly undoing them. I was reaching for the zipper when Simon's hand curled into the back of my hair, drawing my lips to his. He kissed a fiery path over my shoulder, tugging the strap of my bra down. Not wanting anything between us any longer, I reached my hands behind my back. As soon as I unclasped my bra, Simon lifted his gaze to my eyes.

His eyes lowered to my chest as I removed the bra and I trembled at the hunger in them. "You're perfect," he murmured huskily, gently cupping my cheek as he tenderly kissed me.

Simon began moving down the bed, kissing every inch of me as he went. When he reached below my belly, he undid my shorts. I raised my hips to help him take them off. He dragged the shorts down my legs and I kicked them off the rest of the way.

Simon's hands ran up my legs, over my knees and thighs. When his eyes found mine again, his mouth was dangerously close to where I was aching for him. He dipped his chin, placing his lips against the thin fabric of my underwear. My body trembled as I moaned at the contact. He continued kissing me.

"You like that, sweetheart?" His voice was barely audible.

"Yes," I managed to whisper as he ran his tongue along my center while guiding my legs farther apart.

He lifted up suddenly, tugging my panties down. One minute, I felt the cloth sliding down my legs, and the next I was clutching the sheets as he worked his lips over me once again. I'd never experienced this before and it was the most wonderfully, terrifying feeling.

"God, you're so sweet." Simon groaned. "So fucking perfect."

My hips moved on their own accord, bucking up to meet his mouth as I rode the high of what he was doing. Within seconds, I was screaming his name and gripping at the sheet as I found release.

As I came down from the intensity, I felt Simon lift up quickly from the bed. My eyes darted to his hands that deftly undid the zipper of his jeans, pulling them down. I swear I'd never seen anything more amazing in my entire life. He stood before me in black boxer briefs that did little to hide what was underneath. His eyes wandered over my naked body as he sauntered toward me. I sat up on my knees, facing him as he stood at the side of the bed. My hand ran over his shoulder, his chest, and then his oh so perfect abs.

The scar from the gunshot didn't mar the sight at all. If anything, it made him even more beautiful to me. I felt his muscles twitch under my hand and I lifted my eyes to his as I ran it over his hard length. He pushed his hips toward my palm, grunting in approval as I lightly grasped him through the fabric. A thrill ran through me, knowing just what my touch did to him. It turned me on even more. I was so ready to feel him inside me.

Simon wound his fingers in my hair, tilting my head back as he bent down, kissing me fiercely while backing me onto the bed. I tugged at the waistband of his underwear. He lifted slightly, helping me remove them. We tasted and explored one another, reveling in this blissful feeling. I sucked in a breath when I felt him press against my entrance.

"Holy shit, you're so ready for me," he growled.

I nodded as I licked up his neck to his ear. "I need you. Now."

He placed an arm between us, grabbing himself before sliding against me again. I moaned and braced my hands against his shoulders as he slowly sunk inside. I tensed briefly and he stopped. I drew in a breath as my body adjusted to him.

"Jesus, you feel good." He groaned, moving inside me.

I wrapped my legs around him as he leaned into me, his lips hovering over mine. I was captivated and consumed by Simon. We moved together, watching each other's faces, getting used to this new connection we shared. My heart hammered in my chest, squeezing tight as I let myself get lost in these new sensations. I never knew it could be like this. I didn't want it to end.

"So amazing," he whispered, cupping my cheek as he leaned in to kiss me. We continued to move with each other, breathing heavier. A light sheen of sweat formed across our bodies.

Simon suddenly guided my body upright matching his own. With his hand at the small of my back, he held me tight as our movements became faster and more intense. I could feel myself beginning to lose control again.

Just as my mind and body soared in pure ecstasy, I felt Simon's body tense and then shudder violently as he rasped out my name.

Chapter 29

Mackaela

I felt Simon's breath, steady in sleep, against my neck. His skin was warm, but it didn't make me feel uncomfortable. It was peaceful having him wrapped around me. I had a sense of clarity I hadn't experienced in years. I felt incredibly content, reveling in this marvelous feeling as I thought about the night before and the intensity of making love for the first time.

We'd lost ourselves in each other all night long. I was exhausted but sated and ridiculously happy. I wasn't sure what time it was, but the sun was blaring through my window so it had to be later in the day. I heard my phone ringing in the distance from inside my purse before Simon's started ringing. Apparently, Mickey wasn't joking about having us come help him clean up.

I sighed and attempted to wriggle free from Simon's hold. He groaned and mumbled something, then gripped my waist, pulling me back against him.

"Stay with me," he whispered softly.

I let out a gasp as his hand slid up my side, cupping one of my breasts. His lips traveled along the back of my neck and down, following the line of my spine. Heat spread through me at the contact. He pressed against me from behind and suddenly I didn't care about our phones anymore.

I rolled to my back, his emerald gaze piercing straight to my soul. His dark hair was slightly disheveled, going every which way, and the stubble along his jaw along with the tattoo on his chest, made him look every bit like a bad boy. Overcome with a sudden urge of desire, I wrapped my arms around his neck and drew his lips to mine. I was intoxicated by the scent of him. A mix of whatever soap or cologne he had and his skin.

Simon moved over me, positioning himself so that he could slip inside. He let out a groan as he sunk in slowly, sucking air through his clenched teeth.

"So. Damn. Good," he murmured before dipping his head down to mine, tasting me with his tongue and teasing me with his lips.

*

Eventually, the real world called and it was time to leave my bed. Simon went to take a shower and I grabbed my cell seeing that I had not only a huge amount of missed calls, but ten text messages all from Mickey. Each one said the same thing, "Call me now!" I immediately dialed his number, falling back on the bed.

"It's about damn time!" Mickey growled into the phone.

"Sorry, we overslept."

"Yeah right, I know exactly what you two were doing."

I couldn't help the annoying shade of crimson my cheeks turned at his words, even though I was alone at the moment.

"Were you safe?" Mickey asked. His voice was a little calmer.

"Mickey Silver, I am not talking to you about this!" I shrieked.

I was on the pill and knew that Simon and I were both clean, but I wasn't about to divulge that information to him. My face flamed hotter.

"I know you're blushing right now. Hey, I'm just looking out for my brother and best friend."

I rolled my eyes even though he couldn't see it.

"We were perfectly safe and that's the last time I'm discussing it with you."

Mickey sighed. "Fine, I won't bring up your guys' sex life again."

"Mickey!"

"Sorry, Mack, I just like teasing you." He chuckled.

"So what's with blowing up our phones?"

Mickey was silent a moment.

"I got a call from Jack this morning. He's going to be back in town for a few days. He wants to see Simon and talk to him and he'd like to take us all out for dinner tonight, including you."

"Why do I have to go?" I never was a fan of Jack and wasn't at all close to him.

"Well I sure as hell don't want to go with just him and Simon. You can be a buffer."

"All right, I guess, but you should probably talk to your brother about it."

"Can I talk to him?" Mickey asked.

"He's in the show—" My voice was cut off by the sight of Simon walking in my bedroom, his body damp from the shower and completely bare.

My mouth went dry. Simon smirked at me and in a few strides, he was lying next to me. I still hadn't dressed yet. He slid his hand over the dip in my stomach, up to my chest.

"Mackaela, are you there?"

I swallowed and tried to find my voice.

Simon didn't stop his wandering hands as I spoke.

"Yeah, yeah, sorry I got ... distracted."

Simon grinned wide and placed a kiss on the inside of my wrist.

"Well is Simon there? I'll just talk to him now."

"Sure, hang on a second." I pulled the phone away and held it out to Simon.

"Is it Mick?" he asked softly.

"Yeah, apparently your dad is coming into town tonight." I watched Simon's jaw clench as he grabbed the phone out of my hand, placing a swift kiss on my forehead.

I knew he wasn't going to be happy about the dinner thing. If it were my dad, I wouldn't be too ecstatic either.

Simon

I wasn't looking forward to spending one on one time with Jack Silver. I would much rather prefer to be spending the day with Mackaela and Mick. I was itching to go to the beach now that the weather was warm and I was healthy enough. But my father wanted to talk to me and I agreed that it was time to discuss my past and how his abandonment affected me.

Dinner a few nights ago was less than pleasant, but I could tell Jack was trying. Maybe it was the fact that I'd been shot or that Mick was selling off his half of the business, but it seemed like our father was acting more sentimental than usual. Of course, I really didn't know one way or the other considering I didn't really know the man. Even Mick said there was something different about him. I was glad that Mackaela was there for me. I literally held tight to her throughout the entire meal. She was what grounded me, she brought me peace.

We'd been staying at her place the last few days. I was able to enjoy her a lot more that way. And I enjoyed her often. I knew I had to set an example, considering she too had daddy issues. It might take a little more time for her since the man didn't really seem interested in speaking with her, either.

Holly, her therapist, had wanted Mackaela to invite him to her counseling session today, but he never answered her call. I could tell she was upset, but she played it off like it was no big deal. It pissed me off though and I told her that. My sweet and beautiful, broken girl was everything to me. Knowing that someone, especially her own dad, didn't want her, made my heart break. It also made me want to punch something.

Mackaela wrapped her arms around my neck and I gripped her waist, pulling her closer to me.

"Can't I just hold you like this forever?" I whispered, grinning at the way her body responded to me.

Her body trembled against mine before she leaned back to press her lips to mine. "Mm, I would love that," she said. "But you have to meet your dad and I have my appointment with Holly."

I cupped her cheek, nibbling on her lower lip. "I want you. Right now, I want you." I pleaded in between kisses.

She clutched me tighter but shook her head. I reluctantly pulled away from her and sighed. "It's good for you to talk to him. Are you nervous?" she asked as she slipped on a pair of sandals.

"Not really nervous, I'm just not sure what to say. All these years, I thought I had it all planned out in my head. Now that I have the opportunity, I'm not sure."

"Just relax and go with the conversation, Simon. Don't over-think too much, you know?"

I raised a brow at her and smirked. "Aren't we awful insightful all of a sudden?"

Mackaela smiled.

"I guess it's all that counseling rubbing off on me." She gave me another lingering hug and then I kissed her soundly, trying to convince her one last time to not make me do this. It didn't work of course, and we both left her apartment.

I sat in my Range Rover and watched her start up her Mustang before driving away. I let out a long breath, turning the ignition.

"Here goes nothing," I muttered to myself.

*

We'd agreed to meet up at a restaurant of Jack's choosing in Downtown Seattle. To be honest, I didn't have much of an appetite. Jack was waiting for me at the entrance, dressed in a gray suit without a tie. He always appeared to be ever the business-man. Too bad his business was shady as shit and not at all relatable to the high-class people in this establishment. He played the part well though, I'll give him that.

"Hey, son, how are you?" he asked as he clapped me on the shoulder.

"I'm great," I replied.

I followed him to a table as the hostess led the way. He tipped her after she handed us our menus and I had to stifle an eye roll in his direction. Sensing my coldness I assumed, Jack narrowed his eyes at me.

"Always so harsh and angry ... " he said as he shook his head. I matched his look.

"I just don't get it. You told Mick that I was living it up. You made me out to be a spoiled brat when it was him who had every-thing."

"When Layla said she was taking you, I was angry. I remember the day you were born, Simon. Despite what you think, I was be-yond happy to have a son. You were my first-born boy and I loved you. I still do."

I snorted.

"Right. Enough to let my drug addicted mother take me away. I never heard from you. You never showed up or wrote letters. What do you expect from me, *Dad*?"

Jack sighed. "I understand how you must feel, how you felt back then even. Simon, I didn't stay away to hurt you. I guess I was so upset with your mom that you happened to get hurt in the process. I absolutely loved her whether you believe that or not. She wasn't a saint by any means."

I pinned him with a livid glare, my hands clenching into fists in my lap.

"You don't know a damn thing about how I felt, let's get that perfectly clear, Jack. My mother loved me. She wasn't perfect, I know that, but I never doubted that she loved me."

My throat grew tight. Talking about her brought on the pain of losing her all over again. I refused to show him any weakness.

"Maybe I don't know how you felt, and I am sorry for what Todd did to you. If I'd known, I wouldn't have just sat back. Your mother told me she was taking you to a better home and a better man. I called every week for the first year. But every time, she said you guys were great and that you didn't want to speak with me."

I rolled my eyes.

"A small child really has no sense of why they should or shouldn't talk on the phone." I cocked my head to the side thoughtfully. "Come to think of it, I never heard about you calling."

Jack nodded.

"She was trying to protect you from me. Layla knew the business I was in and didn't want you around it. Since she seemed clean, I figured you were better off. I didn't know that she relapsed and had health issues until it was too late."

I closed my eyes, shaking my head to clear the vivid images of my sick mother that rattled in my brain. Watching somebody go through cancer was probably the worst experience imaginable. You know that the inevitable is coming and there is nothing you can do about it.

"I had to watch her die," I said in a choked whisper. I could feel tears forming behind my eyes and I squeezed them shut to try and force them away.

"Son, you have to believe me when I say that I'm terribly sorry. I hate myself for telling Mick that you were better off. I'm glad that you two are so close now." Jack's own voice was full of conviction.

I slowly opened my eyes and let out a steady breath. "Why didn't you come for me after she died? I was so scared and so alone. I was in jail for a year."

My father's eyes looked wary as he stretched his arm across the table and placed a hand on my shoulder. "Simon, it wasn't until after Mick found you that I knew what happened. I was so busy, wrapped up in the business. I guess I figured that if you were in a bad spot you would have called."

"You took that choice away from me when you let her take me away. As far as I knew, I had no one to call, nobody to comfort me.

The one person that I knew could help me was the one that had died."

Jack nodded and squeezed my shoulder before drawing his hand back.

"I'm honestly sorry, son. I wish I could take the years back. I would if I could. Please understand that."

I saw the look of remorse on my dad's face as he spoke to me. Everything he was saying made sense and though it hurt and I would need time to forgive him, I knew that I couldn't cut him out of my life. Not if he genuinely tried. It wouldn't be easy and it'd take a long time to connect with him, but I didn't want to lose another parent. There was no changing what happened to me. I thought about Mackaela and the horrible things that she went through. If she could be strong, I could do the same.

The waitress came at that moment to take our orders and we both decided on beers and burgers. After she left, Jack spoke again.

"I know it might take a while, but I want a relationship with you, Simon. Mick says that you're staying in Seattle."

I nodded and tried to relax a little bit.

"That's the plan for now. I've grown attached to him. I missed him a lot growing up."

A faint smile touched my father's lips. "I'm sure Mackaela has something to do with your decision, too." He quirked a brow and I clenched my jaw automatically.

I really didn't want to talk about her with him. I kept my reply as simple and short as possible.

"I care about her a lot, so yeah, she's a big reason for me wanting to stay."

"She's a good girl, a little rough around the edges at times, but I always liked her." I furrowed my brow at him, not sure what to say. He smiled. "She and Mick have been attached at the hip for a long time now. I know a bit about her past and it's a shame about what happened to her mom." I nodded.

The waitress came back with our beers and food which silenced our conversation for a few minutes. The rest of our lunch was spent talking about my plans for starting a garage and working with Mick.

By the end of the meal, I was starting to understand Jack Silver a little better. We were surprisingly quite a bit alike and though it wasn't the best of circumstances between us, we even joked and laughed occasionally. I wished that I had been able to have more time with him growing up.

"I really appreciate you meeting with me today," Jack said as we stood out on the sidewalk of the restaurant.

I ran a hand through my hair and nodded. "I don't know what to say other than I hope we can spend more time together."

"I'm sure of that, Simon. Portland isn't too far away and if you ever feel the urge to come and visit, you are more than welcome."

"Thanks."

Jack put his hand out for me to shake and I reluctantly took it.

I saw the apologetic look in his eyes as he met my gaze and smiled. Suddenly he pulled me into a hug and held me tightly for a moment.

"I love you, Simon. I'm really sorry."

"I know," I said, nodding. "Me too." Something shifted between my father and I in that moment and I knew that everything would eventually be okay.

Truth be told, I think he needed me just as much as I needed him.

Chapter 30

Mackaela

I found myself lying on the bed in Simon's room, curled up on my side with my knees to my chest, lost in thought. Jack Silver had gone back down to Portland one week ago. Simon didn't hang out with him again after their one on one meal. That wasn't too surprising considering Jack was always focused on business and Ricky was still on the loose. We knew he wasn't in Seattle thanks to that new guy, Hawks, who had men in Seattle keeping an eye out. But where he was beyond that, was a mystery.

Simon would be back from his doctor's appointment soon. I was thinking about the smile on his face as he got in his car and drove away earlier. It was funny to watch him get so excited over little tasks like that since the shooting.

Lately he was trying to start working out again. I would go on walks with him and he would take off running, wanting to race me. The last few weeks, we pretty much always spent time at my apartment. He'd even moved most of his clothes over to my place instead of Mickey's.

Part of me was wary at first that maybe Simon and I were moving too fast, but with him it just felt right. He was like the other half of me, a part of my heart that had been missing. He knew everything about me inside and out. Basically living together felt natural.

We'd stayed at Mickey's last night because he and Simon wanted to discuss their plans for the garage that they'd be starting up soon. Mickey knew a guy who found an old run down garage for a steal and after checking the place out, Simon agreed it was the one. After the business discussions, we ate pizza and drank some beers and the three of us just hung out.

I enjoyed being able to spend time with my best friend and the man who had my heart. I knew that I loved him, but we had yet to officially say it to each other. I wasn't used to telling someone that I loved them other than Mickey and even that was few and far between. I was holding out for that moment when you simply said it and knew that you meant it. The girly parts of me wanted it to be special.

I was progressing nicely with Holly at the counseling sessions. It was a few days into July now and we were discussing college courses for me to start in the fall. I was a little apprehensive considering I was older than a normal freshman, but Holly assured me it was common for people to start college later in life. I wasn't that old yet. I was sort of excited at the prospect of meeting new people and possibly making new friends. I wasn't at all sure what I wanted to major in yet, but I was leaning toward business considering I liked the idea of being my own boss. Maybe I would start an art studio or something.

The issues with my father had yet to change, but it didn't really bother me. I'd talked to him last week and he turned me down to come to counseling again. He'd said maybe some other time but didn't seem too enthused. I didn't let it get me down though. I knew that with certain people it took time. Sometimes a whole hell of a lot of it, but there was nothing I could do about him other than move forward for now. I heard footsteps approach the doorway and I turned slightly.

Mickey was leaning against the wall, arms crossed over his chest casually. His dirty blond hair was getting longer, curling slightly over his ears. I smiled at him as he stepped toward me. I untucked my legs so that he could sit on the bed beside me.

"Tired?" he asked. My shoulder briefly lifted in a shrug.

"We stayed up way too late last night." Mickey nodded and then smirked. "Don't even ..." I started to say as he quirked his brow.

He chuckled. I pinched his thigh and he winced, laughing harder. I rolled my eyes. Mickey seemed to enjoy teasing me about being with Simon. I don't know why it made me blush and get embarrassed. I definitely wasn't a prude before Simon. I think it was just because I genuinely cared about him and what we shared was distinctive and sacred. Mickey was silent for a few minutes, softening his expression.

"You really care about him, don't you?" he asked quietly.

A small smile formed as I sat up, extending my hand to his. "I know it might be weird for you. I didn't think in a million years I would ever have what Simon and I have."

Mickey stared down at our hands. His brow furrowed. "To be honest, I never thought I'd ever see you happy again." He lifted his gaze to mine and I could see a thousand different emotions in his face.

A lump formed in my throat.

"You used to laugh all the time when we were younger. You were carefree and easy going. I loved that about you."

I squeezed Mickey's hand.

It was only recently that I realized how much I'd changed from a typical teenage girl to the hard shell of a woman. I let life get the best of me and wished I could take back how I reacted to the situations more than the actual situations themselves.

"I missed you every day as you slipped further away to that cold, cautious version of yourself. I didn't know what to do for you other than keep you near me. Sometimes I feel like I was too overprotective. Maybe if I pushed you more, you could have healed better. And then I turned you into a prostitute." He clenched his free hand into a fist, scowling. "I didn't realize at the time how that would affect you. It wasn't until Simon pointed out just how selfish I was being. I used you, my best friend, to better my business for more money. I'm so sorry, Mackaela. I feel like I let you down in the worst way. I helped in creating the person you became. I hurt you."

I sat silently, absorbing all he said as his eyes filled with tears. Mickey Silver didn't cry. He let his guard down with me more than anyone, but not like this.

"Mickey, no." I choked out a sob.

How could he ever blame himself for what I went through?

"No part of what happened to me was your fault." I wrapped my arms around his middle and hugged him tightly. I felt his own arms come around me as he sobbed along with me. I'd damaged more than myself all these years. He had to know it wasn't him.

"I'm just so sorry, Mackaela."

I had no words, so I just held him tighter, soothing both of us as best I could.

I clung to my best friend as we both grieved for the innocence lost and the things that shaped the both of us into who we''d become. After a while, we pulled apart from each other. Mickey wiped his eyes with the sleeve of his shirt.

"I love you, Mackaela. I'm really glad you can finally be at peace."

"I love you, too, Mickey. You're my best friend. I know you feel guilty, but I wouldn't be here right now if it wasn't for you. You're an amazing friend, Mickey Silver, and you'll never know how much I appreciate you."

He smiled at me and then shook his head with a light chuckle.

Raising a brow, he gazed at me slyly. "Amazing, huh?" I rolled my eyes.

"Don't get too cocky, Silver." I playfully punched his arm. "How are you doing by the way? I feel like we don't talk as much anymore."

"Maybe that's because you're so enamored with my brother," he teased, poking me in the ribs. "No, honestly you two are perfect for each other. I wouldn't want you with anyone else. It just fits."

I smiled. "Sometimes it's scary how connected Simon and I are," I admitted. "Have you ever felt that way before?"

Mickey pursed his lips in thought. I had no idea how many girls were running through his mind at the moment. His gaze shifted back to me and he shook his head slowly.

"Nope, I've never felt what you seem to feel."

"I'm not used to it," I said quietly.

"But you like it?"

"Yeah," I nodded. "I like it." He smiled and put his hand on my shoulder.

"That's all that matters. Don't question it, Mackaela, just go with it."

Simon

Complete and utter perfection.

There was no other word I could use to describe the way Mackaela made me feel, the way she looked. Everything about this woman was exactly what I needed in every single way.

Holding her hand as we drove down the scenic highway, the feel of the wind against us with the windows rolled down, was liberating. The fact she allowed me to drive her car as long as she got reign of the stereo was absolute bliss. We were headed to the beach on a sunny Sunday afternoon.

The doctor's told me that I was fully healed this week, and I wanted to celebrate. Mackaela was surprised when I showed up at her apartment with a basket full of food and a bottle of champagne. The smile on her face made me kiss her before I could even tell her what my plans were. Once I was able to explain that we were going to have a picnic dinner on the beach, she agreed it sounded like a great idea.

"Do you think we'll be able to find a place that isn't too crowded?" She asked as she fumbled with the radio.

"I'm sure of it."

She shot me a wary look and narrowed her eyes.

"How are you so sure?"

I shrugged. "I know a spot."

Her golden eyes looked deep into mine and a smirk formed on those pretty little lips. "You never cease to amaze me, Simon Silver."

I lifted her hand to my lips, placing a kiss on the back. "Likewise, sweetheart."

Within twenty minutes, we were turning off the highway and onto a dirt road that led toward the beach. Mackaela sat up, eyes wide in anticipation. A few miles down, the road came to an end in front of some large boulders. Just on the other side of them was a secluded alcove of sand where we could be alone.

As soon as I stopped the car and shut it off, she got out and took in the view of the Sound. I walked back to the trunk, pulling out a blanket, along with the food and champagne. She followed me as we stepped around the boulders onto the sand.

The weather couldn't have been better. There was a slight breeze to keep us cool, not a single cloud in the sky. I laid out the blanket in the shade from one of the larger boulders and kicked off my shoes.

"Are you hungry?" I asked.

Mackaela nodded as she knelt down on the blanket. "This is amazing, Simon."

I sat beside her, taking out the salads and sandwiches that I brought. Once they were placed, I grabbed two plastic cups and poured the champagne.

"You're amazing. I'm glad you agreed to come with me."

"I'd go anywhere with you."

I brushed a stray strand of hair away from her face and tucked it behind her ear, then I leaned in and kissed her softly. Pulling away, I held my cup up to hers.

"We need to make a toast," I declared.

"Okay, what are we toasting to?"

"Hmm ... " I pursed my lips in thought. I smiled, staring directly in her eyes. "To fate." Smiling, she tapped her cup against mine.

"It really was fate that brought you to me," she said matter of fact as she began eating her salad.

"Or it brought you to me, but either way I'm not arguing. You know what I was thinking on the way over here?" She'd just taken a bite so she shook her head in response. "I was thinking how perfect you are for me." A slow smile crept up her lips.

"You really know all the right things to say. How do you do that?" She laughed.

I laughed, too. "Honestly, I've told you it just comes out when I'm with you."

"So you were never charming and romantic for other girls?" Mackaela raised a brow at me and then bit into her sandwich.

I took a sip of the champagne, gazing back at her with a lazy smile. "I'm charming and romantic?"

"Don't act like you don't know that," she teased, tossing a piece of bread at me.

I caught it easily and threw it back at her. Surprisingly, it happened to go right down the front of the loose fitting shirt she was wearing.

Her mouth opened in shock and her eyes widened, sparkling playfully.

I quirked a brow and smiled. "Was that charming and romantic?"

She giggled, digging in her shirt, trying to get the bread out. "That definitely wasn't what I would call romantic." She finally removed the bread. "Nice shot though."

"Thanks."

We finished our food and packed everything away when we were done. After that, I grabbed her hands and pulled her up from the blanket to take a walk with me. I didn't let go of her the entire time we strolled along the shoreline.

We watched the water, trying to sight a whale or a seal but didn't get lucky enough. She searched for shells and when her hands got full, she handed them to me.

The past few months had been extremely emotional for both of us. Things were finally beginning to settle down and fall into place. I couldn't shake the feeling this was where I belonged. When the sun began to set, we wandered back to the blanket and lay down to watch the sky change colors.

I tucked one hand behind my head and held my other arm out so that she could rest against my chest. I absently played with her hair, running my fingers through the silky strands. As the sky darkened and stars began peeking through, I closed my eyes, tightening my arm around her shoulders, tucking her closer to my side.

I kissed her hair and whispered, "I love you, Mackaela."

A few moments went by before her arm around my waist tightened and she slowly lifted her head. Her golden eyes were laced with tears.

"I love you, Simon. I've never been more in love with anyone."

I withdrew my hand from behind my head and cupped her cheek, running my thumb against her bottom lip.

We gazed at each other silently and then I kissed her. I continued to declare my love for her in whispers against her skin as my lips traveled down her jaw to her neck. I ran my hand down her arm to her hip where I pulled her closer and rocked my hips against hers. She moaned and wrapped her leg around my waist as I settled on top of her.

"I love you so much." I groaned in her ear as she nibbled along my neck.

My hand dove into the hair at the nape of her neck and tugged gently. Her hips lifted to meet mine. I could feel the heat between her legs against me, driving me crazy. I couldn't get enough of her. Drawing back, I pinned her with an intense look, a growl rumbling from my chest.

"I need you. Now."

We continued to make out, teasing and tasting each other. When I couldn't take anymore, I lifted myself off her abruptly. My heart was hammering in my chest as I knelt in front of her. I knew that we were pretty secluded, but I wouldn't risk somebody walking up on us in the open.

"Give me your hand," I urged gently.

Mackaela sat up, placing her hand in mine without question. I pulled her to her feet, holding tight to her as I marched toward the car.

"Simon, what are you doing?" she asked warily as she turned to peer at the area we just left.

I didn't respond until we got to the Mustang. I yanked open the driver's door and reached in to push the seat down. Stepping back, I swept my hand toward the back seat. A slow smirk formed on her face. I winked at her.

"If this is okay with you of course."

She nodded excitedly. "Definitely."

I climbed in behind her and shut the door. It wasn't the most spacious area, but at least we weren't out in the open. I turned to face Mackaela as she fisted my shirt in her hands, eagerly kissing me. I leaned forward, sliding her underneath me again.

My hands roamed over her body, grabbing the hem of her top and tugging it off easily. I took in the sight of the dark purple bra she was wearing and then lowered my lips to her skin. She pulled at my shirt and within seconds, it was gone, too. I pushed down the fabric of her bra, sliding my tongue around the curve of her, nibbling gently. Her breath caught and she ran her nails down my back, scratching me.

There was a slight prick of pain, but it was more pleasure when I thought of how she was marking me. She was mine and I was undoubtedly hers. I was more than ready for her by now and urgently sought out the button of her shorts. I had them pulled down along with her panties in record time. She clutched at my shorts, but her trembling fingers couldn't work the buttons. I kissed her lips and pulled back, undoing the button myself and gliding the shorts down.

I sucked in a breath and nearly lost it right there when she grabbed me, gliding her hand up and down my length. I groaned and quickly clasped my hand around hers to stop her. Her eyes locked with mine.

"I want to be inside you," I panted breathlessly.

Mackaela didn't let go but began guiding me so that I was positioned against her. We both took in sharp breaths and she moaned as I buried myself inside her. I moved against her slowly, trying to relish in this incredible feeling. Our eyes were still locked as I pulled her hips closer to me.

When her eyes started to close, I pulled her entire body up so that she was straddling me. With one hand on her hip and the other at the back of her neck, my eyes penetrated hers.

"I want you to look at me," I whispered as I kissed her swollen lips. "I want to see you explode around me." I dug my fingers into her hip as she gripped my shoulders, rocking against me.

"I love you," she breathed.

Her eyes were glistening as she stared back at me.

"I love you, sweetheart."

We began moving faster then, finding a rhythm while clinging to each other desperately. Her head fell back and I stared in awe as she fell apart above me. Within seconds, I was following. I placed feather light kisses all over her body as we sat in the back seat of her car, catching our breath.

"I love you so much," I murmured against her skin.

"I love you, Simon." Her hands ran along my chest, brushing the necklace that I kept my mother's ring on.

I caught her hand and met her eyes.

"You're the most important thing in the world to me," I vowed, brushing her hair off her shoulder. "I can't imagine my life without you. I don't know how I lived before. I was lucky to have someone looking out for me. Someone to lead me to you." I ran my lips along her cheek, to the corner of her mouth.

I heard her sigh and I leaned my forehead against hers. Swallowing the lump in my throat, I lifted my hands, removing the necklace. Mackaela's brow furrowed.

"What are you doing?"

"I love everything about you. Your mind, your body, and your soul." Her eyes welled with tears and I could feel the pulse of her heartbeat against my hand clasped around her wrist.

I held my mother's ring in between two fingers, smoothing out her hand so that hers spread apart.

Taking a steady breath, I said, "I won't ask you to marry me yet. I won't do that because we're not ready, but we will be. I'm asking if you'll be mine … unconditionally."

Tears spilled down her cheeks as I slipped the ring on her right ring finger. Nodding, she brought her lips to mine.

"I will," she murmured.

Complete and utter perfection.

Chapter 31

Mackaela

The night Simon told me he loved me turned my entire world upside down in the best way. It was unbelievable to see how drastically my entire life had changed by simply knowing him.

When I met Simon, I was in a low place. If anyone would have told me then that I would be where I was now, I wouldn't have believed it. At the time, I didn't think I'd ever feel pure joy. Sure, there were times that I laughed, but I was never completely happy, never fully content until now. What disappointed me the most was hearing other people like Mickey and Sadie commenting on how broken I'd been. I was in so deep that I couldn't even register how poorly I treated others around me. These were the people that actually cared about me and I let them down, especially Mickey.

Being able to have that conversation with him and assure him it was nothing he'd done, triggered a stronger bond between us. I didn't have a single doubt that Mickey Silver would always be my best friend.

I talked to Holly at my last counseling session about what happened with Simon that night at the beach. Well, I left out the whole back seat in the Mustang romp of course. It didn't seem at all sudden to me that he gave me a ring, his mother's ring. Ever since the day I met Simon, everything that happened between us, the words spoken, the need, the fear, the love, it all felt exceptionally right to me.

I'd waited my entire life for him and there was no doubt that he was that one person for me. The one I was meant to hold onto forever. Holly reiterated that my feelings were justified and I need not worry about whatever length of time took place to develop them.

They say that everything happens for a reason, and I believe that the heartache I went through, every single painful memory, the loss of my mother, was all worth it. Because now, I was a stronger person and the past that once haunted me was now a badge of honor I wore to remind me of who I had become.

The End

Acknowledgements

I would like to start off by thanking all of the readers for taking a chance on me and reading my stories! Without you, I wouldn't be able to continue doing what I love. Thank you!

Next, I'd like to thank my incredible team of women at Aurora Publicity for believing in me and helping me make this series better than I ever could have imagined. I am so incredibly grateful to be working with you all.

To my husband, Jeff, thank you for reading my books and continuing to always encourage me. I keep going for you and the kids and am so grateful to have the unconditional support and love you give.

Here's to creating more stories in the future!

~ Melissa

Contact

K. MORGAN

www.melissakmorgan.com
Facebook: @AuthorMelissaKMorgan
Facebook Group: M.K.'s Book Babes
Instagram: @author_melissa_k_morgan
Email: authormelissakmorgan@gmail.com

Silver Series

Two brothers. Two Women. One dangerous world.

SOMETHING TO BELIEVE IN, BOOK #1

*She's nothing he expected. He's nothing she wanted.
Mackaela Stone is damaged. Haunted by her past, she's worked
hard to wall herself off from ever repeating the mistakes that left
her feeling too filthy for love. But meeting Simon Silver might be
enough to crack those fortifications—if he can overcome his own
turbulent history.
Trusting one another is hard enough, but finding faith, hope
and love may be more than they can manage. Is their connection
enough to give them something to believe in? Or is the damage
done too great to overcome?*

SOMETHING TO HOLD ONTO, BOOK #2

*She was supposed to be the key to everything he ever wanted.
He was the shadow of a past she swore she'd leave behind.
Claire Evan's is risking it all. She knew her new job—working for
the golden boy of Seattle, Mickey Silver—might be too good to be
true. But the perks of playing his game were more than she could
resist, even if the price included being dragged deeper into his*

cruel, dark world. Now his game of revenge may take them both down a path of mutual destruction.

Can working together finally open their eyes to what matters most? Or will the cost of cold ambition leave them both broken and alone?

STANDALONE CONTEMPORARY ROMANCES BY MELISSA K. MORGAN

Always Beautiful

Sometimes fate doesn't just throw you a curve ball, it hits you in the face. Breaking your nose, blackening your eyes, and making you second guess everything you've spent your entire life working toward. Do you ignore that ball and continue in the direction of security and stability? Or do you throw caution to the wind, follow your heart, and potentially become so damaged that you'll never recover?

Experiencing an intensity she's never known, a passion she's never felt, and a way to escape the mundane has Lucky changing her once solid foundation. But seasons change and so do people. When she discovers Zeppelin is hiding something from her, those walls she let fall so easily begin to build back up. Zeppelin finally reveals his devastating secret and Lucky is left with two choices. Walk away and forget him entirely or take his hand and follow him into the darkness and sorrow.

(Available in eBook on Amazon.com and Free in Kindle Unlimited)

Let Me Down

Maria Fredericks is starting over. After nearly a decade of living in the shadows of a deep depression and losing herself, she is finally moving on. Nothing matters anymore as long as her and her six year old daughter are happy and safe.

As a result of the many years being broken down, Maria is struggling to figure out who she is after everything she was made to believe. Knox Allen is no stranger to pain. Though he was able to obtain a second chance at life, not a day goes by that he doesn't remember what it was like to feel like nothing.

Knox and Maria find solace in each other, but the temporary respite is not as serene as they thought it would be. Maria can't trust him or herself for that matter. Knox fears their unexpected bond will end up hurting him in the end.

Can two broken people survive the modern world and all the drama that goes along with it? Or will their fears get the best of them and leave them crashing and burning at the end of it all?

(Available in eBook on Amazon.com and Free in Kindle Unlimited)

www.ingramcontent.com/pod-product-compliance
Lightning Source LLC
Chambersburg PA
CBHW070059120726
47909CB00002B/437